Acclaim for *Naked Lunch*

"William S. Burroughs' *Naked Lunch* . . . is writing of an order that may be cleanly defended not only as a masterpiece of its own *genre*, but as a monumentally moral descent into the hell of narcotic addiction . . . only after the first shock does one realize that what Burroughs is writing about is not only the destruction of depraved men by their drug lust, but the destruction of all men by their consuming addictions, whether the addiction be drugs or over-righteous propriety, lasciviousness or sixteen-year-old girls. Burroughs is not only serious in his intent, but he is a writer of great power and artistic integrity engaged in a profoundly meaningful search for true values. . . ."
—John Ciardi, *Saturday Review*

"**A book of great beauty, great difficulty, and maniacally exquisite insight.**" —Norman Mailer

". . . an absolutely devastating ridicule of all that is false, primitive, and vicious in current American life: the abuses of power, hero worship, aimless violence, materialistic obsession, intolerance, and every form of hypocrisy. . . . Burroughs is first and foremost a poet. His attunement to contemporary language is probably unequalled in American writing. . . . Compared to Burroughs' grasp of modern idiom in almost every form of English—and his ability at distillation and ellipsis—the similar efforts of Ring Lardner, and of Hemingway, appear amateurish and groping. . . . for the new generation of American writers the work of William Burroughs is by far the most influential being done today."
—Terry Southern

William S. Burroughs

NAKED LUNCH

Grove Press, Inc.
New York

First Black Cat Edition 1966

ISBN: 0-394-17108-X
Library of Congress Catalog Card Number: 60-11097

Manufactured in the United States of America

Grove Press, Inc., 920 Broadway, New York, N.Y. 10010

24   23   22

Contents

Naked Lunch on Trial

    The Supreme Court of Massachusetts in a decision handed down on July 7, 1966, declared Naked Lunch *by William S. Burroughs not obscene. In clearing the novel of obscenity charges and finding that it was protected by the First Amendment of the United States Constitution, the highest court of Massachusetts reversed an earlier decision of the Superior Court of Boston and removed the threat of a state-wide ban on the book. Since* Naked Lunch *was first published in the United States in 1962, the only other censorship action against the book outside the State of Massachusetts occurred in Los Angeles, where the novel was cleared of obscenity charges at a trial in 1965.*

    At the Boston trial which preceded the Massachusetts Supreme Court ruling, Norman Mailer, Allen Ginsberg, and John Ciardi were among the witnesses who testified on behalf of Naked Lunch. *The attorney appearing on behalf of the book and its publisher was Edward de Grazia, assisted by Daniel Klubock. Below is the full text of the majority decision of the Supreme Court of Massachusetts, followed by excerpts from the testimonies of Mr. Mailer and Mr. Ginsberg, and a statement from Mr. de Grazia.*

ATTORNEY GENERAL vs.
A BOOK NAMED "NAKED LUNCH"

BY THE COURT. The book was adjudged obscene in the Superior Court, G. L. c. 272, §§ 28C, 28E, 28F (each inserted by St. 1945, c. 278, § 1). The Supreme Court of the United States has held that, to justify a holding of obscenity, "three elements must coalesce: it must be established that (a) the dominant theme of the material taken as a whole appeals to a prurient interest in sex; (b) the material is patently offensive because it affronts contemporary community standards . . . and (c) the material is *utterly* without redeeming social value" (emphasis supplied). *A Book Named "John Cleland's Memoirs of a Woman of Pleasure"* v. *Attorney Gen. of Mass.* 383 U. S. 413, 418-421 (hereafter referred to as the *Memoirs* case). "Naked Lunch" may appeal to the prurient interest of deviants and those curious about deviants. To us, it is grossly offensive and is what the author himself says, "brutal, obscene and disgusting."

As to whether the book has any redeeming social value, the record contains many reviews and articles in literary and other publications discussing seriously this controversial book portraying the hallucinations of a drug addict. Thus it appears that a substantial and intelligent group in the community believes the book to be of some literary significance. Although we are not bound by the opinions of others concerning the book, we cannot ignore the serious acceptance of it by so many persons in the literary community. Hence, we cannot say that "Naked Lunch" has no "redeeming social importance in the hands of those who publish or distribute it on the basis of that value." See the *Memoirs* case at p. 421.

The record does not show that the book has been "commercially exploited for the sake of prurient appeal, to the exclusion of all other values." The question, therefore, is not presented whether the book, or its publication and distribution, are on that account "utterly without redeeming social importance." See the *Memoirs* case at pp. 420-421, which appears to treat the privilege under the First Amendment of publishing material like this as a qualified privilege which may be lost if abused. See also *Ginzburg* v. *United States*, 383 U. S. 463, 467-476; *Mishkin* v. *New York*, 383 U. S. 502, 508-512. Cf. *Galvin* v. *New York, N.H. & H.R.R.*, 341 Mass. 293, 296-298.

The final decree is reversed and a new final decree is to be entered declaring that (without considering whether the book has been commercially exploited for the sake of prurient appeal) the book cannot be declared to be obscene. This new final decree shall be without prejudice to the bringing of new proceedings with respect to this book under the appropriate sections of G. L. c. 272, if it shall appear that, after March 21, 1966, the date of the three recent Supreme Court cases, already cited, any persons have been or are advertising or distributing this book in this Commonwealth in a manner to exploit it for the sake of its possible prurient appeal.

So ordered.

The Chief Justice took no part in the consideration of this case.

EXCERPTS FROM THE BOSTON TRIAL OF *NAKED LUNCH*

EDWARD DE GRAZIA: *Mr. Mailer, you have referred to the fact that in some of your writings you deal with political matters. Would it be unfair to say that in much of your writing, both as a novelist and as an essayist, you deal with moral questions and moral matters?*

NORMAN MAILER: Well, I try to. It's like saying—

Q. *What's good and bad?*

A. If you're a ballplayer you would not like to say you are a good third baseman, you try to play third base. You try to deal with moral questions. Whether you deal with them well is another matter.

Q. *When I use the word "moral," there, I mean, you are trying to deal with questions of good and bad and good and evil?*

A. Yes, I try to deal with such questions.

Q. *You have read* Naked Lunch, *the book before the Court?*

A. Yes, I have.

Q. *Do you have some opinion as to its importance?*

A. I have a changing opinion as to its importance, because I have now read the book, not completely, but I have read the book completely twice. I have read more than two-thirds of the book, in other words, three times. I have encountered the book over a period of about three or four years; or to be more precise, I first encountered it in 1959, in the magazine *Big Table*. I read an excerpt from it; then I read the book entirely about two years ago, when it came out. In the last few days I have read it very slowly and carefully. I have read the first hundred and ten pages.

THE COURT: *What is the association between* Big Table, *and* Naked Lunch?

MAILER: *Big Table* is a magazine.

THE COURT: *I assume it is a trade magazine.*

MAILER: *Big Table* was a magazine that was put out by some editors who had left the *Chicago Review,* which was a literary magazine of the University of Chicago.

DE GRAZIA: *Mr. Mailer, would you now tell us, in your own words, the importance that you see in the novel, changing as it may be?*

MAILER: Well, the change I have mentioned, the change —because what is interesting about it to me—I started reading the book. I liked the book very much when I read it. The last time I said, "Fine thing." I started to read it with trepidation, whether I didn't like it as much.

THE COURT: *Did that concern you too much?*

MAILER: Well, if I am going to testify on it—

THE COURT: *In that light, pardon me.*

MAILER: So, I found, as I read it—

THE COURT: *If you read a book once and took a fancy to it and read it a second time and didn't like it, you wouldn't want to stake your life under those circumstances, would you?*

MAILER: No, sir. At any rate I found I had more respect for the reading of it this time. I haven't finished it. I had to read slowly and think about it a great deal, as to my respect for it. I have a feeling that it is much more of a literary work than I felt the previous time, even though the previous time I felt it was a work of high talent. The man has extraordinary talent. Possibly he is the most talented writer in America. As a professional writer I don't like to go about bestowing credit on any other writers.

THE COURT: *Have you read him before?*

MAILER: I read a book, *Junky;* and I read it in a paperback; and it is just a very good, hard-boiled sort of novel. It is a false novel. He wrote it to make some money; but it is well-written. Small portions of it, as a matter of fact, appear in *Naked Lunch* as one of the themes.

But I felt, reading it through this last time, I had the feeling that the work presents a kind of complexity which I will not compare to James Joyce's *Ulysses*, I'd say it is not without comparison. It's possible, as a work that would take considerable inquiry and study. I found it considerably less shocking as I read it this time. I felt it more and more, the purpose in the various parts of it. The first time through I thought it was well-written. The man has extraordinary style. He catches just a little of the beauty. I think he catches the beauty, at the same time the viciousness and the meanness and the excitement, you see, of ordinary talk, the talk of criminals, of soldiers, athletes, junkies.

There is a kind of speech that is referred to as gutter talk that often has a very fine, incisive, dramatic line to it; and Burroughs captures that speech like no American writer I know. He also—and this makes it impressive to me as a writer—he also has an exquisite poetic sense. His poetic images are intense. They are often disgusting; but at the same time there is a sense of collision in them, of montage that is quite unusual. And, as I say, all this together gives me great respect for his style. But I also began to feel that really this time there is more to his intent than I had ever recognized before; that the work was more of a deep work, a calculated work, a planned work. In other words, the artistry in it was more deliberate and more profound than I thought before. So, as a matter of fact, after this case is over, I am looking forward to finishing it. As I say, I have read just the first half this time through.

DE GRAZIA: *Mr. Mailer, while you are on that subject, there was a reference earlier by Mr. Cowin (Assistant Attorney General) to the question of the notes, of his notes of which he has no precise memory of having written, which later became the basis of* Naked Lunch; *and I was wondering, as a writer, if you could give us your opinion what may have been involved here?*

A. Yes. I listened to that very carefully because I remembered reading that in the beginning of the book; and it seemed to me, as I was reading the book, I started thinking about a matter that is one of the mysteries of writing. It is very often you can wake up in the morning and start writing and you have this experience: what you are writing about is what you haven't been thinking about. It will come out in detail. One's best writing seems to bear no relation to what one is thinking about. There is an unconscious calculation that seems to go on in one's sleep. The work is done while you sleep; and the discipline of writing is almost to keep from interfering with that creative work that is done by the unconscious. In other words, if a man is working on a novel, that his habits are regular and precise—I am getting long-winded here for a point. The best of his habits are regular because he doesn't portray the work he is performing while conscious.

In Burroughs' work I think something quite extraordinary is going on here, since the man is a self-confessed drug addict. I have heard various versions of how he wrote *Naked Lunch*. He seems to have been writing—he wrote somewhere, he used to write coming out of drug addictions, at other times he says he wrote it in drug addictions, while he was a drug addict. It is possible he wrote this book in all three phases. I am just guessing this. Possibly it was written while an addict, while withdrawing, and while he was withdrawn from addiction.

But what is fascinating to me is that there is a structure to the book, you see, which is doubtless imperfect. I think one reason we can't call it a great book like *Remembrance of Things Past* or *Ulysses*, is the imperfection of this structure. There is no doubt as to the man's talent; while it was, perhaps, excited and inflamed by drug addiction, it was also hurt. This man might have been one of the greatest geniuses of the English language if he had never been an addict. Through this there is a feeling of great torture in the composition of the book. What comes through to me is that there also is style, the subconscious going through all the various trials and ordeals of addiction, he still holds on to a scheme in the book; and there is a deep meaning. It is curious the way these themes keep recurring.

I have no idea how the book was put together. The ingredients are so exceptional, like you have a banquet of thirty, forty components. You may eat in any order. You may shift them. The themes are so deeply entwined; any page put with another page creates an aura. It was so profoundly conceived.

Well, it may be this book was so—as I say, has no other structure than the profundity of the experience that the author had, the particular ordeal the man went through in his life; or it may be that there is a firm structure to it. It is just on the basis of these three readings. I feel the work is sufficiently complex I couldn't begin to see—I found it absolutely fascinating because it draws me to read it further and further, the way *Ulysses* did when I read that in college, as if there are mysteries to be uncovered when I read it.

Q. *When you use the words, "absolutely fascinating," and so on, do you mean also, it has importance to you as a writer and other writers? Are you expressing a notion of its importance?*

A. It has enormous importance to me as a writer.

Q. *Before, you mentioned the unconscious and subconscious. Do you have a feeling, as a writer, that one of the important tests of a writer is to be able to summon up, to evoke unconscious material and put it into artistic form, and that in order to make his contribution, as a writer, to society? Is this part of your feeling of one of the writer's tasks or problems? And if so, has Burroughs done this very well?*

A. Well, I think that I don't want to go to great length about what I think.

Q. *Let me rephrase the question more simply. Do you think that Burroughs in this book has drawn up out of the unconscious, in one way or another, a great deal of material which has become useful, which by being placed in artistic form, has become unique?*

A. I think it is not only unique and useful, but I think that he has given a portrait in this work. I think this work, as one of the gentlemen who testified earlier spoke of St. Augustine, I wouldn't begin to think of St. Augustine. To me this is a simple portrayal of Hell. It is Hell precisely. In fact, Your Honor, I have written a little bit about that to bring in— Should I read that, if you wish?

Q. *You have some notes, I think?*

THE COURT: *You have some notes?*

MAILER: I have some notes.

THE COURT: *You may.*

MAILER: Well, in these notes, I said—

THE COURT: *Incidentally, when did you draw up these notes?*

MAILER: I wrote them on Sunday. I have written about William Burroughs before; and I wrote about him in *Esquire* two years ago, I think, a year and a half ago. But I felt I didn't want to even look back at that. The remarks were complimentary, but I felt I wanted it freshly. If you wish I can give this to you?

Q. *Go ahead, Mr. Mailer.*

A. William Burroughs is in my opinion—whatever his

conscious intention may be—a religious writer. There is a sense in *Naked Lunch* of the destruction of soul, which is more intense than any I have encountered in any other modern novel. It is a vision of how mankind would act if man was totally divorced from eternity. What gives this vision a machine-gun-edged clarity is an utter lack of sentimentality. The expression of sentimentality in religious matters comes forth usually as a sort of saccharine piety which revolts any idea of religious sentiment in those who are sensitive, discriminating, or deep of feeling. Burroughs avoids even the possibility of such sentimentality (which would, of course, destroy the value of his work), by attaching a stringent, mordant vocabulary to a series of precise and horrific events, a species of gallows humor which is a defeated man's last pride, the pride that he has, at least, not lost his bitterness. So it is the sort of humor which flourishes in prisons, in the Army, among junkies, race tracks and pool halls, a graffiti of cool, even livid wit, based on bodily functions and the frailties of the body, the slights, humiliations and tortures a body can undergo. It is a wild and deadly humor, as even and implacable as a sales tax; it is the small coin of communication in every one of those worlds. Bitter as alkali, it pickles every serious subject in the caustic of the harshest experience; what is left untouched is as dry and silver as a bone. It is this sort of fine, dry residue which is the emotional substance of Burroughs' work for me.

Just as Hieronymus Bosch set down the most diabolical and blood-curdling details with a delicacy of line and a Puckish humor which left one with a sense of the mansions of horror attendant upon Hell, so, too, does Burroughs leave you with an intimate, detailed vision of what Hell might be like, a Hell which may be waiting as the culmination, the final product, of the scientific revolution. At the end of medicine is dope; at the end of life is death; at the end of man may be the Hell which arrives from the vanities of the mind. Nowhere, as in *Naked Lunch*'s collection of monsters, half-mad geniuses, cripples, mountebanks, criminals, perverts, and putrefying beasts is there such a modern panoply of the vanities of the human will, of the excesses of evil which occur when the idea of personal or intellectual power reigns superior to the compassions of the flesh.

We are richer for that record; and we are more impressive as a nation because a publisher can print that record and sell it in an open bookstore, sell it legally. It even offers a hint that the "Great Society," which Lyndon Johnson speaks of, may not be merely a politician's high wind, but indeed may have the hard seed of a new truth; for no ordinary society could have the bravery and moral honesty to stare down into the abyss of *Naked Lunch*. But a Great Society can look into the chasm of its own potential Hell and recognize that it is stronger as a nation for possessing an artist who can come back from Hell with a portrait of its dimensions.

And I would add, and so warrants all, perhaps.

DE GRAZIA: *I have no more questions.*

* * *

DE GRAZIA: *Mr. Ginsberg, have you read the book entitled* Naked Lunch *by William Burroughs?*

ALLEN GINSBERG: Yes.

Q. *More than once?*

A. Yes, a number of times.

Q. *Would you specify before me, for the Court, a few examples or illustrations of ideas having social importance which you feel are expressed in this book?*

A. Yes. Well, there are a great number of ideas in it that have social importance; and they are all interrelated in the presentation of the book. One of the main ideas is a theory of junk addiction or a theory of heroin addiction applied as a model for addiction to many other things besides drugs. It is usually referred to in the book as "The Algebra of Need," and the other addictions which are mentioned in the book, are treated dramatically—addiction to homosexuality, which is considered by Burroughs also a sort of addiction; and, on a larger scale, what he conceives of as the United States addiction to materialistic goods and properties. Addiction to money is mentioned in the book a number of times; and most of all, an addiction to power or addiction to controlling other people by having power over them. So throughout the book there are dramatic illustrations of people whose obsession or lust is for control over the minds and hearts and souls of other people.

At the very beginning of the book this general theory of addiction, "The Algebra of Need," is mentioned in the Introduction, Latin numbers v to xvi*; and it is referred to again on page 21 and on page 168 of the book.

Q. *Just before you referred thus to the pages of the book,*

* All page references are to the hardcover edition of *Naked Lunch.*

where "The Algebra of Need" is referred to, you indicated Burroughs—that this book is concerned with the problems of control of individuals over other individuals, of institutions over individuals. Did you mean to limit the reference—I think you said—to spiritual?

A. This would be political controls.

Q. I think you may not have mentioned sexual and I wonder if you meant to?

A. Yes.

Q. That is, Mr. Jackson a few minutes ago testified to a couple of episodes where the horror of the situation seemed to involve the homosexual relation, almost enforced, socially enforced homosexual relationship. Well then, going back to your last answer—

A. This theme that you are referring to, of sexual control, certainly plays a very large part in the book and is referred to at great length in the episodes involving Carl and also in the practices of Dr. Benway in brainwashing some of his patients.

Q. Have you found in the book, among the many ideas that you have indicated, the book contains an idea relating to the issue, the social issue of whether punitive or medical psychiatric treatment of addicts is the wiser or better method?

A. Yes. The book treats this problem from any number of different angles. I think it is the opinion of the author of the book, as he expresses it very directly in the Introduction and also, I believe, in the Appendix, at the conclusion, that a medical treatment for heroin addiction is to be preferred over punitive treatment. And he illustrates, or gives examples of, his opinions, by dramatic representations of addicts being treated punitively and carrying these representations to fantastical or weird extremes: such as the pictures that he gives on page 16 and thereafter of Bradley the Buyer, who is an agent for the punitive forces, who finally becomes addicted to being an agent and takes pleasure in the power that he has over the junkie, and finally can get no pleasure at all unless he is in direct physical contact with a junkie.

THE COURT: *Mr. Ginsberg, do you consider that this book is obscene?*

GINSBERG: Not really, no, sir.

THE COURT: *Well, would you be surprised if the author himself admitted it was obscene and must be necessarily obscene in order to convey his thoughts and impressions?*

GINSBERG: The sentence you are referring to—

THE COURT: *Well, it's on page xii of the Introduction: "Since* Naked Lunch *treats this health problem, it is necessarily brutal, obscene and disgusting. Sickness is often repulsive details not for weak stomachs."*

GINSBERG: Yes, he has said that. I don't think he intends that to be obscene in any legal sense or even obscene as seen through his own eyes or through the eyes of a sympathetic reader. He is dealing with matters very basic and very frightening.

THE COURT: *What do you understand him to mean by the phrase: "As always the lunch is naked"? Do you mind my asking these questions?*

DE GRAZIA: *No, Your Honor.*

GINSBERG: That phrase occurs when he is discussing capital punishment, I think.

THE COURT: *Where does he discuss capital punishment?*

GINSBERG: Right in *that*.

THE COURT: *He discusses it in the Foreword, or the Introduction?*

GINSBERG: In the paragraph on the same page. "Let them see what is on the end of that long newspaper spoon."

THE COURT: *What is a "newspaper spoon"?*

GINSBERG: We are presented or spoonfed with news about death, about capital punishment, or executions.

THE COURT: *Does he use the expression, "newspaper spoon"?*

GINSBERG: Yes.

THE COURT: *What page is that?*

GINSBERG: The same page you were reading from, page xii, "Since *Naked Lunch* treats this health problem," —the next paragraph beginning: "Certain passages in the book,"—the end of the paragraph: "Let them see what is on the end of that long newspaper spoon."

THE COURT: *You think the title*, Naked Lunch, *relates to capital punishment?*

GINSBERG: No, no. It relates to nakedness of seeing, to being able to see clearly without any confusing disguises, to see through the disguise.

THE COURT: *That is your interpretation of the title?*

GINSBERG: Yes.

THE COURT: *Or the meaning of the title?*

GINSBERG: Of the word, "Naked," in the title; and "Lunch" would be a complete banquet of all this naked awareness.

THE COURT: *All right.*

DE GRAZIA: *Among the ideas you have noticed in this book, you have spoken of the idea of control and the problems surrounding control, individual over individual, institution over individual. Does this have some relationship to the control of the addict as it is used in the book, the term, "control addict"?*

A. Yes. The concept of addiction is carried out to include, in Burroughs' phrase, "control addicts," or people who are habituated or pushing other people around. What it boils down to: controlling them sexually, politically, socially. From page 21 on we have a picture of Dr. Benway, who is specifically referred to as a very highly specialized, scientifically prepared, technologically adept control addict. There is one who, in *this* case, is one who is addicted to controlling and brainwashing large social groups. He is sort of a—this is a parody in a sense of a super, modern, efficient bureaucrat. And also in the pages that follow page 21 and later on, throughout the book, in the Freeland and in the next sections there are almost scientific expositions given by the author of techniques of mass brainwash and mass control, and theories of modern dictatorships, theories of modern police states, presented suggestions for the possibility of using both drugs and electrical shock— somewhere else nerve gasses.

Q. *When these suggestions appear or are dealt with, are they dealt with in the sense of being recommended or being fearful things?*

A. No. I think he is laconically, satirically analyzing them and presenting evidences of these activities in our modern culture, now and then in a science-fiction style, projecting them into the future, nightmare situations if control addicts took over.

THE COURT: *Mr. Ginsberg, have you the book in front of you?*

GINSBERG: Yes, I have a copy, sir.

THE COURT: *Will you refer to page xiv in the Foreword?*

GINSBERG: The Preface?

THE COURT: *Yes. The third paragraph: "And some of us are on Different Kicks and that's a thing out in the open the way I like to see what I eat and visa versa mutatis mutandis as the case may be.* Bill's Naked Lunch Room. . . . *Step right up. . . . Good for young and old, man and bestial. Nothing like a little snake oil to grease the wheels and get a show on the track Jack. Which side are you on? Fro-Zen Hydraulic? Or you want to take a look around with Honest Bill?"*

Now, is there any association between that and the title? And if so, what does it mean to you?

A. He is referring, I think *here* he is referring to the whole book as Bill Burroughs' *Naked Lunch* Room, a lunch room, so, "Step right up," or step in, take a look around. These are the goods he is offering, or these are the ideas he is offering; and he is doing it here in a funny, carnival pitchman style when he is talking about "snake oil" and "good for young and old, man and bestial." The goods he is offering in this paragraph, the ideas he is referring to, are ideas about which he speaks in the next paragraph, the number one World Health Problem, which, he feels, is this tendency on the part of—the tendency in a mechanized civilization for very few people to get control of enormous amounts of power.

THE COURT: *You wouldn't even remotely associate the title with any incidents in this book which portray unnatural acts?*

GINSBERG: Yes, that part of it, too. The unnatural acts portrayed are part of exhibitions of control.

THE COURT: *Would you go so far as to say it is associated with a description of a person eating excrement, served on a plate here in the front part of the book?*

GINSBERG: That particular association had not literally ever occurred to me.

THE COURT: *Well, what do you say now?*

GINSBERG: I am sure that could be included, too. Certainly that would be included also. All levels in the title would be acceptable, I think.

THE COURT: *All right.*

DE GRAZIA: *Is there a discussion in this book of ideas which may be associated with present or future political parties, perhaps, somewhat in the nature of H. G. Wells' and Kafka's writings?*

A. Yes.

*   *   *

Q. *Well, in terms of the question I had begun to ask, or you had begun to answer, concerning political parties or imaginary political parties or projected political parties of the future. Would you identify for us some of these parties as they appear in* Naked Lunch?

A. Yes. From page 144 on, maybe to, say, page 165 or 169, you have a complete and very detailed exposition of about four imaginary political parties. This is the political meat of the book; and I think, ultimately, the most, one of the most interesting parts of the book, and the most significant.

THE COURT: *Is there a conservative party?*

GINSBERG: Oh, yes, there are two conservative parties.

THE COURT: *Would you mind pointing that out to me?*

GINSBERG: It depends upon your definition of "conservative." If you want a really respectable conservative party, there is the Factualists. They are the ones who were against future police state control. They warned of control of the whole, control of the public, as with Dr. Benway. They take, in a sense, a very anti-State or anti-creeping-State position.

THE COURT: *Under what guise does the radical party travel in this book?*

GINSBERG: Since Mr. Burroughs, himself, considers himself a Factualist, then the Factualists might also be considered radical. Burroughs considers himself a Factualist. The extremist party would be both of the left and the right. They would be the Liquefactionists.

THE COURT: *The Birch Society deals with factuality, doesn't it?*

GINSBERG: Actually I haven't read their *prose.*

THE COURT: *All right.*

DE GRAZIA: *Are there extremist parties here?*

A. Yes. There are two extremist parties. There's the Liquefactionists. They are dealt with on page 163.

Q. *In commonsense terms might these be compared with Fascists?*

A. Very much so. The word *liquefy* comes from Fascists or Communists, the liquidation policies spoken of by Stalin. They want to liquidate or liquefy all opposition and everybody is to be liquefied or eliminated except one controlling personality to run the whole world.

Q. *How about Divisionists?*

A. They have a different method of taking over. They have one faction or one man who they refer to as the Sender, who is going to survive by inundating the world with his own replicas. He will divide in two and make replicas of himself. Wherever he travels he will have someone to talk to. He won't feel lonesome any more.

THE COURT: *Divisionists are the homosexuals?*

GINSBERG: Yes. The Divisionist is a parody of a homosexual situation also; but Burroughs *is* attacking the homosexuals in this book also.

THE COURT: *Do the conservatives fall into any particular sex class in this book?*

GINSBERG: Well, I think the conservatives, if we consider the Factualist to be conservative, I think they have a feeling of laissez-faire, whatever is natural, whatever does no harm will be acceptable. When the homosexuality becomes an obsession or a compulsion or an attempt to control other people, then it is to be disapproved of. And I think the Factualists, as a conservative party, have issued several tentative bulletins which are given, I think, on page 167, dealing with this matter.

THE COURT: *Lest anyone take this seriously, of course, obviously it is fantasy.*

GINSBERG: Yes.

THE COURT: *And I think it should be certainly pointed out here, there is absolutely no connection with any political party in the United States, as you and I understand.*

DE GRAZIA: *I think it is futuristic.*

GINSBERG: Yes, as I say, these are anecdotes of imaginary political parties. I think Burroughs would say these *are* representative of major forces moving in the world today. Perhaps that can be justified, inasmuch as there are places in the world that are police states.

THE COURT: *Is there some serious relevance on futuristic political parties?*

GINSBERG: Even present political patterns, not necessarily in America, but all over, *also* in America.

DE GRAZIA: *Do you think, for example, when he speaks of the Divisionist party or the Divisionist group that's been mentioned a few moments ago, that although he is speaking of it, or projecting a kind of futuristic party, political party, that he is really, that he is dealing with, not political parties, but groups today, social groups today that are involved in political struggles in the United States?*

A. Yes.

THE COURT: *What political struggles are homosexuals involved in?*

GINSBERG: That may be a matter of opinion, sir.

DE GRAZIA: *I think he testified they were only a part of the Divisionists.*

GINSBERG: Homosexuality, as seen here, is only one attempt to control other people. There are other ways of doing it besides direct sexual manipulation; another is by brainwashing, equating a brainwasher who tries to—who is sadistically trying to dominate another person—with a homosexual who tries to physically dominate another person.

THE COURT: *Let me ask again: Do you think that he is seriously suggesting that some time in the future* that a political party will be in some way concerned with sex?

GINSBERG: I think so, yes, yes.

DE GRAZIA: *Did 1984—*

THE COURT: *Excuse me. When I say, "Concerned with sex," I don't mean in an attempt to reform perversion. I am not talking about any crusade to make the world a better world in which to live, as you and I understand it today; but I am suggesting that from your answer, what he is trying to portray here, is that some time in the future there will be a political party, for instance, made up of homosexuals?*

GINSBERG: Well, I think, saying that, this has already happened in a sense,—or of sex perverts—and we can point to Hitler, Germany under Hitler, that was a political party that was sexually not right.

THE COURT: *There may be homosexuals in every political party, but I don't think they are predominant.*

DE GRAZIA: *I don't think Mr. Ginsberg is trying to testify to the truth as to whether or not Hitler was perverse or whether or not Fascism or Hitler's political party was homosexual or anything of this kind; but I think that what we are trying, what Mr. Ginsberg is trying to point out is that as the author deals with these questions and some of these categories of people and of parties that he is involved in; and he is dealing with issues of political importance and issues which have a bearing and a relationship to things like even present political parties or political parties of the recent past.*

GINSBERG: May I make a comment, sir?

THE COURT: *Yes.*

GINSBERG: It might clear some of this up. A party, an imaginary party like Divisionists, though homosexuality is one aspect of Divisionism, there are other political aspects. It is not just exclusively—Divisionists are not exclusively another name for homosexuality. The Divisionists in the book have other intentions, like, they are involved in a lot of dealing, with international deals with defective produce, back and forth at one point with the other group, the Liquefactionists. For instance, I think he would compare them, not with the sexual group, but with a race group. He would compare the Liquefactionists with the racists. The Liquefactionists want everybody to be liquefied or eliminated except themselves. They want their image to be dominant over the group here. There would be no sexual connection between the political parties; and the names here, as Liquefactionists—I am saying it applies to *more* than a sexual level. That is one of the puns that is intended.

DE GRAZIA: *Mr. Ginsberg, there are references in the book to the character, the County Clerk?*

A. Yes.

Q. *Which was mentioned—*

THE COURT: *That is within those pages 144 to 165?*

GINSBERG: The County Clerk follows immediately on page 169. We have, I would say, an example of one of the Liquefactionists. It is a complete portrait; but down to modern-down-to-earth newspaper terms, in terms of kinds of people that we have read about in the newspaper—of anti-Negro, and anti-Northern, anti-Semitic, the Southern, white racist bureaucrat. The portrait is perhaps set here as a contemporary example of what Burroughs would refer to as Liquefactionist. I think this is actually one of the most funny and brilliant sections of the book, because it was written, you must remember, before these people came so much into prominence in the newspapers; and it is written in a very beautiful prose style, in the sense that the actual kind of vulgarism and slang of language of the character portrayed is set down very accurately by the author.

THE COURT: *Particularly with reference to the Dalton Street Drugstore.*

GINSBERG: Well, the section goes on, I think, 169 to 177. It's a long monologue by a Southern Sheriff or County Clerk, on page 177, at the end, beginning with: "The Clerk looked at the card suspiciously: 'You don't look like a bone feed mast-fed Razor Back to me. . . . What you think about the Jeeeeews . . .?'
" 'Well, Mr. Anker, you know yourself all a Jew wants to do is doodle a Christian girl. . . . One of these days we'll cut the rest of it off.' "

THE COURT: *What page are you on now?*

GINSBERG: Page 177. It's very funny actually.

THE COURT: *Well, let me ask you this: Is that sentence offensive, grossly offensive to you?*

GINSBERG: I am Jewish; and I should be offended. What Burroughs is doing, he is parodying this monster; he is parodying this anti-Semite.

THE COURT: *It is not offensive to you?*

GINSBERG: No. Burroughs is defending the Jews here. Don't you realize he is making a parody of the monstrous speech and thought processes of a red-necked Southern, hate-filled type, who hates everybody,

Jews, Negroes, Northerners. Burroughs is taking a very moral position, like defending the good here, I think.

* * *

DE GRAZIA: *Would you, Mr. Ginsberg, please tell the Court whether or not, or to what extent* Naked Lunch, *the book, as a book has had importance for your own creative work?*

A. It has had a great deal.

Q. *Whether in its experimental or other forms.*

A. It's had a great deal of effect and influence on me over the many years that I have read and reread the book—and other books—by the writer; this time, particularly, because it was an enormous breakthrough into truthful expression of exactly really what was going on inside his head, with no holds barred. He really confessed completely, put everything down so that anybody could see it.

He found a way to put it down as economically as possible. He found a sort of mosaic method to place all these different elements in order. But the important thing that struck me was the enormous courage it took to make such a total confession. There is absolutely nothing hidden or left out.

Q. *What about the art involved?*

THE COURT: *The literary art.*

A. So far as literary art—

Q. *In answering that question, when you are saying the "enormous courage," etc.*

A. That is part of the literary art, really, I think.

Q. *That he was able to put [it] into artistic form?*

A. Yes. That kind of courage and that kind of impulse as a kind of idealism on the part of the author, I feel is an integral part of literary art. On a more superficial level there is the question of style of composition, like mosaic, I was saying. The passages have been put in place like a mosaic, dealt out with great finesse and great beauty in this book. That the main literary qualities that I have noticed and many other people have noticed have been, first of all—he's got a fantastic ear for common speech, like a doctor giving a lecture on medicine, a junkie dunking poundcake, a narcotics officer confronting the District Supervisor, an Arab street boy in North Africa, a middle aged suburban housewife, a southern County Clerk. This is a fantastic gamut of speech rhythms, diction and still-life style, to be able to reproduce with great, short, economic exactness.

Q. *In this way and the other ways you have indicated you, as a poet, have learned from this book, and others like you, others you know have also learned from it?*

A. Yes. And also there is another thing which is—there is a great deal of very pure language and pure poetry in this book that is as great as any poetry being written in America in my opinion, specifically one line which I would like to read. "Motel . . . Motel . . . Motel . . . broken neon arabesque . . . loneliness moans across the continent like fog horns over still oily water of tidal rivers. . . ."

Q. *Didn't you once write a poem about* Naked Lunch?

A. Yes, a long time ago.

Q. *Do you have it?*

A. Yes.

Q. *What does this appear in?*

A. A book of my own that is called *Reality Sandwiches*.

THE COURT: *Where will I find that book?*

GINSBERG: Probably in Cambridge. It's a poem I wrote early on reading passages here. That was "On Burroughs' Work." May I read it?

Q. *Yes, please do.*

A. The method must be purest meat
   and no symbolic dressing,
actual visions & actual prisons
   as seen then and now.

Prisons and visions presented
   with rare descriptions
corresponding exactly to those
   of Alcatraz and Rose.

A naked lunch is natural to us,
   we eat reality sandwiches.
But allegories are so much lettuce.
   Don't hide the madness.

DE GRAZIA: *No more questions.*

❊ ❊ ❊

DE GRAZIA: . . . . With Your Honor's permission, I would like at this point to read from a letter I received not very long ago from William Burroughs. "The question: What is sex? And the concomitant questions as to what is obscene, impure, is not asked, let alone answered, precisely because of barriers of semantic anxiety which precludes our free or, I think, objective scientific examination of sexual phenomena. How can these phenomena be studied if one is forbidden to write or think about them?

"Unless and until a free examination of sexual manifestations is allowed, man will continue to be controlled by sex rather than controlling. A phenomena totally unknown because deliberately ignored and ruled out as a subject for writing and research.

"What we are dealing with here is a barrier of what can only be termed medieval superstition and fear, precisely the same barrier that held up the natural sciences for some hundreds of years with dogma rather than examination and research. In short, the same objective methods that have been applied to natural science should now be applied to sexual phenomena with a view to understand and control these manifestations. A doctor is not criticized for describing the manifestations and symptoms of an illness, even though the symptoms may be disgusting.

"I feel that a writer has the right to the same freedom. In fact, I think that the time has come for the line between literature and science, a purely arbitrary line, to be erased."

That is the end of the quote.

Your Honor, we were taught this long ago—that is the sentiment expressed by Mr. Burroughs, which I have adopted in my concluding argument—a long time ago, that artists and writers had contributions to make to civilization's knowledge and learning, as great, perhaps, as our scientists do.

Let me quote once more, very briefly this time,

from the founder of modern psychiatric science, Sigmund Freud: "Imaginative writers are valuable colleagues and their testimony is to be rated very highly because they draw on sources that we have not yet made accessible to science. The portrayal of the psychic life of human beings is, of course, the imaginative writer's most special demand. He has always been the forerunner of science and thus scientific psychology, too." A very similar expression was made by one of this country's leading educators, John Dewey; and I quote: "The freeing of the artist in literary presentation is as much a precondition of the desirable creation of adequate opinion on public matters as is the freeing of social inquiry. Artists have always been the real purveyors of news, for it is not the outward happening in itself which is news, but the kindling by it of emotion, perception and appreciation."

Your Honor, I agree, I think the witnesses we heard today, who have read *Naked Lunch*, and have testified for the Court and for us and for you, also agree; I am sure the United States Supreme Court will, if necessary, agree; I hope you agree.

Introduction

I awoke from The Sickness at the age of forty-five,
calm and sane, and in reasonably good health except
for a weakened liver and the look of borrowed flesh
common to all who survive The Sickness. . . . Most
survivors do not remember the delirium in detail. I
apparently took detailed notes on sickness and delirium.
I have no precise memory of writing the notes which
have now been published under the title *Naked Lunch*.
The title was suggested by Jack Kerouac. I did not
understand what the title meant until my recent recovery. The title means exactly what the words say:
NAKED Lunch—a frozen moment when everyone sees
what is on the end of every fork.

The Sickness is drug addiction and I was an addict
for fifteen years. When I say addict I mean an addict
to junk (generic term for opium and/or derivatives in-
cluding all synthetics from demerol to palfium. I have
used junk in many forms: morphine, heroin, delaudid,
eukodal, pantopon, diocodid, diosane, opium, demerol,
dolophine, palfium. I have smoked junk, eaten it,

sniffed it, injected it in vein-skin-muscle, inserted it in rectal suppositories. The needle is not important. Whether you sniff it smoke it eat it or shove it up your ass the result is the same: addiction. When I speak of drug addiction I do not refer to keif, marijuana or any preparation of hashish, mescaline, *Bannisteria Caapi*, LSD6, Sacred Mushrooms or any other drug of the hallucinogen group. . . . There is no evidence that the use of any hallucinogen results in physical dependence. The action of these drugs is physiologically opposite to the action of junk. A lamentable confusion between the two classes of drugs has arisen owing to the zeal of the U. S. and other narcotic departments.

I have seen the exact manner in which the junk virus operates through fifteen years of addiction. The pyramid of junk, one level eating the level below (it is no accident that junk higher-ups are always fat and the addict in the street is always thin) right up to the top or tops since there are many junk pyramids feeding on peoples of the world and all built on basic principles of monopoly:

      1—Never give anything away for nothing.
      2—Never give more than you have to give (always catch the buyer hungry and always make him wait).
      3—Always take everything back if you possibly can.

The Pusher always gets it all back. The addict needs more and more junk to maintain a human form . . . buy off the Monkey.

Junk is the mold of monopoly and possession. The addict stands by while his junk legs carry him straight in on the junk beam to relapse. Junk is quantitative and accurately measurable. The more junk you use the less you have and the more you have the more you use. All the hallucinogen drugs are considered sacred by those who use them—there are Peyote Cults and Bannisteria Cults, Hashish Cults and Mushroom Cults—"the Sacred Mushrooms of Mexico enable a man to see God"—but no one ever suggested that junk is sacred. There are no opium cults. Opium is profane and quantitative like money. I have heard that there was once a beneficent non-habit-forming junk in India. It was called *soma* and is pictured as a beautiful blue tide. If *soma* ever existed the Pusher was there to bottle it and monopolize it and sell it and it turned into plain old time JUNK.

Junk is the ideal product . . . the ultimate merchandise. No sales talk necessary. The client will crawl through a sewer and beg to buy. . . . The junk merchant does not sell his product to the consumer, he sells the consumer to his product. He does not improve and simplify his merchandise. He degrades and simplifies the client. He pays his staff in junk.

Junk yields a basic formula of "evil" virus: *The Algebra of Need*. The face of "evil" is always the face of total need. A dope fiend is a man in total need of dope. Beyond a certain frequency need knows absolutely no limit or control. In the words of total need: *"Wouldn't you?"* Yes you would. You would lie, cheat, inform on your friends, steal, do *anything* to satisfy total need. Because you would be in a state of total sickness, total possession, and not in a position to act in any other way. Dope fiends are sick people who cannot act other than they do. A rabid dog cannot choose but bite. Assuming a self-righteous position is nothing to the purpose unless your purpose be to keep the junk virus in operation. And junk is a big industry. I recall talking to an American who worked for the Aftosa Commission in Mexico. Six hundred a month plus expense account:

"How long will the epidemic last?" I enquired.

"As long as we can keep it going. . . . And yes . . . maybe the aftosa will break out in South America," he said dreamily.

If you wish to alter or annihilate a pyramid of numbers in a serial relation, you alter or remove the bottom number. If we wish to annihilate the junk pyramid, we must start with the bottom of the pyramid: *the Addict in the Street*, and stop tilting quixotically for the "higher ups" so called, all of whom are immediately replaceable. *The addict in the street who must have junk to live is the one irreplaceable factor in the junk equation.* When there are no more addicts to buy junk there will be no junk traffic. As long as junk need exists, someone will service it.

Addicts can be cured or quarantined—that is, allowed a morphine ration under minimal supervision like typhoid carriers. When this is done, junk pyramids of the world will collapse. So far as I know, England is the only country to apply this method to the junk problem. They have about five hundred quarantined addicts in the U.K. In another generation when the quarantined addicts die off and pain killers operating on a non-junk principle are discovered, the junk virus will be like smallpox, a closed chapter—a medical curiosity.

The vaccine that can relegate the junk virus to a

land-locked past is in existence. This vaccine is the Apomorphine Treatment discovered by an English doctor whose name I must withhold pending his permission to use it and to quote from his book covering thirty years of apomorphine treatment of addicts and alcoholics. The compound apomorphine is formed by boiling morphine with hydrochloric acid. It was discovered years before it was used to treat addicts. For many years the only use for apomorphine which has no narcotic or pain-killing properties was as an emetic to induce vomiting in cases of poisoning. It acts directly on the vomiting center in the back brain.

I found this vaccine at the end of the junk line. I lived in one room in the Native Quarter of Tangier. I had not taken a bath in a year nor changed my clothes or removed them except to stick a needle every hour in the fibrous grey wooden flesh of terminal addiction. I never cleaned or dusted the room. Empty ampule boxes and garbage piled to the ceiling. Light and water long since turned off for non-payment. I did absolutely nothing. I could look at the end of my shoe for eight hours. I was only roused to action when the hourglass of junk ran out. If a friend came to visit—and they rarely did since who or what was left to visit— I sat there not caring that he had entered my field of vision—a grey screen always blanker and fainter— and not caring when he walked out of it. If he had died on the spot I would have sat there looking at my shoe waiting to go through his pockets. Wouldn't you? Because I never had enough junk—no one ever does. Thirty grains of morphine a day and it still was not enough. And long waits in front of the drugstore. Delay is a rule in the junk business. The Man is never on time. This is no accident. There are no accidents in the junk world. The addict is taught again and again exactly what will happen if he does not score for his junk ration. Get up that money or else. And suddenly my habit began to jump and jump. Forty, sixty grains a day. And it still was not enough. And I could not pay.

I stood there with my last check in my hand and realized that it was my last check. I took the next plane for London.

The doctor explained to me that apomorphine acts on the back brain to regulate the metabolism and normalize the blood stream in such a way that the enzyme system of addiction is destroyed over a period of four or five days. Once the back brain is regulated apomorphine can be discontinued and only used in case of relapse. (No one would take apomorphine for kicks. *Not one case of addiction to apomorphine has ever been recorded.*) I agreed to undergo treatment and entered a nursing home. For the first twenty-four hours I was literally insane and paranoid as many addicts are in severe withdrawal. This delirium was dispersed by twenty-four hours of intensive apomorphine treatment. The doctor showed me the chart. I had received minute amounts of morphine that could not possibly account for my lack of the more severe withdrawal symptoms such as leg and stomach cramps, fever and my own special symptom, The Cold Burn, like a vast hive covering the body and rubbed with menthol. Every addict has his own special symptom that cracks all control.

There was a missing factor in the withdrawal equation —that factor could only be apomorphine.

I saw the apomorphine treatment really work. Eight days later I left the nursing home eating and sleeping normally. I remained completely off junk for two full years—a twelve year record. I did relapse for some months as a result of pain and illness. Another apomorphine cure has kept me off junk through this writing.

The apomorphine cure is qualitatively different from other methods of cure. I have tried them all. Short reduction, slow reduction, cortisone, antihistamines, tranquilizers, sleeping cures, tolserol, reserpine. None of these cures lasted beyond the first opportunity to relapse. I can say definitely that I was never *metabolically* cured until I took the apomorphine cure. The overwhelming relapse statistics from the Lexington Narcotic Hospital have led many doctors to say that addiction is not curable. They use a dolophine reduction cure at Lexington and have never tried apomorphine so far as I know. In fact, this method of treatment has been largely neglected. No research has been done with variations of the apomorphine formula or with synthetics. No doubt substances fifty times stronger than apomorphine could be developed and the side effect of vomiting eliminated.

Apomorphine is a metabolic and psychic regulator that can be discontinued as soon as it has done its work. The world is deluged with tranquilizers and energizers but this unique regulator has not received attention. No research has been done by any of the large pharmaceutical companies. I suggest that research with variations of apomorphine and synthesis of it will open a new medical frontier extending far beyond the problem of addiction.

The smallpox vaccine was opposed by a vociferous lunatic group of anti-vaccinationists. No doubt a scream of protest will go up from interested or unbalanced individuals as the junk virus is shot out from under them. Junk is big business; there are always cranks and operators. They must not be allowed to interfere with the essential work of inoculation treatment and quarantine. *The junk virus is public health problem number one of the world today.*

Since *Naked Lunch* treats this health problem, it is necessarily brutal, obscene and disgusting. Sickness is often repulsive details not for weak stomachs.

Certain passages in the book that have been called pornographic were written as a tract against Capital Punishment in the manner of Jonathan Swift's *Modest Proposal.* These sections are intended to reveal capital punishment as the obscene, barbaric and disgusting anachronism that it is. As always the lunch is naked. If civilized countries want to return to Druid Hanging Rites in the Sacred Grove or to drink blood with the Aztecs and feed their Gods with blood of human sacrifice, let them see what they actually eat and drink. Let them see what is on the end of that long newspaper spoon.

I have almost completed a sequel to *Naked Lunch.* A mathematical extension of the Algebra of Need beyond the junk virus. Because there are many forms of addiction I think that they all obey basic laws. In the words of Heiderberg: "This may not be the best of all possible universes but it may well prove to be one of the simplest." If man can *see*.

Post Script. . . . Wouldn't You?

And speaking *Personally* and if a man speaks any other way we might as well start looking for his Protoplasm Daddy or Mother Cell. . . . *I Don't Want To Hear Any More Tired Old Junk Talk And Junk Con.* . . . The same things said a million times and more and there is no point in saying anything because *NOTHING Ever Happens* in the junk world.

Only excuse for this tired death route is THE KICK when the junk circuit is cut off for the non-payment and the junk-skin dies of junk-lack and overdose of time and the Old Skin has forgotten the skin game simplifying a way under the junk cover the way skins will. . . . A condition of total exposure is precipitated when the Kicking Addict cannot choose but see smell and listen. . . . Watch out for the cars. . . .

It is clear that junk is a Round-the-World-Push-an-Opium-Pellet-with-Your-Nose-Route. Strictly for Scarabs—stumble bum junk heap. And as such report to disposal. Tired of seeing it around.

Junkies always beef about *The Cold* as they call it, turning up their black coat collars and clutching their withered necks . . . pure junk con. A junky does not want to be warm, he wants to be Cool-Cooler-COLD. But he wants The Cold like he wants His Junk—NOT OUTSIDE where it does him no good but INSIDE so he can sit around with a spine like a frozen hydraulic jack . . . his metabolism approaching Absolute ZERO. TERMINAL addicts often go two months without a bowel move and the intestines make with sit-down-adhesions—Wouldn't you?—requiring the intervention of an apple corer or its surgical equivalent. . . . Such is life in The Old Ice House. Why move around and waste TIME?

Room for One More Inside, Sir.

Some entities are on thermodynamic kicks. They invented thermodynamics. . . . Wouldn't you?

And some of us are on Different Kicks and that's a thing out in the open the way I like to see what I eat and visa versa mutatis mutandis as the case may be. *Bill's Naked Lunch Room*. . . . Step right up. . . . Good for young and old, man and bestial. Nothing like a little snake oil to grease the wheels and get a show on the track Jack. Which side are you on? Fro-Zen Hydraulic? Or you want to take a look around with Honest Bill?

So that's the World Health Problem I was talking about back in The Article. The Prospect Before Us Friends of MINE. Do I hear muttering about a personal razor and some bush league short con artist who is known to have invented The Bill? Wouldn't You? The razor belonged to a man named Occam and he was not a scar collector. Ludwig Wittgenstein *Tractatus Logico-Phlilosophicus*: "If a proposition is NOT NECESSARY it is MEANINGLESS and approaching MEANING ZERO."

"And what is More UNNECESSARY than junk if You Don't Need it?"

Answer: "Junkies, if you are not ON JUNK."

I tell you boys, I've heard some tired conversation

but no other OCCUPATION GROUP can approximate that old thermodynamic junk Slow-DOWN. Now your heroin addict does not say hardly anything and that I can stand. But your Opium "Smoker" is more active since he still has a tent and a Lamp . . . and maybe 7-9-10 lying up in there like hibernating reptiles keep the temperature up to Talking Level: How low the other junkies are "whereas We—WE have this tent and this lamp and this tent and this lamp and this tent and nice and warm in here nice and warm nice and IN HERE and nice and OUTSIDE ITS COLD. . . . ITS COLD OUTSIDE where the dross eaters and the needle boys won't last two years not six months hardly won't last stumble bum around and there is no class in them. . . . But WE SIT HERE and never increase the DOSE . . . never—never increase the dose never except TONIGHT is a SPECIAL OCCASION with all the dross eaters and needle boys out there in the cold. . . . And we never eat it never never never eat it. . . . Excuse please while I take a trip to The Source Of Living Drops they all have in pocket and opium pellets shoved up the ass in a finger stall with the Family Jewels and the other shit.

Room for one more inside, Sir.

Well when that record starts around for the billionth light year and never the tape shall change us non-junkies take drastic action and the men separate out from the Junk boys.

Only way to protect yourself against this horrid peril is come over HERE and shack up with Charybdis. . . . Treat you right kid. . . . Candy and cigarettes.

I am after fifteen years in that tent. In and out in

and out in and OUT. *Over* and *Out*. So listen to Old Uncle Bill Burroughs who invented the Burroughs Adding Machine Regulator Gimmick on the Hydraulic Jack Principle no matter how you jerk the handle result is always the same for given co-ordinates. Got my training early . . . wouldn't you?

Paregoric Babies of the World Unite. We have nothing to lose but Our Pushers. And THEY are NOT NECESSARY.

Look down LOOK DOWN along that junk road before you travel there and get in with the Wrong Mob. . . .

A word to the wise guy.

—William S. Burroughs

I can feel the heat closing in, feel them out there making their moves, setting up their devil doll stool pigeons, crooning over my spoon and dropper I throw away at Washington Square Station, vault a turnstile and two flights down the iron stairs, catch an uptown A train . . . Young, good looking, crew cut, Ivy League, advertising exec type fruit holds the door back for me. I am evidently his idea of a character. You know the type comes on with bartenders and cab drivers, talking about right hooks and the Dodgers, call the counterman in Nedick's by his first name. A real asshole. And right on time this narcotics dick in a white trench coat (imagine tailing somebody in a white trench coat—trying to pass as a fag I guess) hit the platform. I can hear the way he would say it holding my outfit in his left hand, right hand on his piece: "I think you dropped something, fella."

But the subway is moving.

"So long flatfoot!" I yell, giving the fruit his B production. I look into the fruit's eyes, take in the white teeth, the Florida tan, the two hundred dollar sharkskin suit, the button-down Brooks Brothers shirt and carrying *The News* as a prop. "Only thing I read is Little Abner."

A square wants to come on hip. . . . Talks about "pod," and smoke it now and then, and keeps some around to offer the fast Hollywood types.

"Thanks, kid," I say, "I can see you're one of our own." His face lights up like a pinball machine, with stupid, pink effect.

"Grassed on me he did," I said morosely. (Note: Grass is English thief slang for inform.) I drew closer and laid my dirty junky fingers on his sharkskin sleeve. "And us blood brothers in the same dirty needle. I can tell you in confidence he is due for a hot shot." (Note: This is a cap of poison junk sold to addict for liquidation purposes. Often given to informers. Usually the hot shot is strychnine since it tastes and looks like junk.)

"Ever see a hot shot hit, kid? I saw the Gimp catch one in Philly. We rigged his room with a one-way whorehouse mirror and charged a sawski to watch it. He never got the needle out of his arm. They don't if the shot is right. That's the way they find them, dropper full of clotted blood hanging out of a blue arm. The look in his eyes when it hit—Kid, it was tasty. . . .

"Recollect when I am traveling with the Vigilante, best Shake Man in the industry. Out in Chi . . . We is working the fags in Lincoln Park. So one night the Vigilante turns up for work in cowboy boots and a black vest with a hunka tin on it and a lariat slung over his shoulder.

"So I says: 'What's with you? You wig already?'

"He just looks at me and says: 'Fill your hand stranger' and hauls out an old rusty six shooter and I take off across Lincoln Park, bullets cutting all around me. And he hangs three fags before the fuzz nail him. I mean the Vigilante earned his moniker. . . .

"Ever notice how many expressions carry over from queers to con men? Like 'raise,' letting someone know you are in the same line?

" 'Get her!'

" 'Get the Paregoric Kid giving that mark the build up!'

" 'Eager Beaver wooing him much too fast.'

"The Shoe Store Kid (he got that moniker shaking down fetishists in shoe stores) say: 'Give it to a mark with K.Y. and he will come back moaning for more.' And when the Kid spots a mark he begin to breathe heavy. His face swells and his lips turn purple like an Eskimo in heat. Then slow, slow he comes on the mark, feeling for him, palpating him with fingers of rotten ectoplasm.

"The Rube has a sincere little boy look, burns through him like blue neon. That one stepped right off a *Saturday Evening Post* cover with a string of bullheads, and preserved himself in junk. His marks never beef and the Bunko people are really carrying a needle for the Rube. One day Little Boy Blue starts to slip, and what crawls out would make an ambulance attendant puke. The

Rube flips in the end, running through empty automats and subway stations, screaming: 'Come back, kid!! Come back!!' and follows his boy right into the East River, down through condoms and orange peels, mosaic of floating newspapers, down into the silent black ooze with gangsters in concrete, and pistols pounded flat to avoid the probing finger of prurient ballistic experts."

And the fruit is thinking: "What a character!! Wait till I tell the boys in Clark's about this one." He's a character collector, would stand still for Joe Gould's seagull act. So I put it on him for a sawski and make a meet to sell him some "pod" as he calls it, thinking, "I'll catnip the jerk." (Note: Catnip smells like marijuana when it burns. Frequently passed on the incautious or uninstructed.)

"Well," I said, tapping my arm, "duty calls. As one judge said to another: 'Be just and if you can't be just, be arbitrary.'"

I cut into the automat and there is Bill Gains huddled in someone else's overcoat looking like a 1910 banker with paresis, and Old Bart, shabby and inconspicuous, dunking pound cake with his dirty fingers, shiny over the dirt.

I had some uptown customers Bill took care of, and Bart knew a few old relics from hop smoking times, spectral janitors, grey as ashes, phantom porters sweeping out dusty halls with a slow old man's hand, coughing and spitting in the junk-sick dawn, retired asthmatic fences in theatrical hotels, Pantopon Rose the old madam from Peoria, stoical Chinese waiters never show sickness. Bart sought them out with his old junky walk, patient and cautious and slow, dropped into their blood-less hands a few hours of warmth.

I made the round with him once for kicks. You know how old people lose all shame about eating, and it makes you puke to watch them? Old junkies are the same about junk. They gibber and squeal at sight of it. The spit hangs off their chin, and their stomach rumbles and all their guts grind in peristalsis while they cook up, dissolving the body's decent skin, you expect any moment a great blob of protoplasm will flop right out and surround the junk. Really disgust you to see it.

"Well, my boys will be like that one day," I thought philosophically. "Isn't life peculiar?"

So back downtown by the Sheridan Square Station in case the dick is lurking in a broom closet.

Like I say it couldn't last. I knew they were out there powowing and making their evil fuzz magic, putting dolls of me in Leavenworth. "No use sticking needles in that one, Mike."

I hear they got Chapin with a doll. This old eunuch dick just sat in the precinct basement hanging a doll of him day and night, year in year out. And when Chapin hanged in Connecticut, they find this old creep with his neck broken.

"He fell downstairs," they say. You know the old cop bullshit.

Junk is surrounded by magic and taboos, curses and amulets. I could find my Mexico City connection by radar. "Not this street, the next, right . . . now left. Now right again," and there he is, toothless old woman face and cancelled eyes.

I know this one pusher walks around humming a tune and everybody he passes takes it up. He is so grey and spectral and anonymous they don't see him and think it is their own mind humming the tune. So the customers come in on *Smiles,* or *I'm in the Mood for Love,* or *They Say We're Too Young to Go Steady,* or whatever the song is for that day. Sometime you can see maybe fifty ratty-looking junkies squealing sick, running along behind a boy with a harmonica, and there is The Man on a cane seat throwing bread to the swans, a fat queen drag walking his Afghan hound through the East Fifties, an old wino pissing against an El post, a radical Jewish student giving out leaflets in Washington Square, a tree surgeon, an exterminator, an advertising fruit in Nedick's where he calls the counterman by his first name. The world network of junkies, tuned on a cord of rancid jissom, tying up in furnished rooms, shivering in the junk-sick morning. (Old Pete men suck the black smoke in the Chink laundry back room and Melancholy Baby dies from an overdose of time or cold turkey withdrawal of breath.) In Yemen, Paris, New Orleans, Mexico City and Istanbul—shivering under the air hammers and the steam shovels, shrieked junky curses at one another neither of us heard, and The Man leaned out of a passing steam roller and I coped in a bucket of tar. (Note: Istanbul is being torn down and rebuilt, especially shabby junk quarters. Istanbul has more heroin junkies than NYC.) The living and the dead, in sickness or on the nod, hooked or kicked or hooked again, come in on the junk beam and the Connection is eating Chop Suey on Dolores Street, Mexico D.F., dunking pound cake in the automat, chased up Exchange Place by a baying pack of People. (Note: People is New Orleans slang for narcotic fuzz.)

The old Chinaman dips river water into a rusty tin can, washes down a yen pox hard and black as a cinder. (Note: Yen pox is the ash of smoked opium.)

Well, the fuzz has my spoon and dropper, and I know they are coming in on my frequency led by this blind pigeon known as Willy the Disk. Willy has a round, disk mouth lined with sensitive, erectile black hairs. He is blind from shooting in the eyeball, his nose and palate eaten away sniffing H, his body a mass of scar tissue hard and dry as wood. He can only eat the shit now with that mouth, sometimes sways out on a long tube of ectoplasm, feeling for the silent frequency of junk. He follows my trail all over the city into rooms I move out already, and the fuzz walks in some newlyweds from Sioux Falls.

"All right, Lee!! Come out from behind that strap-on! We know you" and pull the man's prick off straight-away.

Now Willy is getting hot and you can hear him always out there in darkness (he only functions at night) whimpering, and feel the terrible urgency of that blind, seeking mouth. When they move in for the bust, Willy goes all out of control, and his mouth eats a hole right through the door. If the cops weren't there to restrain him with a stock probe, he would suck the juice right out of every junky he ran down.

I knew, and everybody else knew they had the Disk on me. And if my kid customers ever hit the stand: "He force me to commit all kinda awful sex acts in return for junk" I could kiss the street good-bye.

So we stock up on H, buy a second-hand Studebaker, and start West.

The Vigilante copped out as a schizo possession case:
"I was standing outside myself trying to stop those hangings with ghost fingers. . . . I am a ghost wanting what every ghost wants—a body—after the Long Time moving through odorless alleys of space where no life is only the colorless no smell of death. . . . Nobody can breathe and smell it through pink convolutions of gristle laced with crystal snot, time shit and black blood filters of flesh."

He stood there in elongated court room shadow, his face torn like a broken film by lusts and hungers of larval organs stirring in the tentative ectoplasmic flesh of junk kick (ten days on ice at time of the First Hearing) flesh that fades at the first silent touch of junk.

I saw it happen. Ten pounds lost in ten minutes standing with the syringe in one hand holding his pants up with the other, his abdicated flesh burning in a cold yellow halo, there in the New York hotel room . . . night table littter of candy boxes, cigarette butts cascading out of three ashtrays, mosaic of sleepless nights and sudden food needs of the kicking addict nursing his baby flesh. . . .

The Vigilante is prosecuted in Federal Court under a lynch bill and winds up in a Federal Nut House specially designed for the containment of ghosts: precise, prosaic impact of objects . . . washstand . . . door . . . toilet . . . bars . . . there they are . . . this is it . . . all lines cut . . . nothing beyond . . . Dead End . . . And the Dead End in every face. . . .

The physical changes were slow at first, then jumped forward in black klunks, falling through his slack tissue, washing away the human lines. . . . In his place of total darkness mouth and eyes are one organ that leaps forward to snap with transparent teeth . . . but no organ is constant as regards either function or position . . . sex organs sprout anywhere . . . rectums open, defecate and close . . . the entire organism changes color and consistency in split-second adjustments. . . .

The Rube is a social liability with his attacks as he calls them. The Mark Inside was coming up on him and that's a rumble nobody can cool; outside Philly he jumps out to con a prowl car and the fuzz takes one look at his face and bust all of us.

Seventy-two hours and five sick junkies in the cell with us. Now not wishing to break out my stash in front of these hungry coolies, it takes maneuvering and laying of gold on the turnkey before we are in a separate cell.

Provident junkies, known as squirrels, keep stashes against a bust. Every time I take a shot I let a few drops fall into my vest pocket, the lining is stiff with stuff. I had a plastic dropper in my shoe and a safety-pin stuck in my belt. You know how this pin and dropper routine is put down: "She seized a safety pin caked with blood and rust, gouged a great hole in her leg which seemed to hang open like an obscene, festering mouth waiting for unspeakable congress with the dropper which she now plunged out of sight into the gaping wound. But her hideous galvanized need (hunger of insects in dry places) has broken the dropper off deep in the flesh of her ravaged thigh (looking rather like a poster on soil

erosion). But what does she care? She does not even
bother to remove the splintered glass, looking down at
her bloody haunch with the cold blank eyes of a meat
trader. What does she care for the atom bomb, the bed
bugs, the cancer rent, Friendly Finance waiting to re-
possess her delinquent flesh. . . . Sweet dreams, Pantopon Rose."

The real scene you pinch up some leg flesh and make
a quick stab hole with a pin. Then fit the dropper *over*,
not in the hole and feed the solution slow and careful
so it doesn't squirt out the sides. . . . When I grabbed
the Rube's thigh the flesh came up like wax and stayed
there, and a slow drop of pus oozed out the hole. And
I never touched a living body cold as the Rube there in
Philly. . . .

I decided to lop him off if it meant a smother party.
(This is a rural English custom designed to eleminate
aged and bedfast dependents. A family so afflicted
throws a "smother party" where the guests pile mat-
tresses on the old liability, climb up on top of the mat-
tresses and lush themselves out.) The Rube is a drag on
the industry and should be led out into the skid rows of
the world. (This is an African practice. Official known
as the "Leader Out" has the function of taking old
characters out into the jungle and leaving them there.)

The Rube's attacks become an habitual condition.
Cops, doormen, dogs, secretaries snarl at his approach.
The blond God has fallen to untouchable vileness. Con
men don't change, they break, shatter—explosions of
matter in cold interstellar space, drift away in cosmic
dust, leave the empty body behind. Hustlers of the

world, there is one Mark you cannot beat: The Mark Inside. . . .

I left the Rube standing on a corner, red brick slums to the sky, under a steady rain of soot. "Going to hit this croaker I know. Right back with that good pure drug-store M. . . . No, you wait here—don't want him to rumble you." No matter how long, Rube, wait for me right on that corner. Goodbye, Rube, goodbye kid. . . . Where do they go when they walk out and leave the body behind?

Chicago: invisible hierarchy of decorticated wops, smell of atrophied gangsters, earthbound ghost hits you at North and Halstead, Cicero, Lincoln Park, pan-handler of dreams, past invading the present, rancid magic of slot machines and roadhouses.

Into the Interior: a vast subdivision, antennae of tele-vision to the meaningless sky. In lifeproof houses they hover over the young, sop up a little of what they shut out. Only the young bring anything in, and they are not young very long. (Through the bars of East St. Louis lies the dead frontier, riverboat days.) Illinois and Mis-souri, miasma of mound-building peoples, groveling worship of the Food Source, cruel and ugly festivals, dead-end horror of the Centipede God reaches from Moundville to the lunar deserts of coastal Peru.

America is not a young land: it is old and dirty and evil before the settlers, before the Indians. The evil is there waiting.

And always cops: smooth college-trained state cops, practiced, apologetic patter, electronic eyes weigh your car and luggage, clothes and face; snarling big city dicks, soft-spoken country sheriffs with something black and menacing in old eyes color of a faded grey flannel shirt. . . .

And always car trouble: in St. Louis traded the 1942 Studebaker in (it has a built-in engineering flaw like the Rube) on an old Packard limousine heated up and barely made Kansas City, and bought a Ford turned out to be an oil burner, packed it in on a jeep we push too hard (they are no good for highway driving)—and burn something out inside, rattling around, went back to the old Ford V-8. Can't beat that engine for getting there, oil burner or no.

And the U.S. drag closes around us like no other drag in the world, worse than the Andes, high mountain towns, cold wind down from postcard mountains, thin air like death in the throat, river towns of Ecuador, malaria grey as junk under black Stetson, muzzle loading shotguns. vultures pecking through the mud streets—and what hits you when you get off the Malmo Ferry in (no juice tax on the ferry) Sweden knocks all that cheap, tax free juice right out of you and brings you all the way down: averted eyes and the cemetery in the middle of town (every town in Sweden seems to be built around a cemetery), and nothing to do in the afternoon, not a bar not a movie and I blasted my last stick of Tangier tea and I said, "K.E. let's get right back on that ferry."

But there is no drag like U.S. drag. You can't see it, you don't know where it comes from. Take one of those cocktail lounges at the end of a subdivision street—every block of houses has its own bar and drugstore and market and liquorstore. You walk in and it hits you. But where does it come from?

Not the bartender, not the customers, nor the cream-colored plastic rounding the bar stools, nor the dim neon. Not even the TV.

And our habits build up with the drag, like cocaine will build you up staying ahead of the C bring-down. And the junk was running low. So there we are in this no-horse town strictly from cough syrup. And vomited up the syrup and drove on and on, cold spring wind whistling through that old heap around our shivering sick sweating bodies and the cold you always come down with when the junk runs out of you. . . . On through the peeled landscape, dead armadillos in the road and vultures over the swamp and cypress stumps. Motels with beaverboard walls, gas heater, thin pink blankets.

Itinerant short con and carny hyp men have burned down the croakers of Texas. . . .

And no one in his right mind would hit a Louisiana croaker. State Junk Law.

Came at last to Houston where I know a druggist. I haven't been there in five years but he looks up and makes me with one quick look and just nods and says: "Wait over at the counter. . . ."

So I sit down and drink a cup of coffee and after a while he comes and sits beside me and says, "What do you want?"

"A quart of PG and a hundred nembies."

He nods, "Come back in half an hour."

So when I come back he hands me a package and says, "That's fifteen dollars. . . . Be careful."

Shooting PG is a terrible hassle, you have to burn out the alcohol first, then freeze out the camphor and draw this brown liquid off with a dropper—have to shoot it in the vein or you get an abscess, and usually end up with an abscess no matter where you shoot it. Best deal is to drink it with goof balls. . . . So we pour it in a Pernod bottle and start for New Orleans past iridescent lakes and orange gas flares, and swamps and garbage heaps, alligators crawling around in broken bottles and tin cans, neon arabesques of motels, marooned pimps scream obscenities at passing cars from islands of rubbish. . . .

New Orleans is a dead museum. We walk around Exchange Place breathing PG and find The Man right away. It's a small place and the fuzz always knows who is pushing so he figures what the hell does it matter and sells to anybody. We stock up on H and backtrack for Mexico.

Back through Lake Charles and the dead slot-machine country, south end of Texas, nigger-killing sheriffs look us over and check the car papers. Something falls off you when you cross the border into Mexico, and suddenly the landscape hits you straight with nothing between you and it, desert and mountains and vultures; little wheeling specks and others so close you can hear wings cut the air (a dry husking sound), and when they spot something they pour out of the blue sky, that shattering bloody blue sky of Mexico, down in a black funnel. . . . Drove all night, came at dawn to a warm misty place, barking dogs and the sound of running water.

"Thomas and Charlie," I said.

"What?"

"That's the name of this town. Sea level. We climb straight up from here ten thousand feet." I took a fix and went to sleep in the back seat. She was a good driver. You can tell as soon as someone touches the wheel.

Mexico City where Lupita sits like an Aztec Earth Goddess doling out her little papers of lousy shit.

"Selling is more of a habit than using," Lupita says. Nonusing pushers have a contact habit, and that's one you can't kick. Agents get it too. Take Bradley the Buyor. Best narcotics agent in the industry. Anyone would make him for junk. (Note: Make in the sense of dig or size up.) I mean he can walk up to a pusher and score direct. He is so anonymous, grey and spectral the pusher don't remember him afterwards. So he twists one after the other. . . .

Well the Buyer comes to look more and more like a junky. He can't drink. He can't get it up. His teeth fall out. (Like pregnant women lose their teeth feeding the stranger, junkies lose their yellow fangs feeding the monkey.) He is all the time sucking on a candy bar. Baby Ruths he digs special. "It really disgust you to see the Buyer sucking on them candy bars so nasty," a cop says.

The Buyer takes on an ominous grey-green color. Fact is his body is making its own junk or equivalent. The Buyer has a steady connection. A Man Within you might say. Or so he thinks. "I'll just set in my room," he says. "Fuck 'em all. Squares on both sides. I am the only complete man in the industry."

But a yen comes on him like a great black wind

through the bones. So the Buyer hunts up a young junky and gives him a paper to make it.

"Oh all right," the boy says. "So what you want to make?"

"I just want to rub up against you and get fixed."

"Ugh . . . Well all right. . . . But why cancha just get physical like a human?"

Later the boy is sitting in a Waldorf with two colleagues dunking pound cake. "Most distasteful thing I ever stand still for," he says. "Some way he make himself all soft like a blob of jelly and surround me so nasty. Then he gets wet all over like with green slime. So I guess he come to some kinda awful climax. . . . I come near wigging with that green stuff all over me, and he stink like a old rotten canteloupe."

"Well it's still an easy score."

The boy sighed resignedly; "Yes, I guesss you can get used to anything. I've got a meet with him again tomorrow."

The Buyer's habit keeps getting heavier. He needs a recharge every half hour. Sometimes he cruises the precincts and bribes the turnkey to let him in with a cell of junkies. It get to where no amount of contact will fix him. At this point he receives a summons from the District Supervisor:

"Bradley, your conduct has given rise to rumors—and I hope for your sake they are no more than that—so unspeakably distasteful that . . . I mean Caesar's wife . . . hrump . . . that is, the Department must be above suspicion . . . certainly above such suspicions as you have seemingly aroused. You are lowering the entire tone of the industry. We are prepared to accept your immediate resignation."

The Buyer throws himself on the ground and crawls over to the D.S. "No, Boss Man, no . . . The Department is my very lifeline."

He kisses the D.S.'s hand thrusting his fingers into his mouth (the D.S. must feel his toothless gums) complaining he has lost his teeth "inna thervith." "Please Boss Man. I'll wipe your ass, I'll wash out your dirty condoms, I'll polish your shoes with the oil on my nose. . . ."

"Really, this is most distasteful! Have you no pride? I must tell you I feel a distinct revulsion. I mean there is something, well, rotten about you, and you smell like a compost heap." He put a scented handkerchief in front of his face. "I must ask you to leave this office at once."

"I'll do anything, Boss, *anything*." His ravaged green face splits in a horrible smile. "I'm still young, Boss, and I'm pretty strong when I get my blood up."

The D.S. retches into his handkerchief and points to the door with a limp hand. The Buyer stands up looking at the D.S. dreamily. His body begins to dip like a dowser's wand. He flows forward. . . .

"No! No!" screams the D.S.

"Schlup . . . schlup schlup." An hour later they find the Buyer on the nod in the D.S.'s chair. The D.S. has disappeared without a trace.

The Judge: "Everything indicates that you have, in some unspeakable manner uh . . . assimilated the District Supervisor. Unfortunately there is no proof. I would recommend that you be confined or more accurately contained in some institution, but I know of no place suitable for a man of your caliber. I must reluctantly order your release."

"That one should stand in an aquarium," says the arresting officer.

The Buyer spreads terror throughout the industry. Junkies and agents disappear. Like a vampire bat he gives off a narcotic effluvium, a dank green mist that anesthetizes his victims and renders them helpless in his enveloping presence. And once he has scored he holes up for several days like a gorged boa constrictor. Finally he is caught in the act of digesting the Narcotics Commissioner and destroyed with a flame thrower—the court of inquiry ruling that such means were justified in that the Buyer had lost his human citizenship and was, in consequence, a creature without species and a menace to the narcotics industry on all levels.

In Mexico the gimmick is to find a local junky with a government script whereby they are allowed a certain quantity every month. Our Man was Old Ike who had spent most of his life in the States.

"I was travelling with Irene Kelly and her was a sporting woman. In Butte, state of Montany, she gets the coke horors and run through the hotel screaming Chinese coppers chase her with meat cleavers. I knew this cop in Chicago sniff coke used to come in form of crystals, blue crystals. So he go nuts and start screaming the Federals is after him and run down this alley and stick his head in the garbage can. And I said, 'What you think you are doing?' and he say, 'Get away or I shoot you. I got myself hid good.' "

We are getting some C on RX at this time. Shoot it in the mainline, son. You can smell it going in, clean and cold in your nose and throat then a rush of pure pleasure right through the brain lighting up those C connections. Your head shatters in white explosions. Ten minutes later you want another shot . . . you will walk across town for another shot. But if you can't score for C you eat, sleep and forget about it.

This is a yen of the brain alone, a need without feeling and without body, earthbound ghost need, rancid ectoplasm swept out by an old junky coughing and spitting in the sick morning.

One morning you wake up and take a speed ball, and feel bugs under your skin. 1890 cops with black mustaches block the doors and lean in through the windows snarling their lips back from blue and bold embossed badges. Junkies march through the room singing the Moslem Funeral Song, bear the body of Bill Gains, stigmata of his needle wounds glow with a soft blue flame. Purposeful schizophrenic detectives sniff at your chamber pot.

It's the coke horrors. . . . Sit back and play it cool and shoot in plenty of that GI M.

Day of the Dead: I got the chucks and ate my little Willy's sugar skull. He cried and I had to go out for another. Walked past the cocktail lounge where they blasted the Jai Lai bookie.

In Cuernavaca or was it Taxco? Jane meets a pimp trombone player and disappears in a cloud of tea smoke.

The pimp is one of these vibration and dietary artists —which is a means he degrades the female sex by forcing his chicks to swallow all this shit. He was continually enlarging his theories . . . he would quiz a chick and threaten to walk out if she hadn't memorized every nuance of his latest assault on logic and the human image.

"Now, baby. I got it here to give. But if you won't receive it there's just nothing I can do."

He was a ritual tea smoker and very puritanical about junk the way some teaheads are. He claimed tea put him in touch with supra blue gravitational fields. He had ideas on every subject: what kind of underwear was healthy, when to drink water, and how to wipe your ass. He had a shiny red face and great spreading smooth nose, little red eyes that lit up when he looked at a chick and went out when he looked at anything else. His shoulders were very broad and suggested deformity. He acted as if other men did not exist, conveying his restaurant and store orders to male personnel through a female intermediary. And no Man ever invaded his blighted, secret place.

So he is putting down junk and coming on with tea. I take three drags, Jane looked at him and her flesh crystallized. I leaped up screaming "I got the fear!" and ran out of the house. Drank a beer in a little restaurant —mosaic bar and soccer scores and bullfight posters— and waited for the bus to town.

A year later in Tangier I heard she was dead.

BENWAY

So I am assigned to engage the services of Doctor Benway for Islam Inc.

Dr. Benway had been called in as advisor to the Freeland Republic, a place given over to free love and continual bathing. The citizens are well adjusted, co-operatives, honest, tolerant and above all clean. But the invoking of Benway indicates all is not well behind that hygienic façade: Benway is a manipulator and coordinator of symbol systems, an expert on all phases of interrogation, brainwashing and control. I have not seen Benway since his precipitate departure from Annexia, where his assignment had been T.D.—Total Demoralization. Benway's first act was to abolish concentration camps, mass arrest and, except under certain limited and special circumstances, the use of torture.

"I deplore brutality," he said. "It's not efficient. On the other hand, prolonged mistreatment, short of physical violence, gives rise, when skillfully applied, to anxiety and a feeling of special guilt. A few rules or rather guiding principles are to be borne in mind. The subject must not realize that the mistreatment is a deliberate attack of an anti-human enemy on his personal identity. He must be made to feel that he deserves *any* treatment he receives because there is something (never specified) horribly wrong with him. The naked need of the control addicts must be decently covered by an arbitrary and intricate bureaucracy so that the subject cannot contact his enemy direct."

Every citizen of Annexia was required to apply for and carry on his person at all times a whole portfolio of documents. Citizens were subject to be stopped in the street at any time; and the Examiner, who might be in plain clothes, in various uniforms, often in a bathing suit or pyjamas, sometimes stark naked except for a badge pinned to his left nipple, after checking each paper, would stamp it. On subsequent inspection the citizen was required to show the properly entered stamps of the last inspection. The Examiner, when he stopped a large group, would only examine and stamp the cards of a few. The others were then subject to arrest because their cards were not properly stamped. Arrest meant "provisional detention"; that is, the prisoner would be released if and when his Affidavit of Explanation, properly signed and stamped, was approved by the Assistant Arbiter of Explanations. Since this official hardly ever came to his office, and the Affidavit of Explanation had to be presented in person, the explainers spent weeks and months waiting around in unheated offices with no chairs and no toilet facilities.

Documents issued in vanishing ink faded into old pawn tickets. New documents were constantly required. The citizens rushed from one bureau to another in a frenzied attempt to meet impossible deadlines.

All benches were removed from the city, all fountains turned off, all flowers and trees destroyed. Huge electric buzzers on the top of every apartment house (everyone lived in apartments) rang the quarter hour. Often the vibrations would throw people out of bed. Searchlights played over the town all night (no one was permitted to use shades, curtains, shutters or blinds).

No one ever looked at anyone else because of the strict law against importuning, with or without verbal approach, anyone for any purpose, sexual or otherwise. All cafés and bars were closed. Liquor could only be obtained with a special permit, and the liquor so obtained could not be sold or given or in any way transferred to anyone else, and the presence of anyone else in the room was considered *prima facie* evidence of conspiracy to transfer liquor.

No one was permitted to bolt his door, and the police had pass keys to every room in the city. Accompanied by a mentalist they rush into someone's quarters and start "looking for it."

The mentalist guides them to whatever the man wishes to hide: a tube of vaseline, an enema, a handkerchief with come on it, a weapon, unlicensed alcohol. And they always submitted the suspect to the most humiliating search of his naked person on which they make sneering and derogatory comments. Many a latent homosexual was carried out in a straitjacket when they planted vaseline in his ass. Or they pounce on any object. A pen wiper or a shoe tree.

"And what is this supposed to be for?"

"It's a pen wiper."

"A pen wiper, he says."

"I've heard everything now."

"I guess this is all we need. Come on, you."

After a few months of this the citizens cowered in corners like neurotic cats.

Of course the Annexia police processed suspected agents, saboteurs and political deviants on an assembly line basis. As regards the interrogation of suspects, Benway has this to say:

"While in general I avoid the use of torture—torture

locates the opponent and mobilizes resistance—the threat of torture is useful to induce in the subject the appropriate feeling of helplessness and gratitude to the interrogator for withholding it. And torture can be employed to advantage as a penalty when the subject is far enough along with the treatment to accept punishment as deserved. To this end I devised several forms of disciplinary procedure. One was known as The Switchboard. Electric drills that can be turned on at any time are clamped against the subject's teeth; and he is instructed to operate an arbitrary switchboard, to put certain connections in certain sockets in response to bells and lights. Every time he makes a mistake the drills are turned on for twenty seconds. The signals are gradually speeded up beyond his reaction time. Half an hour on the switchboard and the subject breaks down like an overloaded thinking machine.

"The study of thinking machines teaches us more about the brain than we can learn by introspective methods. Western man is externalizing himself in the form of gadgets. Ever pop coke in the mainline? It hits you right in the brain, activating connections of pure pleasure. The pleasure of morphine is in the viscera. You listen down into yourself after a shot. But C is electricity through the brain, and the C yen is of the brain alone, a need without body and without feeling. The C-charged brain is a berserk pinball machine, flashing blue and pink lights in electric orgasm. C pleasure could be felt by a thinking machine, the first stirrings of hideous insect life. The craving for C lasts only a few hours, as long as the C channels are stimulated. Of course the effect of C could be produced by an electric current activating the C channels. . . .

"So after a bit the channels wear out like veins, and the addict has to find new ones. A vein will come back in time, and by adroit vein rotation a junky can piece out the odds if he don't become an oil burner. But brain cells don't come back once they're gone, and when the addict runs out of brain cells he is in a terrible fucking position.

"Squatting on old bones and excrement and rusty iron, in a white blaze of heat, a panorama of naked idiots stretches to the horizon. Complete silence—their speech centers are destroyed—except for the crackle of sparks and the popping of singed flesh as they apply electrodes up and down the spine. White smoke of burning flesh hangs in the motionless air. A group of children have tied an idiot to a post with barbed wire and built a fire between his legs and stand watching with bestial curiosity as the flames lick his thighs. His flesh jerks in the fire with insect agony.

"I digress as usual. Pending more precise knowledge of brain electronics, drugs remain an essential tool of the interrogator in his assault on the subject's personal identity. The barbiturates are, of course, virtually useless. That is, anyone who can be broken down by such means would succumb to the puerile methods used in an American precinct. Scopolamine is often effective in dissolving resistance, but it impairs the memory: an agent might be prepared to reveal his secrets but quite unable to remember them, or cover story and secret life info might be inextricably garbled. Mescaline, harmaline, LSD6, bufotenine, muscarine successful in many cases. Bulbocapnine induces a state approximating schizophrenic catatonia . . . instances of automatic obedience have been observed. Bulbocapnine is a backbrain depressant probably putting out of action the centers of motion in the hypothalamus. Other drugs that have produced experimental schizophrenia—mescaline, harmaline, LSD6—are backbrain stimulants. In schizophrenia the backbrain is alternately stimulated and depressed. Catatonia is often followed by a period of excitement and motor activity during which the nut rushes through the wards giving everyone a bad time. Deteriorated schizos sometimes refuse to move at all and spend their lives in bed. A disturbance of the regulatory function of the hypothalamus is indicated as the 'cause' (causal thinking never yields accurate description of metabolic process—limitations of existing language) of schizophrenia. Alternate doses of LSD6 and bulbocapnine—the bulbocapnine potientiated with curare—give the highest yield of automatic obedience.

"There are other procedures. The subject can be reduced to deep depression by administering large doses of benzedrine for several days. Psychosis can be induced by continual large doses of cocaine or demerol or by the abrupt withdrawal of barbiturates after prolonged administration. He can be addicted by dihydro-oxy-heroin and subjected to withdrawal (this compound should be five times as addicting as heroin, and the withdrawal proportionately severe).

"There are various 'psychological methods,' compulsory psychoanalysis, for example. The subject is requested to free-associate for one hour every day (in cases where time is not of the essence). 'Now, now. Let's not be negative, boy. Poppa call nasty man. Take baby walkabout switchboard.'

"The case of a female agent who forgot her real identity and merged with her cover story—she is still a fricoteuse in Annexia—put me onto another gimmick. An agent is trained to deny his agent identity by asserting his cover story. So why not use psychic jiu-jitsu and go along with him? Suggest that his cover story is his identity and that he has no other. His agent identity becomes unconscious, that is, out of his control; and you can dig it with drugs and hypnosis. You can make a square heterosex citizen queer with this angle ... that is, reinforce and second his rejection of normally latent homosexual trends—at the same time depriving him of cunt and subjecting him to homosex stimulation. Then drugs, hypnosis, and—" Benway flipped a limp wrist.

"Many subjects are vulnerable to sexual humiliation. Nakedness, stimulation with aphrodisiacs, constant supervision to embarrass subject and prevent relief of masturbation (erections during sleep automatically turn on an enormous vibrating electric buzzer that throws the subject out of bed into cold water, thus reducing the incidence of wet dreams to a minimum). Kicks to hypnotize a priest and tell him he is about to consummate a hypostatic union with the Lamb—then steer a randy old sheep up his ass. After that the Interrogator can gain complete hypnotic control—the subject will come at his whistle, shit on the floor if he but say Open Sesame. Needless to say, the sex humiliation angle is contraindicated for overt homosexuals. (I mean let's keep our eye on the ball here and remember the old party line . . . never know who's listening in.) I recall this one kid, I condition to shit at sight of me. Then I wash his ass and screw him. It was real tasty. And he was a lovely fellah too. And some times a subject will burst into boyish tears because he can't keep from ejaculate when you screw him. Well, as you can plainly see, the possibilities are endless like meandering paths in a great big beautiful garden. I was just scratching that lovely surface when I am purged by Party Poops. . . . Well, 'son cosas de la vida.' "

I reach Freeland, which is clean and dull my God. Benway is directing the R.C., Reconditioning Center. I drop around, and "What happened to so and so?" sets in like: "Sidi Idriss 'The Nark' Smithers crooned to the Senders for a longevity serum. No fool like an old queen." "Lester Stroganoff Smuunn—'El Hassein'—turned himself into a Latah trying to perfect A.O.P., Automatic Obedience Processing. A martyr to the industry . . ." (Latah is a condition occurring in South East Asia. Otherwise sane, Latahs compulsively imitate every motion once their attention is attracted by snapping the fingers or calling sharply. A form of compulsive involuntary hypnosis. They sometimes injure themselves trying to imitate the motions of several people at once.)

"Stop me if you've heard this atomic secret. . . ."

Benway's face retains its form in the flash bulb of urgency, subject at any moment to unspeakable cleavage or metamorphosis. It flickers like a picture moving in and out of focus.

"Come on," says Benway, "and I'll show you around the R.C."

We are walking down a long white hall. Benway's voice drifts into my consciousness from no particular place . . . a disembodied voice that is sometimes loud and clear, sometimes barely audible like music down a windy street.

"Isolated groups like natives of the Bismarck Archipelago. No overt homosexuality among them. God damned matriarchy. All matriarchies anti-homosexual, conformist and prosaic. Find yourself in a matriarchy walk don't run to the nearest frontier. If you run, some frustrate latent queer cop will likely shoot you. So somebody wants to establish a beach head of homogeneity in a shambles of potentials like West Europe and U.S.A.? Another fucking matriarchy, Margaret Mead notwithstanding . . . Spot of bother there. Scalpel fight with a colleague in the operating room. And my baboon assistant leaped on the patient and tore him to pieces. Baboons always attack the weakest party in an altercation. Quite right too. We must never forget our glorious simian heritage. Doc Browbeck was party inna second part. A retired abortionist and junk pusher (he was a veterinarian actually) recalled to service during the manpower shortage. Well, Doc had been in the hospital kitchen all morning goosing the nurses and tanking up on coal gas and Klim—and just before the operation he sneaked a double shot of nutmeg to nerve himself up."

(In England and especially in Edinburgh the citizens bubble coal gas through Klim—a horrible form of powdered milk tasting like rancid chalk—and pick up on the results. They hock everything to pay the gas bill, and when the man comes around to shut it off for the non-payment, you can hear their screams for miles. When a citizen is sick from needing it he says "I got the klinks" or "That old stove climbing up my back."

Nutmeg. I quote from the author's article on narcotic drugs in the *British Journal of Addiction* (see Appendix): "Convicts and sailors sometimes have recourse to nutmeg. About a tablespoon is swallowed with water. Result vaguely similar to marijuana with side effects of headache and nausea. There are a number of narcotics of the nutmeg family in use among the Indians of South America. They are usually administered by sniffing a dried powder of the plant. The medicine men take these noxious substances and go into convulsive states. Their twitchings and mutterings are thought to have prophetic significance.")

"I had a Yage hangover, me, and in no condition to take any of Browbeck's shit. First thing he comes on with I should start the incision from the back instead of the front, muttering some garbled nonsense about being sure to cut out the gall bladder it would fuck up the meat. Thought he was on the farm cleaning a chicken. I told him to go put his head back in the oven, whereupon he had the effrontery to push my hand severing the patient's femoral artery. Blood spurted up and blinded the anesthetist, who ran out through the halls screaming. Browbeck tried to knee me in the groin, and I managed to hamstring him with my scalpel. He crawled about the floor stabbing at my feet and legs. Violet, that's my baboon assistant—only woman I ever cared a damn about—really wigged. I climbed up on the table and poise myself to jump on Browbeck with both feet and stomp him when the cops rushed in.

"Well, this rumble in the operating room, 'this unspeakable occurrence' as the Super called it, you might say was the blow off. The wolf pack was closing for the kill. A crucifixion, that's the only word for it. Of course I'd made a few 'dumheits' here and there. Who hasn't? There was the time me and the anesthetist drank up all the ether and the patient came up on us, and I was accused of cutting the cocaine with Saniflush. Violet did it actually. Had to protect her of course. . . .

"So the wind-up is we are all drummed out of the industry. Not that Violet was a *bona fide* croaker, neither was Browbeck for that matter, and even my own certificate was called in question. But Violet knew more medicine than the Mayo Clinic. She had an extraordinary intuition and a high sense of duty.

"So there I was flat on my ass with no certificate. Should I turn to another trade? No. Doctoring was in my blood. I managed to keep up my habits performing cutrate abortions in subway toilets. I even descended to hustling pregnant women in the public streets. It was positively unethical. Then I met a great guy, Placenta Juan the After Birth Tycoon. Made his in slunks during the war. (Slunks are underage calves trailing afterbirths and bacteria, generally in an unsanitary and unfit condition. A calf may not be sold as food until it reaches a minimum age of six weeks. Prior to that time it is classified as a slunk. Slunk trafficking is subject to a heavy penalty.) Well, Juanito controlled a fleet of cargo boats he register under the Abyssinian flag to avoid bothersome restrictions. He gives me a job as ship's doctor on the *S.S. Filiarisis*, as filthy a craft as ever sailed the seas. Operating with one hand, beating the rats offa my patient with the other and bedbugs and scorpions rain down from the ceiling.

"So somebody wants homogeneity at this juncture. Can do but it costs. Bored with the whole project, me. . . . Here we are . . . . Drag Alley."

Benway traces a pattern in the air with his hand and a door swings open. We step through and the door closes. A long ward gleaming with stainless steel, white tile floors, glass brick walls. Beds along one wall. No one smokes, no one reads, no one talks.

"Come and take a close look," says Benway. "You won't embarrass anybody."

I walk over and stand in front of a man who is sitting on his bed. I look at the man's eyes. Nobody, nothing looks back.

"IND's," says Benway, "Irreversible Neural Damage. Overliberated, you might say . . . a drag on the industry."

I pass a hand in front of the man's eyes.

"Yes," says Benway, "they still have reflexes. Watch this." Benway takes a chocolate bar from his pocket, removes the wrapper and holds it in front of the man's nose. The man sniffs. His jaws begin to work. He makes snatching motions with his hands. Saliva drips from his mouth and hangs off his chin in long streamers. His stomach rumbles. His whole body writhes in peristalsis. Benway steps back and holds up the chocolate. The man drops to his knees, throws back his head and barks. Benway tosses the chocolate. The man snaps at it, misses, scrambles around on the floor making slobbering noises. He crawls under the bed, finds the chocolate and crams it into his mouth with both hands.

"Jesus! These ID's got no class to them."

Benway calls over the attendant who is sitting at one end of the ward reading a book of J. M. Barrie's plays.

"Get these fucking ID's outa here. It's a bring down already. Bad for the tourist business."

"What should I do with them?"

"How in the fuck should I know? I'm a scientist. A *pure* scientist. Just get them outa here. I don't hafta look at them is all. They constitute an albatross."

"But what? Where?"

"Proper channels. Buzz the District Coordinator or whatever he calls himself   new title every week. Doubt if he exists."

Doctor Benway pauses at the door and looks back at the IND's. "Our failures," he says. "Well, it's all in the day's work."

"Do they ever come back?"

"They don't come back, won't come back, once they're gone," Benway sings softly. "Now this ward has some innarest."

The patients stand in groups talking and spitting on the floor. Junk hangs in the air like a grey haze.

"A heart-warming sight," says Benway, "those junkies standing around waiting for the Man. Six months ago they were all schizophrenic. Some of them hadn't been out of bed for years. Now look at them. In all the course of my practices, I have never seen a schizophrenic junky, and junkies are mostly of the schizo physical type. Want to cure anybody of anything, find out who doesn't have it. So who don't got it? Junkies don't got it. Oh, incidentally, there's an area in Bolivia with no psychosis. Right sane folk in them hills. Like to get in there, me, before it is loused up by literacy, advertising, TV and drive-ins. Make a study strictly from metabolism: diet, use of drugs and alcohol, sex, etc. Who cares what they think? Same nonsense everybody thinks, I daresay.

"And why don't junkies got schizophrenia? Don't know yet. A schizophrenic can ignore hunger and starve to death if he isn't fed. No one can ignore heroin withdrawal. The fact of addiction imposes contact.

"But that's only one angle. Mescaline, LSD6, deteriorated adrenalin, harmaline can produce an approximate schizophrenia. The best stuff is extracted from the blood of schizos; so schizophrenia is likely a drug psychosis. They got a metabolic connection, a Man Within you might say. (Interested readers are referred to Appendix.)

"In the terminal stage of schizophrenia the backbrain is permanently depressed, and the front brain is almost without content since the front brain is only active in response to backbrain stimulation.

"Morphine calls forth the antidote of backbrain stimulation similar to schizo substance. (Note similarity between withdrawal syndrome and intoxication with Yage or LSD6.) Eventual result of junk use—especially true of heroin addiction where large doses are available to the addict—is permanent backbrain depression and a state much like terminal schizophrenia: complete lack of affect, autism, virtual absence of cerebral event. The addict can spend eight hours looking at a wall. He is conscious of his surroundings, but they have no emotional connotation and in consequence no interest. Remembering a period of heavy addiction is like playing back a tape recording of events experienced by the front brain alone. Flat statements of external events. 'I went to the store and bought some brown sugar. I came home and ate half the box. I took a three grain shot etc.' Complete absence of nostalgia in these memories. However, as soon as junk intake falls below par, the withdrawal substance floods the body.

"If all pleasure is relief from tension, junk affords relief from the whole life process, in disconnecting the hypothalamus, which is the center of psychic energy and libido.

"Some of my learned colleagues (nameless assholes) have suggested that junk derives its euphoric effect from direct stimulation of the orgasm center. It seems more probable that junk suspends the whole cycle of tension, discharge and rest. The orgasm has no function in the junky. Boredom, which always indicates an undischarged tension, never troubles the addict. He can look at his shoe for eight hours. He is only roused to action when the hourglass of junk runs out."

At the far end of the ward an attendant throws up an iron shutter and lets out a hog call. The junkies rush up grunting and squealing.

"Wise guy," says Benway. "No respect for human dignity. Now I'll show you the mild deviant and criminal ward. Yes, a criminal is a mild deviant here. He doesn't deny the Freeland contract. He merely seeks to circumvent some of the clauses. Reprehensible but not too serious. Down this hall . . . We'll skip wards 23, 86, 57 and 97 . . . and the laboratory."

"Are homosexuals classed as deviants?"

"No. Remember the Bismarck Archipelago. No overt

homosexuality. A *functioning* police state needs no police. Homosexuality does not occur to anyone as conceivable behaviour. . . . Homosexuality is a *political*
crime in a matriarchy. No society tolerates overt rejection of its basic tenets. We aren't a matriarchy here,
Insh'allah. You know the experiment with rats where
they are subject to this electric shock and dropped in
cold water if they so much as move at a female. So they
all become fruit rats and that's the way it is with the
etiology. And shall such a rat squeak out, 'I'm queah
and I luuuuuuuuve it' or 'Who cut yours off, you two-
holed freak?' 'twere a square rat so to squeak. During
my rather brief experience as a psychoanalyst—spot of
bother with the Society—one patient ran amok in Grand
Central with a flame thrower, two committed suicide
and one died on the couch like a jungle rat (jungle rats
are subject to die if confronted suddenly with a hopeless situation). So his relations beef and I tell them, 'It's
all in the day's work. Get this stiff outa here. It's a
bring down for my live patients'—I noticed that all my
homosexual patients manifested strong unconscious
heterosex trends and all my hetero patients unconscious homosexual trends. Makes the brain reel, don't
it?"

"And what do you conclude from that?"

"Conclude? Nothing whatever. Just a passing obser-
vation."

We are eating lunch in Benway's office when he gets
a call.

"What's that? . . . Monstrous! Fantastic! . . . Carry on
and stand by."

He puts down the phone. "I am prepared to accept

immediate assignment with Islam Incorporated. It seems the electronic brain went berserk playing six-dimensional chess with the Technician and released every subject in the R.C. Leave us adjourn to the roof. Operation Helicopter is indicated."

From the roof of the R.C. we survey a scene of unparalleled horror. IND's stand around in front of the café tables, long streamers of saliva hanging off their chins, stomachs noisily churning, others ejaculate at the sight of women. Latahs imitate the passers-by with monkey-like obscenity. Junkies have looted the drugstores and fix on every street corner. . . . Catatonics decorate the parks. . . . Agitated schizophrenics rush through the streets with mangled, inhuman cries. A group of P.R.'s—Partially Reconditioned—have surrounded some homosexual tourists with horrible knowing smiles showing the Nordic skull beneath in double exposure.

"What do you want?" snaps one of the queens.

"We want to *understand* you."

A contingent of howling simopaths swing from chandeliers, balconies and trees, shitting and pissing on passers-by. (A simopath—the technical name for this disorder escapes me—is a citizen convinced he is an ape or other simian. It is a disorder peculiar to the army, and discharge cures it.) Amoks trot along cutting off heads, faces sweet and remote with a dreamy half smile. . . . Citizens with incipient Bang-utot clutch their penises and call on the tourists for help. . . . Arab rioters yipe and howl, castrating, disembowelling, throw burning gasoline. . . . Dancing boys strip-tease with intestines, women stick severed genitals in their cunts, grind, bump and flick it at the man of their choice. . . . Religious fanatics harangue the crowd from helicopters and rain stone tablets on their heads, inscribed with meaningless messages. . . . Leopard Men tear people to pieces with iron claws, coughing and grunting. . . . Kwakiutl Cannibal Society initiates bite off noses and ears. . . .

A coprophage calls for a plate, shits on it and eats the shit, exclaiming, "Mmmm, that's my rich substance."

A battalion of rampant bores prowls the streets and hotel lobbies in search of victims. An intellectual avant-gardist—"Of course the only writing worth considering now is to be found in scientific reports and periodicals" —has given someone a bulbocapnine injection and is preparing to read him a bulletin on "the use of neo-hemoglobin in the control of multiple degenerative granuloma." (Of course, the reports are all gibberish he has concocted and printed up.)

His opening words: "You look to me like a man of intelligence." (Always ominous words, my boy . . . When you hear them stay not on the order of your going but go at once.)

An English colonial, assisted by five police boys, has detained a subject in the club bar: "I say, do you know Mozambique?" and he launches into the endless saga of his malaria. "So the doctor said to me, 'I can only advise you to leave the area. Otherwise I shall bury you. This croaker does a little undertaking on the side. Piecing out the odds you might say, and throwing himself a spot of business now and then." So after the third pink gin when he gets to know you, he shifts to dysentery. "Most extraordinary discharge. More or less of a white yellow color like rancid jism and stringy you know."

An explorer in sun helmet has brought down a citizen with blow gun and curare dart. He administers artificial respiration with one foot. (Curare kills by paralyzing the lungs. It has no other toxic effect, is not, strictly speaking, a poison. If artificial respiration is administered the subject will not die. Curare is eliminated with great rapidity by the kidneys.) "That was the year of the rindpest when everything died, even the hyenas. . . . So there I was completely out of K.Y. in the headwaters of the Baboonsasshole When it came through by air drop my gratitude was indescribable. . . . As a matter of fact, and I have never told this before to a living soul—elusive blighters"—his voice echoes through a vast empty hotel lobby in 1890 style, red plush, rubber plants, gilt and statues—"I was the only white man ever initiated into the infamous Agouti Society, witnessed and participated in their unspeakable rites."

(The Agouti Society has turned out for a Chimu Fiesta. (The Chimu of ancient Peru were much given to sodomy and occasionally staged bloody battles with clubs, running up several hundred casualties in the course of an afternoon.) The youths, sneering and goosing each other with clubs, troop out to the field. Now the battle begins.

Gentle reader, the ugliness of that spectacle buggers description. Who can be a cringing pissing coward, yet vicious as a purple-assed mandril, alternating these deplorable conditions like vaudeville skits? Who can shit on a fallen adversary who, dying, eats the shit and screams with joy? Who can hang a weak passive and catch his sperm in mouth like a vicious dog? Gentle reader, I fain would spare you this, but my pen hath its will like the Ancient Mariner. Oh Christ what a scene is this! Can tongue or pen accommodate these scandals? A beastly young hooligan has gouged out the eye of his confrere and fuck him in the brain. "This brain atrophy already, and dry as grandmother's cunt."

He turns into Rock and Roll hoodlum. "I screw the old gash—like a crossword puzzle what relation to me is the outcome if it outcome? My father already or not yet? I can't screw you, Jack, you is about to become my father, and better 'twere to cut your throat and screw my mother playing it straight than fuck my father or *vice versa mutatis mutandis* as the case may be, and cut my mother's throat, that sainted gash, though it be the best way I know to stem her word horde and freeze her asset. I mean when a fellow be caught short in the switches and don't know is he to offer up his ass to 'great big daddy' or commit a torso job on the old lady. Give me two cunts and a prick of steel and keep your dirty finger out of my sugar bum what you think I am a purple-assed reception already fugitive from Gibraltar? Male and female castrated he them. Who can't distinguish between the sexes? I'll cut your throat you white mother fucker. Come out in the open like my grandchild and meet thy unborn mother in dubious battle. Confusion hath fuck his masterpiece. I have cut the janitor's throat quite by mistake of identity, he being such a horrible fuck like the old man. And in the coal bin all cocks are alike."

So leave us return to the stricken field. One youth

hath penetrate his comrade, whilst another youth does amputate the proudest part of that cock's quivering beneficiary so that the visiting member projects to fill the vacuum nature abhors and ejaculate into the Black Lagoon where impatient piranha snap up the child not yet born nor—in view of certain well established facts—at all likely.)

Another bore carries around a suitcase full of trophies and medals, cups and ribbons: "Now this I won for the Most Ingenious Sex Device Contest in Yokohama. (Hold him, he's desperate.) The Emperor gave it to me himself and there were tears in his eyes, and the runners up all castrated theirselves with harakiri knives. And I won this ribbon in a Degradation Contest at the Teheran meeting of Junkies Anonymous."

"Shot up my wife's M.S. and her down with a kidney stone big as the Hope Diamond. So I give her half a Vagamin and tell her, "You can't expect too much relief. . . . Shut up awready. I wanta enjoy my medications.'"

"Stole an opium suppository out of my grandmother's ass."

The hypochondriac lassoes the passer-by and administers a straitjacket and starts talking about his rotting septum: "An awful purulent discharge is subject to flow out . . . just wait till you see it."

He does a strip tease to operation scars, guiding the reluctant fingers of a victim. "Feel that suppurated swelling in my groin where I got the lymphogranulomas. . . . And now I want you to palpate my internal haemorrhoids."

(The reference is to lymphogranuloma, "climactic

buboes." A virus venereal disease indigenous to Ethiopia. "Not for nothing are we known as feelthy Ethiopians," sneers an Ethiopian mercenary as he sodomizes Pharaoh, venomous as the King's cobra. Ancient Egyptian papyrus talk all the time about them feelthy Ethiopians.

So it started in Addis Ababa like the Jersey Bounce, but these are modern times, One World. Now the climactic buboes swell up in Shanghai and Esmeraldas, New Orleans and Helsinki, Seattle and Capetown. But the heart turns home and the disease shows a distinct predilection for Negroes, is in fact the whitehaired boy of white supremacists. But the Mau Mau voodoo men are said to be cooking up a real dilly of a VD for the white folks. Not that Caucasians are immune: five British sailors contracted the disease in Zanzibar. And in Dead Coon County, Arkansas ("Blackest Dirt, Whitest People in the U.S.A.—Nigger, Don't Let The Sun Set On You Here") the County Coroner come down with the buboes fore and aft. A vigilante committee of neighbours apologetically burned him to death in the Court House privy when his interesting condition came to light. "Now, Clem, just think of yourself as a cow with the aftosa." "Or a poltroon with the fowl pest." "Don't crowd too close, boys. His intestines is subject to explode in the fire." The disease in short arm hath a gimmick for going places unlike certain unfortunate viruses who are fated to languish unconsummate in the guts of a tick or a jungle mosquito, or the saliva of a dying jackal slobbering silver under the desert moon. And after an initial lesion at the point of infection the disease passes to the lymph glands of the groin, which swell and burst in suppurating fissures, drain for days, months, years, a purulent stringy discharge streaked with blood and putrid lymph. Elephantiasis of the genitals is a frequent complication, and cases of gangrene have been recorded where the amputation *in medio* of the patient from the waist down was indicated but hardly worth while. Women usually suffer secondary infection of the anus. Males who resign themselves up for passive intercourse to infected partners like weak and soon to be purple-assed baboons, may also nourish a little stranger. Initial proctitis and the inevitable purulent discharge—which may pass unnoticed in the shuffle—is followed by stricture of the rectum requiring intervention of an apple corer or its surgical equivalent, lest the unfortunate patient be reduced to fart and shit in his teeth giving rise to stubborn cases of halitosis and unpopularity with all sexes, ages and conditions of *homo sapiens*. In fact a blind bugger was deserted by his seeing eye police dog—copper at heart. Until quite recently there was no satisfactory treatment. "Treatment is symptomatic" —which means in the trade there is none. Now many cases yield to intensive therapy with aureomycin, terramycin and some of the newer molds. However a certain appreciable percentage remain refractory as mountain gorillas. . . . So, boys, when those hot licks play over your balls and prick and dart up your ass like an invisible blue blow torch of orgones, in the words of I. B. Watson, *Think*. Stop panting and start palpating . . . and if you palpate a bubo draw your-

self back in and say in a cold nasal whine: "You think
I am innarested to contact your horrible old condition?
I am not innarested at all.")

Rock and Roll adolescent hoodlums storm the streets
of all nations. They rush into the Louvre and throw
acid in the Mona Lisa's face. They open zoos, insane
asylums, prisons, burst water mains with air hammers,
chop the floor out of passenger plane lavatories, shoot
out lighthouses, file elevator cables to one thin wire,
turn sewers into the water supply, throw sharks and
sting rays, electric eels and candiru into swimming
pools (the candiru is a small eel-like fish or worm
about one-quarter inch through and two inches long
patronizing certain rivers of ill repute in the Greater
Amazon Basin, will dart up your prick or your asshole
or a woman's cunt *faute de mieux*, and hold himself
there by sharp spines with precisely what motives is
not known since no one has stepped forward to observe
the candiru's life-cycle *in situ*), in nautical costumes
ram the *Queen Mary* full speed into New York Harbor,
play chicken with passenger planes and busses, rush
into hospitals in white coats carrying saws and axes and
scalpels three feet long; throw paralytics out of iron
lungs (mimic their suffocations flopping about on the
floor and rolling their eyes up), administer injections
with bicycle pumps, disconnect artificial kidneys, saw
a woman in half with a two-man surgical saw, they
drive herds of squealing pigs into the Curb, they shit
on the floor of the United Nations and wipe their ass
with treaties, pacts, alliances.

By plane, car, horse, camel, elephant, tractor, bicycle
and steam roller, on foot, skis, sled, crutch and pogo-

stick the tourists storm the frontiers, demanding with inflexible authority asylum from the "unspeakable conditions obtaining in Freeland," the Chamber of Commerce striving in vain to stem the debacle: "Please to be restful. It is only a few crazies who have from the crazy place outbroken."

JOSELITO

And Joselito who wrote had, class-conscious poetry began to cough. The German doctor made a brief examination, touching Joselito's ribs with long, delicate fingers. The doctor was also a concert violinist, a mathematician, a chess master, and a Doctor of International Jurisprudence with license to practice in the lavatories of the Hague. The doctor flicked a hard, distant glance across Joselito's brown chest. He looked at Carl and smiled—one educated man to another smile—and raised his eyebrow, saying without words:

"Alzo for the so stupid peasant we must avoid use of the word is it not? Otherwise he shit himself with fear. Koch and spit they are *both* nasty words I think?"

He said aloud: "It is a catarro de los pulmones."

Carl talked to the doctor outside under the narrow arcade with rain bouncing up from the street against his pant legs, thinking how many people he tell it to, and the stairs, porches, lawns, driveways, corridors and streets of the world there in the doctor's eyes . . . stuffy German alcoves, butterfly trays to the ceiling, silent portentous smell of uremia seeping under the door, suburban lawns to sound of the water sprinkler, in calm jungle night under silent wings of the Anopheles mosquito. (Note: This is not a figure. Anopheles mosquitoes *are* silent.) Thickly carpeted, discreet nursing home in Kensington: stiff brocade chair and a cup of tea, the Swedish modern living room with water hyacinths in a yellow bowl—outside the China blue Northern sky and drifting clouds, under bad watercolors of the dying medical student.

"A schnaps I think Frau Underschnitt."

The doctor was talking into a phone with a chess board in front of him. "Quite a severe lesion I think . . . of course without to see the fluoroscope." He picks up the knight and then replaces it thoughtfully. "Yes . . . Both lungs . . . quite definitely." He replaces the receiver and turns to Carl. "I have observed these people show amazingly quick wound recovery, with low incidence of infection. It is always the lungs here . . . pneumonia and, of course, Old Faithful." The doctor grabs Carl's cock, leaping into the air with a coarse peasant guffaw. His European smile ignores the misbehavior of a child or an animal. He goes on smoothly in his eerily unaccented, disembodied English. "Our Old Faithful Bacillus Koch." The doctor clicks his heels and bows his head. "Otherwise they would multiply their stupid peasant asshole into the sea, is it not?" He shrieks, thrusting his face into Carl's. Carl retreats sideways with the grey wall of rain behind him.

"Isn't there some place where he can be treated?"

"I think there is some sort of *sanitarium*," he drags out the word with ambiguous obscenity, "up at the District Capital. I will write for you the address."

"Chemical therapy?"

His voice falls flat and heavy in the damp air.

"Who can say. They are all stupid peasants, and the worst of all peasants are the so-called educated. These people should not only be prevented from learning to read, but from learning to talk as well. No need to prevent them from thinking; nature has done that."

"Here is the *address*," the doctor whispered without moving his lips.

He dropped a pill of paper into Carl's hand. His dirty fingers, shiny over the dirt, rested on Carl's sleeve.

"There is the matter of my fee."

Carl slipped him a wadded banknote . . . and the doctor faded into the grey twilight, seedy and furtive as an old junky.

Carl saw Joselito in a big clean room full of light, with private bath and concrete balcony. And nothing to talk about there in the cold empty room, water hyacinths growing in a yellow bowl and the China blue sky and drifting clouds, fear flickering in and out of his eyes. When he smiled the fear flew away in little pieces of light, lurked enigmatically in the high cool corners of the room. And what could I say feeling death around me, and the little broken images that come before sleep, there in the mind?

"They will send me to the new sanitarium tomorrow. Come and visit me. I will be there alone."

He coughed and took a codeineeta.

"Doctor I understand, that is I have been given to understand, I have read and heard—not a medical man myself—don't pretend to be—that the concept of sanitarium treatment has been more or less supplanted, or at least very definitely supplemented, by chemical therapy. Is this accurate in your opinion? What I mean to say is, Doctor, please tell me in all sincerity, as one human being to another, what is your opinion of chemical versus sanitarium therapy? Are you a *partisan*?"

The doctor's liver sick Indian face was blank as a dealer's.

"Completely modern, as you can see," he gestures toward the room with the purple fingers of bad circulation. "Bath . . . water . . . flowers. The lot." He finished in Cockney English with a triumphant smirk. "I will write for you a letter."

"This letter? For the sanitarium?"

The doctor was speaking from a land of black rocks and great, iridescent brown lagoons. "The furniture . . . modern and comfortable. You *find* it so of course?"

Carl could not see the sanitarium owing to a false front of green stucco topped by an intricate neon sign dead and sinister against the sky, waiting for darkness. The sanitarium was evidently built on a great limestone promontory, over which flowering trees and vine tendrils broke in waves. The smell of flowers was heavy in the air.

The commandante sat at a long wooden trestle under a vine trellis. He was doing absolutely nothing. He took the letter that Carl handed him and whispered through it, reading his lips with the left hand. He stuck the letter on a spike over a toilet. He began transcrbing from a ledger full of numbers. He wrote on and on.

Broken images exploded softly in Carl's head, and he was moving out of himself in a silent swoop. Clear and sharp from a great distance he saw himself sitting in a lunchroom. Overdose of H. His old lady shaking him and holding hot coffee under his nose.

Outside an old junky in Santa Claus suit, selling Christmas seals. "Fight tuberculosis, folks," he whispers in his disembodied, junky voice. Salvation Army choir of sincere, homosexual football coaches sings: "In the Sweet Bye and Bye."

Carl drifted back into his body, an earthbound junk ghost.

"I could bribe him, of course."

The commandante taps the table with one finger and hums "Coming Through the Rye." Far away, then urgently near like a foghorn a split second before the grinding crash.

Carl pulled a note half out of his trouser pocket. . . . The commandante was standing by a vast panel of lockers and deposit boxes. He looked at Carl, sick animal eyes gone out, dying inside, hopeless fear reflecting the face of death. In the smell of flowers a note half out of his pocket, the weakness hit Carl, shutting off his breath, stopping his blood. He was in a great cone spinning down to a black point.

"Chemical therapy?" The scream shot out of his flesh through empty locker rooms and barracks, musty resort hotels, and spectral, coughing corridors of T.B. sanitariums, the muttering, hawking, grey dishwater smell of flophouses and Old Men's Homes, great, dusty custom sheds and warehouses, through broken porticoes and smeared arabesques, iron urinals worn paper thin by the urine of a million fairies, deserted weed-grown privies with a musty smell of shit turning back to the soil, erect wooden phallus on the grave of dying peoples plaintive as leaves in the wind, across the great brown river where whole trees float with green snakes in the branches and sad-eyed lemurs watch the shore out over a vast plain (vulture wings husk in the dry air). The way is strewn with broken condoms and empty H caps and K.Y. tubes squeezed dry as bone meal in the summer sun.

"*My furniture.*" The commandante's face burned like metal in the flash bulb of urgency. His eyes went out. A whiff of ozone drifted through the room. The "novia" muttered over her candles and altars in one corner.

"It is all Trak . . . modern, excellent . . ." he is nodding idiotically and drooling. A yellow cat pulls at Carl's pant leg and runs onto a concrete balcony. Clouds drift by.

"I could get back my deposit. Start me a little business someplace." He nods and smiles like a mechanical toy.

"Joselito!!!" Boys look up from street ball games, bull rings and bicycle races as the name whistles by and slowly fades away.

"Joselito! . . . Paco! . . . Pepe! . . . Enrique! . . ." The plaintive boy cries drift in on the warm night. The Trak sign stirs like a nocturnal beast, and bursts into blue flame.

THE BLACK MEAT

"We friends, yes?"

The shoe shine boy put on his hustling smile and looked up into the Sailor's dead, cold, undersea eyes, eyes without a trace of warmth or lust or hate or any feeling the boy had ever experienced in himself or seen in another, at once cold and intense, impersonal and predatory.

The Sailor leaned forward and put a finger on the boy's inner arm at the elbow. He spoke in his dead, junky whisper.

"With veins like that, Kid, I'd have myself a time!"

He laughed, black insect laughter that seemed to serve some obscure function of orientation like a bat's squeak. The Sailor laughed three times. He stopped laughing and hung there motionless listening down into himself. He had picked up the silent frequency of junk. His face smoothed out like yellow wax over the high cheek-bones. He waited half a cigarette. The Sailor knew how to wait. But his eyes burned in a hideous dry hunger. He turned his face of controlled emergency in a slow half pivot to case the man who had just come in. "Fats" Terminal sat there sweeping the café with blank, periscope eyes. When his eyes passed the Sailor he nodded minutely. Only the peeled nerves of junk sickness would have registered a movement.

The Sailor handed the boy a coin. He drifted over to Fat's table with his floating walk and sat down. They sat a long time in silence. The café was built into one side of a stone ramp at the bottom of a high white canyon of masonry. Faces of The City poured through silent as fish, stained with vile addictions and insect lusts. The lighted café was a diving bell, cable broken, settling into black depths.

The Sailor was polishing his nails on the lapels of his glen plaid suit. He whistled a little tune through his shiny, yellow teeth.

When he moved an effluvia of mold drifted out of his clothes, a musty smell of deserted locker rooms. He studied his nails with phosphorescent intensity.

"Good thing here, Fats. I can deliver twenty. Need an advance of course."

"On spec?"

"So I don't have the twenty eggs in my pocket. I tell you it's jellied consommé. One little whoops and a push." The Sailor looked at his nails as if he were studying a chart. "You know I always deliver."

"Make it thirty. And a ten tube advance. This time tomorrow."

"Need a tube now, Fats."

"Take a walk, you'll get one."

The Sailor drifted down into the Plaza. A street boy was shoving a newspaper in the Sailor's face to cover his hand on the Sailor's pen. The Sailor walked on. He pulled the pen out and broke it like a nut in his thick, fibrous, pink fingers. He pulled out a lead tube. He cut one end of the tube with a little curved knife. A black mist poured out and hung in the air like boiling fur. The Sailor's face dissolved. His mouth undulated forward on a long tube and sucked in the black fuzz, vibrating in supersonic peristalsis disappeared in a silent, pink explosion. His face came back into focus unbearably sharp and clear, burning yellow brand of junk searing the grey haunch of a million screaming junkies.

"This will last a month," he decided, consulting an invisible mirror.

All streets of the City slope down between deepening canyons to a vast, kidney-shaped plaza full of darkness. Walls of street and plaza are perforated by dwelling cubicles and cafés, some a few feet deep, others extending out of sight in a network of rooms and corridors.

At all levels criss cross of bridges, cat walks, cable cars. Catatonic youths dressed as women in gowns of burlap and rotten rags, faces heavily and crudely painted in bright colors over a strata of beatings, arabsques of broken, suppurating scars to the pearly bone, push against the passer-by in silent clinging insistence.

Traffickers in the Black Meat, flesh of the giant aquatic black centipede—sometimes attaining a length of six feet—found in a lane of black rocks and iridescent, brown lagoons, exhibit paralyzed crustaceans in camouflage pockets of the Plaza visible only to the Meat Eaters.

Followers of obsolete unthinkable trades, doodling in Etruscan, addicts of drugs not yet synthesized, black marketeers of World War III, excisors of telepathic sensitivity, osteopaths of the spirit, investigators of infractions denounced by bland paranoid chess players, servers of fragmentary warrants taken down in hebephrenic shorthand charging unspeakable mutilations of the spirit, officials of unconstituted police states, brokers of exquisite dreams and nostalgias tested on the sensitized cells of junk sickness and bartered for raw materials of the will, drinkers of the Heavy Fluid sealed in translucent amber of dreams.

The Meet Café occupies one side of the Plaza, a maze of kitchens, restaurants, sleeping cubicles, perilous iron balconies and basements opening into the underground baths.

On stools covered in white satin sit naked Mugwumps sucking translucent, colored syrups through alabaster straws. Mugwumps have no liver and nourish themselves exclusively on sweets. Thin, purple-blue lips cover a razor-sharp beak of black bone with which they frequently tear each other to shreds in fights over clients. These creatures secrete an addicting fluid from their erect penises which prolongs life by slowing metabolism. (In fact all longevity agents have proved addicting in exact ratio to their effectiveness in prolonging life.) Addicts of Mugwump fluid are known as Reptiles. A number of these flow over chairs with their flexible bones and black-pink flesh. A fan of green cartilage covered with hollow, erectile hairs through which the Reptiles absorb the fluid sprouts from behind each ear. The fans, which move from time to time touched by invisible currents, serve also some form of communication known only to Reptiles.

During the biennial Panics when the raw, pealed Dream Police storm the City, the Mugwumps take refuge in the deepest crevices of the wall sealing themselves in clay cubicles and remain for weeks in biostasis. In those days of grey terror the Reptiles dart about faster and faster, scream past each other at supersonic speed, their flexible skulls flapping in black winds of insect agony.

The Dream Police disintegrate in globs of rotten ectoplasm swept away by an old junky, coughing and spitting in the sick morning. The Mugwump Man comes with alabaster jars of fluid and the Reptiles get smoothed out.

The air is once again still and clear as glycerine.

The Sailor spotted his Reptile. He drifted over and ordered a green syrup. The Reptile had a little, round disk mouth of brown gristle, expressionless green eyes almost covered by a thin membrane of eyelid. The Sailor waited an hour before the creature picked up his presence.

"Any eggs for Fats?" he asked, his words stirring through the Reptile's fan hairs.

It took two hours for the Reptile to raise three pink transparent fingers covered with black fuzz.

Several Meat Eaters lay in vomit, too weak to move. (The Black Meat is like a tainted cheese, overpoweringly delicious and nauseating so that the eaters eat and vomit and eat again until they fall exhausted.)

A painted youth slithered in and seized one of the great black claws sending the sweet, sick smell curling through the café.

HOSPITAL

Disintoxication Notes. Paranoia of early withdrawal. . . . Everything looks blue. . . . Flesh dead, doughy, toneless.

Withdrawal Nightmares. A mirror-lined café. Empty.
. . . Waiting for something. . . . A man appears in a side
door. . . . A slight, short Arab dressed in a brown jellaba
with grey beard and grey face . . . There is a pitcher of
boiling acid in my hand. . . . Seized by a convulsion of
urgency, I throw it in his face. . . .

Everyone looks like a drug addict. . . .

Take a little walk in the hospital patio. . . . In my
absence someone has used my scissors, they are stained
with some sticky, red brown gick. . . . No doubt that
little bitch of a criada trimming her rag.

Horrible-looking Europeans clutter up the stairs, in-
tercept the nurse when I need my medicine, empty
piss into the basin when I am washing, occupy the
toilet for hours on end—probably fishing for a finger
stall of diamonds they have stached up their asshole. . . .

In fact the whole clan of Europeans has moved in
next to me. . . .The old mother is having an operation,
and her daughter move right in to see the old gash
receive proper service. Strange visitors, presumably
relatives . . . One of them wears as glasses those gadgets jewellers screw into their eyes to examine stones.
. . . Probably a diamond-cutter on the skids . . . The man
who loused up the Throckmorton Diamond and was
drummed out of the industry. . . . All these jewelers
standing around the Diamond in their frock coats, waiting on The Man. An error of one thousandth of an
inch ruins the rock complete and they have to import
this character special from Amsterdam to do the job.
. . . So he reels in dead drunk with a huge air hammer
and pounds the diamond to dust. . . .

I don't check these citizens. . . . Dope peddlers from

Aleppo? . . . Slunk traffickers from Buenos Aires? Illegal diamond buyers from Johannesburg? . . . Slave traders from Somaliland? Collaborators at the very least . . .

Continual dreams of junk: I am looking for a poppy field. . . . Moonshiners in black Stetsons direct me to a Near East café. . . . One of the waiters is a connection for Yugoslav opium. . . .

Buy a packet of heroin from a Malay Lesbian in white belted trenchcoat. . . . I cop the paper in Tibetan section of a museum. She keeps trying to steal it back. . . . I am looking for a place to fix. . . .

The critical point of withdrawal is not the early phase of acute sickness, but the final step free from the medium of junk. . . . There is a nightmare interlude of cellular panic, life suspended between two ways of being. . . . At this point the longing for junk concentrates in a last, all-out yen, and seems to gain a dream power: circumstances put junk in your way. . . . You meet an old-time Schmecker, a larcenous hospital attendant, a writing croaker. . . .

A guard in a uniform of human skin, black buck jacket with carious yellow teeth buttons, an elastic pullover shirt in burnished Indian copper, adolescent-nordic-sun-tan slacks, sandals from calloused foot soles of young Malayan farmer, an ash-brown scarf knotted and tucked in the shirt. (Ash-brown is a color like grey *under* brown skin. You sometimes find it in mixed Negro and white stock, the mixture did not come off and the colors separated out like oil on water. . . .)

The Guard is a sharp dresser, since he has nothing

to do and saves all his pay to buy fine clothes and changes three times a day in front of an enormous magnifying mirror. He has a Latin handsome-smooth face with a pencil line mustache, small black eyes, blank and greedy, undreaming insect eyes.

When I get to the frontier the Guard rushes out of his casita, a mirror in a wooden frame slung round his neck. He is trying to get the mirror off his neck. . . . This has never happened before, that anyone reached the frontier. The Guard has injured his larynx taking off the mirror frame. . . . He has lost his voice. . . . He opens his mouth, you can see the tongue jumping around inside. The smooth blank young face and the open mouth with the tongue moving inside are incredibly hideous. The Guard holds up his hand. His whole body jerks in convulsive negation. I go over and unhook the chain across the road. It falls with a clank of metal on stone. I walk through. The Guard stands there in the mist looking after me. Then he hooks the chain up again, goes back into the casita and starts plucking at his mustache.

They just bring so-called lunch. . . . A hard-boiled egg with the shell off revealing an object like I never seen it before. . . . A very small egg of a yellow-brown color . . . Perhaps laid by the duck-billed platypus. The orange contained a huge worm and very little else. . . . He really got there firstest with the mostest. . . . In Egypt is a worm gets into your kidneys and grows to an enormous size. Ultimately the kidney is just a thin shell around the worm. Intrepid gourmets esteem the flesh of The Worm above all other delicacies. It is said to be unspeakably toothsome. . . . An Interzone coroner known as Autopsy Ahmed made a fortune trafficking The Worm.

The French school is opposite my window and I dig the boys with my eight-power field glasses. . . . So close I could reach out and touch them. . . . They wear shorts. . . . I can see the goose-pimples on their legs in the cold Spring morning. . . . I project myself out through the glasses and across the street, a ghost in the morning sunlight, torn with disembodied lust.

Did I ever tell you about the time Marv and me pay two Arab kids sixty cents to watch them screw each other? So I ask Marv, "Do you think they will do it?"

And he says, "I think so. They are hungry."

And I say, "That's the way I like to see them."

Makes me feel sorta like a dirty old man but, "Son cosas de la vida," as Soberba de la Flor said when the fuzz upbraids him for blasting this cunt and taking the dead body to the Bar O Motel and fucking it. . . .

"She play hard to get already," he say . . . "I don't hafta take that sound." (Soberba de la Flor was a Mexican criminal convict of several rather pointless murders.)

The lavatory has been locked for three hours solid. . . . I think they are using it for an operating room. . . .

NURSE: "I can't find her pulse, doctor."

DR. BENWAY: "Maybe she got it up her snatch in a finger stall."

NURSE: "Adrenalin, doctor?"

DR. BENWAY: "The night porter shot it all up for kicks." He looks around and picks up one of those rubber vacuum cups at the end of a stick they use to unstop toilets. . . . He advances on the patient. . . . "Make an incision, Doctor Limpf," he says to his appalled assistant. . . . "I'm going to massage the heart."

Dr. Limpf shrugs and begins the incision. Dr. Benway washes the suction cup by swishing it around in the toilet-bowl. . . .

NURSE: "Shouldn't it be sterilized, doctor?"

DR. BENWAY: "Very likely but there's no time." He sits on the suction cup like a cane seat watching his assistant make the incision. . . . "You young squirts couldn't lance a pimple without an electric vibrating scalpel with automatic drain and suture. . . . Soon we'll be operating by remote control on patients we never see. . . . We'll be nothing but button pushers. All the skill is going out of surgery. . . . All the know-how and make-do . . . Did I ever tell you about the time I performed an appendectomy with a rusty sardine can? And once I was caught short without instrument one and removed a uterine tumor with my teeth. That was in the Upper Effendi, and besides . . ."

DR. LIMPF: "The incision is ready, doctor."

Dr. Benway forces the cup into the incision and works it up and down. Blood spurts all over the doctors, the nurse and the wall. . . . The cup makes a horrible sucking sound.

NURSE: "I think she's gone, doctor."

DR. BENWAY: "Well, it's all in the day's work." He walks across the room to a medicine cabinet. . . . "Some fucking drug addict has cut my cocaine with Saniflush! Nurse! Send the boy out to fill this RX on the double!"

Dr. Benway is operating in an auditorium filled with

students: "Now, boys, you won't see this operation performed very often and there's a reason for that. . . . You see it has absolutely no medical value. No one knows what the purpose of it originally was or if it had a purpose at all. Personally I think it was a pure artistic creation from the beginning.

"Just as a bull fighter with his skill and knowledge extricates himself from danger he has himself invoked, so in this operation the surgeon deliberately endangers his patient, and then, with incredible speed and celerity, rescues him from death at the last possible split second. . . . Did any of you ever see Dr. Tetrazzini perform? I say perform advisedly because his operations were performances. He would start by throwing a scalpel across the room into the patient and then make his entrance like a ballet dancer. His speed was incredible: 'I don't give them time to die,' he would say. Tumors put him in a frenzy of rage. 'Fucking undisciplined cells!' he would snarl, advancing on the tumor like a knife-fighter."

A young man leaps down into the operating theatre and, whipping out a scalpel, advances on the patient.

DR. BENWAY: "An espontaneo! Stop him before he guts my patient!"

(Espontaneo is a bull-fighting term for a member of the audience who leaps down into the ring, pulls out a concealed cape and attempts a few passes with the bull before he is dragged out of the ring.)

The orderlies scuffle with the espontaneo, who is finally ejected from the hall. The anesthetist takes advantage of the confusion to pry a large gold filling from the patient's mouth. . . .

I am passing room 10 they moved me out of yester-
day. . . . Maternity case I assume . . . Bedpans full of
blood and Kotex and nameless female substances, enough
to pollute a continent . . . If someone comes to visit me
in my old room he will think I gave birth to a monster
and the State Department is trying to hush it up. . . .

Music from *I Am an American* . . . An elderly man
in the striped pants and cutaway of a diplomat stands
on a platform draped with the American flag. A decayed, corseted tenor—bursting out of a Daniel Boone
costume—is singing the *Star Spangled Banner*, accompanied by a full orchestra. He sings with a slight
lisp. . . .

THE DIPLOMAT (reading from a great scroll of ticker
tape that keeps growing and tangling around his feet):
"And we categorically deny that *any* male citizen of
the United States of America . . ."

TENOR: "Oh thay can you thee . . ." His voice breaks
and shoots up to a high falsetto.

In the control room the Technician mixes a bicarbonate of soda and belches into his hand: "God damned
tenor's a brown artist!" he mutters sourly. "Mike!
rumph," the shout ends in a belch. "Cut that swish
fart off the air and give him his purple slip. He's
through as of right now. . . . Put in that sex-changed
Liz athlete. . . . She's a fulltime tenor at least. . . .
Costume? How in the fuck should I know? I'm no
dress designer swish from the costume department!
What's that? The entire costume department occluded
as a security risk? What am I, an octopus? Let's see . . .
How about an Indian routine? Pocahontas or Hia-

watha? . . . No, that's not right. Some citizen cracks wise about giving it back to the Indians. . . . A Civil War uniform, the coat North and the pants South like it show they got together again? She can come on like Buffalo Bill or Paul Revere or that citizen wouldn't give up the shit, I mean the ship, or a G.I. or a Doughboy or the Unknown Soldier. . . . That's the best deal. . . . Cover her with a monument, that way nobody has to look at her. . . ."

The Lesbian, concealed in a *papier mâché* Arc de Triomphe fills her great lungs and looses a tremendous bellow.

"Oh say do that Star Spangled Banner yet wave . . ."

A great rent rips the Arc de Triomphe from top to bottom. The Diplomat puts a hand to his forehead. . . .

THE DIPLOMAT: "That any male citizen of the United States has given birth in Interzone or at any other place. . . ."

"O'er the land of the FREEEEEEEEEEE . . ."

The Diplomant's mouth is moving but no one can hear him. The Technician clasps his hands over his ears: "Mother of God!" he screams. His plate begins to vibrate like a Jew's harp, suddenly flies out of his mouth. . . . He snaps at it irritably, misses and covers his mouth with one hand.

The Arc de Triomphe falls with a ripping, splintering crash, reveals the Lesbian standing on a pedestal clad only in a leopard-skin jockstrap with enormous falsie basket. . . . She stands there smiling stupidly and flexing her huge muscles. . . . The Technician is crawling around on the control room floor looking for his plate and shouting unitelligible orders: "Thess thupper thonic!! Thut ur oth thu thair!"

THE DIPLOMAT (wiping sweat from his brow): "To any creature of any type or description . . ."

"And the home of the brave."

The diplomat's face is grey. He staggers, trips in the scroll, sags against the rail, blood pouring from eyes, nose and mouth, dying of cerebral hemorrhage.

THE DIPLOMAT (barely audible): "The Department denies . . . un-American . . . It's been destroyed . . . I mean it never was . . . Categor . . ." *Dies.*

In the Control Room instrument panels are blowing out . . . great streamers of electricity crackle through the room. . . . The Technician, naked, his body burned black, staggers about like a figure in Götterdämmerung, screaming: "Thubber thonic!! Oth thu thair!!!" A final blast reduces the Technician to a cinder.

> *Gave proof through the night*
> *That our flag was still there. . . .*

Habit Notes. Shooting Eukodol every two hours. I have a place where I can slip my needle right into a vein, it stays open like a red, festering mouth, swollen and obscene, gathers a slow drop of blood and pus after the shot. . . .

Eukodol is a chemical variation of codeine—dihydro-oxy-codeine.

This stuff comes on more like C than M. . . . When you shoot Coke in the mainline there is a rush of pure pleasure to the head. . . . Ten minutes later you want another shot. . . . The pleasure of morphine is in the viscera. . . . You listen down into yourself after a shot. . . . But intravenous C is electricity through the brain, activating cocaine pleasure connections. . . .There is no withdrawal syndrome with C. It is a need of the brain alone—a need without body and without feeling. Earth-bound ghost need. The craving for C lasts only a few hours as long as the C channels are stimulated. Then you forget it. Eukodol is like a combination of junk and C. Trust the Germans to concoct some really evil shit. Eukodol like morphine is six times stronger than codeine. Heroin six times stronger than morphine. Di-hydro-oxy-heroin should be six times stronger than heroin. Quite possible to develop a drug so habit-form-ing that one shot would cause lifelong addiction.

Habit Note continued: Picking up needle I reach spontaneously for the tie-up cord with my left hand. This I take as a sign I can hit the one useable vein in my left arm. (The movements of tying up are such that you normally tie up the arm with which you reach for the cord.) The needle slides in easily on the edge of a callous. I feel around. Suddenly a thin column of blood shoots up into the syringe, for a moment sharp and solid as a red cord.

The body knows what veins you can hit and conveys this knowledge in the spontaneous movements you make preparing to take a shot. . . . Sometimes the needle points like a dowzer's wand. Sometime I must wait for the message. But when it comes I always hit blood.

A red orchid bloomed at the bottom of the dropper. He hesitated for a full second, then pressed the bulb, watching the liquid rush into the vein as if sucked by the silent thirst of his blood. There was an iridescent, thin coat of blood left in the dropper, and the white paper collar was soaked through with blood like a bandage. He reached over and filled the dropper with water. As he squirted the water out, the shot hit him in the stomach, a soft sweet blow.

Look down at my filthy trousers, haven't been changed in months. . . . The days glide by strung on a syringe with a long thread of blood. . . . I am forgetting sex and all sharp pleasures of the body—a grey, junk-bound ghost. The Spanish boys call me El Hombre Invisible—the Invisible Man. . . .

Twenty push ups every morning. Use of junk removes fat, leaves muscle more or less intact. The addict seems to need less tissue. . . .Would it be possible to isolate the fat-removing molecule of junk?

More and more static at the Drug Store, mutterings of control like a telephone off the hook . . . Spent all day until 8 P.M. to score for two boxes of Eukodol. . . . Running out of veins and out of money.

Keep going on the nod. Last night I woke up with someone squeezing my hand. It was my other hand. . . . Fall asleep reading and the words take on code significance. . . . Obsessed with codes. . . . Man contracts a series of diseases which spell out a code message. . . .

Take a shot in front of D.L. Probing for a vein in

my dirty bare foot. . . . Junkies have no shame. . . . They are impervious to the repugnance of others. It is doubtful if shame can exist in the absence of sexual libido. . . . The junky's shame disappears with his non-sexual sociability which is also dependent on libido. . . . The addict regards his body impersonally as an instrument to absorb the medium in which he lives, evaluates his tissue with the cold hands of a horse trader. "No use trying to hit there." Dead fish eyes flick over a ravaged vein.

Using a new type sleeping pill called Soneryl. . . . You don't feel sleepy. . . . You shift to sleep without transition, fall abruptly into the middle of a dream. . . . I have been years in a prison camp suffering from malnutrition. . . .

The President is a junky but can't take it direct because of his position. So he gets fixed through me. . . . From time to time we make contact, and I recharge him. These contacts look, to the casual observer, like homosexual practices, but the actual excitement is not primarily sexual, and the climax is the separation when the recharge is completed. The erect penises are brought into contact—at least we used that method in the beginning, but contact points wear out like veins. Now I sometimes have to slip my penis under his left eyelid. Of course I can always fix him with an Osmosis Recharge, which corresponds to a skin shot, but that is admitting defeat. An O.R. will put the President in a bad mood for weeks, and might well precipitate an atomic shambles. And the President pays a high price for the Oblique Habit. He has sacrificed all control, and is dependent as an unborn child. The

Oblique Addict suffers a whole spectrum of subjective horror, silent protoplasmic frenzy, hideous agony of the bones. Tensions build up, pure energy without emotional content finally tears through the body throwing him about like a man in contact with high tension wires. If his charge connection is cut off cold, the Oblique Addict falls into such violent electric convulsions that his bones shake loose, and he dies with the skeleton straining to climb out of his unendurable flesh and run in a straight line to the nearest cemetery.

The relation between an O.A. (Oblique Addict) and his R.C. (Recharge Connection) is so intense that they can only endure each other's company for brief and infrequent intervals—I mean aside from recharge meets, when all personal contact is eclipsed by the recharge process.

Reading the paper. . . . Something about a triple murder in the rue de la Merde, Paris: "An adjusting of scores." . . . I keep slipping away. . . . "The police have identified the author . . . Pepe El Culito . . . The Little Ass Hole, an affectionate diminutive." Does it really say that? . . . I try to focus the words . . . they separate in meaningless mosaic. . . .

LAZARUS GO HOME

Fumbling through faded tape at the pick up frontier, a languid grey area of hiatus miasmic with yawns and gaping goof holes, Lee found out that the young junky standing there in his room at 10 A.M. was back from two months skin diving in Corsica and off the junk. . . .

"Here to show off his new body," Lee decided with a shudder of morning junk sickness. He knew that he was seeing—ah yes *Miguel* thank you—three months back sitting in the Metropole nodded out over a stale yellow eclair that would poison a cat two hours later, decided that the effort involved in seeing Miguel at all 10 A.M. was enough without the intolerable chore of correcting an error—("what is this a fucking farm?") which would also entail current picture of Miguel in much used areas like some great, inconvenient beast of an object on top in the suitcase.

"You look marvelous," Lee said, wiping away the more obvious signs of distaste with a sloppy, casual napkin, seeing the grey ooze of junk in Miguel's face, studying patterns of shabbiness as if man and clothes had moved for years through back alleys of time with never a space station to tidy up. . . .

"Besides by the time I could correct the error . . . Lazarus go home. . . . Pay The Man and go home. . . . What I want to see your old borrowed. meat for?"

"Well it's great to see you off. . . .Do yourself a favor." Miguel was swimming around the room spearing fish with his hand. . . .

"When you're down there you never think about horse."

"You're better off like this," said Lee, dreamily caressing a needle scar on the back of Miguel's hand, following the whorls and patterns of smooth purple flesh in a slow twisting movement. . . .

Miguel scratched the back of his hand. . . . He looked

out the window. . . . His body moved in little, galvanized jerks as junk channels lit up. . . . Lee sat there waiting. "One snort never put anybody back on, kid."

"I know what I'm doing."

"They always know."

Miguel took the nail file.

Lee closed his eyes: "It's too tiresome."

"Uh thanks that was great." Miguel's pants fell to his ankles. He stood there in a misshapen overcoat of flesh that turned from brown to green and then colorless in the morning light, fell off in globs onto the floor.

Lee's eyes moved in the substance of his face . . . a little, cold, grey flick. . . . "Clean it up," he said. "Enough dirt in here now."

"Oh uh sure," Miguel fumbled with a dustpan.

Lee put the packet of heroin away.

Lee lived in a permanent third-day kick, with, of course, certain uh essential intermissions to refuel the fires that burned through his yellow-pink-brown gelatinous substance and kept off the hovering flesh. In the beginning his flesh was simply soft, so soft that he was cut to the bone by dust particles, air currents and brushing overcoats while direct contact with doors and chairs seemed to occasion no discomfort. No wound healed in his soft, tentative flesh. . . . Long white tendrils of fungus curled round the naked bones. Mold odors of atrophied testicles quilted his body in a fuzzy grey fog. . . .

During his first severe infection the boiling thermometer flashed a quicksilver bullet into the nurse's brain and she fell dead with a mangled scream. The doctor took one look and slammed steel shutters of survival. He ordered the burning bed and its occupant immediately evicted from the hospital premises.

"Guess he can make his own penicillin!" snarled the doctor.

But the infection burned the mold out. . . . Lee lived now in varying degrees of transparency. . . . While not exactly invisible he was at least difficult to see. His presence attracted no special notice. . . . People covered him with a project or dismissed him as a reflection, shadow: "Some kinda light trick or neon advertisement."

Now Lee felt the first seismic tremors of Old Faithful the Cold Burn. He pushed Miguel's spirit into the hall with a kind, firm tendril.

"Jesus!" said Miguel. "I gotta go!" He rushed out.

Pink fires of histamine spurted from Lee's glowing core and covered his raw periphery. (The room was fireproof, the walls of iron blistered and spotted with moon craters.) He took a large fix and falsified his schedule.

He decided to visit a colleague, NG Joe, who got hooked during a Bang-utot attack in Honolulu.

(Note: Bang-utot, literally, "attempting to get up and groaning . . ." Death occurring in the course of a nightmare . . . The condition occurs in males of S.E. Asiatic extraction. . . . In Manila about twelve cases of death by Bang-utot are recorded each year.

One man who recovered said that "a little man" was sitting on his chest and strangling him.

Victims often know that they are going to die, express the fear that their penis will enter the body and kill them. Sometimes they cling to the penis in a state of shrieking hysteria calling on others for help lest the penis escape and pierce the body. Erections, such as normally occur in sleep, are considered especially dangerous and liable to bring a fatal attack. . . . One man devised a Rube Goldberg contraption to prevent erection during sleep. But he died of Bang-utot.

Careful autopsies of Bang-utot victims have revealed no organic reason for death. There are often signs of strangulation (caused by what?); sometimes slight hemorrhages of pancreas and lungs—not sufficient to cause death and also of unknown origin. It has occurred to the author that the cause of death is a misplacement of sexual energy resulting in a lung erection with consequent strangulation. . . . [See article by Nils Larsen M.D., *The Men with the Deadly Dream* in the *Saturday Evening Post*, December 3, 1955. Also article by Erle Stanley Gardner for *True Magazine*.])

NG lived in constant fear of erection so his habit jumped and jumped. (Note: It is a well known tiresome fact, it is a notoriously dull and long winded fact, that anyone who gets hooked because of any disability whatever, will be presented, during the periods of shortage or deprivation [such a thing as too much fun you know] with an outrageously padded, geometrically progressing, proliferating account.)

An electrode attached to one testicle glowed briefly and NG woke up in the smell of burning flesh and reached for a loaded syringe. He rolled into a foetal position and slid the needle into his spine. He pulled the needle out with a little sigh of pleasure, and realized that Lee was in the room. A long slug undulated out of Lee's right eye and wrote on the wall in iridescent ooze: " The Sailor is in the Ctity buying up TIME."

I am waiting in front of a drugstore for it to open at nine o'clock. Two Arab boys roll cans of garbage up to a high heavy wood door in a whitewashed wall. Dust in front of the door streaked with urine. One of the boys bent over, rolling the heavy cans, pants tight over his lean young ass. He looks at me with the neutral, calm glance of an animal. I wake with a shock like the boy is real and I have missed a meet I had with him for this afternoon.

"We expect additional equalizations," says the Inspector in an interview with Your Reporter. "Otherwise will occur," the Inspector lifts one leg in a typical Nordic gesture, "the bends is it not? But perhaps we can provide the suitable chamber of decompression."

The Inspector opens his fly and begins looking for crabs, applying ointment from a little clay pot. Clearly the·interview is at an end. "You're not going?" he exclaims. "Well, as one judge said to the other, 'Be just and if you can't be just be arbitrary.' Regret cannot observe customary obscenities." He holds up his right hand covered with a foul-smelling yellow ointment.

One's Reporter rushes forward and clasps the soiled hand in both of his. "It's been a pleasure, Inspector, an unspeakable pleasure," he says peeling off his gloves, rolling them into a ball and tossing them into the wastebasket. "Expense account," he smiles.

HASSAN'S RUMPUS ROOM

Gilt and red plush. Rococo bar backed by pink shell. The air is cloyed with a sweet evil substance like decayed honey. Men and women in evening dress sip pousse-cafés through alabaster tubes. A Near East Mugwump sits naked on a bar stool covered in pink silk. He licks warm honey from a crystal goblet with a long black tongue. His genitals are perfectly formed—circumcised cock, black shiny pubic hairs. His lips are thin and purple-blue like the lips of a penis, his eyes blank with insect calm. The Mugwump has no liver, maintaining himself exclusive on sweets. Mugwump push a slender blond youth to a couch and strip him expertly.

"Stand up and turn around," he orders in telepathic pictographs. He ties the boy's hands behind him with a red silk cord. "Tonight we make it all the way."

"No, no!" screams the boy.

"Yes. Yes."

Cocks ejaculate in silent "yes." Mugwump part silk curtains, reveal a teak wood gallows against lighted screen of red flint. Gallows is on a dais of Aztec mosaics.

The boy crumples to his knees with a long "OOOOOOOOH," shitting and pissing in terror. He feels the shit warm between his thighs. A great wave of hot blood swells his lips and throat. His body contracts into a foetal position and sperm spurts hot into his face. The Mugwump dips hot perfumed water from alabaster bowl, pensively washes the boy's ass and

cock, drying him with a soft blue towel. A warm wind
plays over the boys body and the hairs float free. The
Mugwump puts a hand under the boy's chest and
pulls him to his feet. Holding him by both pinioned
elbows, propels him up the steps and under the noose.
He stands in front of the boy holding the noose in
both hands.

The boy looks into Mugwump eyes blank as obsidian
mirrors, pools of black blood, glory holes in a toilet
wall closing on the Last Erection.

An old garbage collector, face fine and yellow as
Chinese ivory, blows The Blast on his dented brass
horn, wakes the Spanish pimp with a hard-on. Whore
staggers out through dust and shit and litter of dead
kittens, carrying bales of aborted foetuses, broken condoms, bloody Kotex, shit wrapped in bright color
comics.

A vast still harbor of iridescent water. Deserted gas
well flares on the smoky horizon. Stink of oil and
sewage. Sick sharks swim through the black water,
belch sulphur from rotting livers, ignore a bloody,
broken Icarus. Naked Mr. America, burning frantic
with self bone love, screams out: "My asshole con-
founds the Louvre! I fart ambrosia and shit pure gold
turds! My cock spurts soft diamonds in the morning
sunlight!" He plummets from the eyeless lighthouse,
kissing and jacking off in face of the black mirror,
glides oblique down with cryptic condoms and mosaic
of a thousand newspapers through a drowned city of
red brick to settle in black mud with tin cans and beer
bottles, gangsters in concrete, pistols pounded flat and

meaningless to avoid short-arm inspection of prurient ballistic experts. He waits the slow striptease of erosion with fossil loins.

The Mugwump slips the noose over the boy's head and tightens the knot caressingly behind the left ear. The boy's penis is retracted, his balls tight. He looks straight ahead breathing deeply. The Mugwump sidles around the boy goosing him and caressing his genitals in hieroglyphs of mockery. He moves in behind the boy with a series of bumps and shoves his cock up the boy's ass. He stands there moving in circular gyrations.

The guests shush each other, nudge and giggle.

Suddenly the Mugwump pushes the boy forward into space, free of his cock. He steadies the boy with hands on the hip bones, reaches up with his stylized hieroglyph hands and snaps the boy's neck. A shudder passes through the boy's body. His penis rises in three great surges pulling his pelvis up, ejaculates immediately.

Green sparks explode behind his eyes. A sweet toothache pain shoots through his neck down the spine to the groin, contracting the body in spasms of delight. His whole body squeezes out through his cock. A final spasm throws a great spurt of sperm across the red screen like a shooting star.

The boy falls with soft gutty suction through a maze of penny arcades and dirty pictures.

A sharp turd shoots clean out his ass. Farts shake his slender body. Skyrockets burst in green clusters across a great river. He hears the faint put-put of a motor boat in jungle twilight. . . . Under silent wings of the anopheles mosquito.

The Mugwump pulls the boy back onto his cock. The boy squirms, impaled like a speared fish. The Mugwump swings on the boy's back, his body contracting in fluid waves. Blood flows down the boy's chin from his mouth, half-open, sweet, and sulky in death. The Mugwump falls with a fluid, sated plop.

Windowless cubicle with blue walls. Dirty pink curtain cover the door. Red bugs crawl on the wall, cluster in corners. Naked boy in the middle of the room twang a two-string ouad, trace an arabesque on the floor. Another boy lean back on the bed smoking keif and blow smoke over his erect cock. They play game with tarot cards on the bed to see who fuck who. Cheat. Fight. Roll on the floor snarling and spitting like young animals. The loser sit on the floor chin on knees, licks a broken tooth. The winner curls up on the bed pretending to sleep. Whenever the other boy come near kick at him. Ali seize him by one ankle, tuck the ankle under his arm pit, lock his arm around the calf. The boy kick desperately at Ali's face. Other ankle pinioned. Ali tilt the boy back on his shoulders. The boy's cock extends along his stomach, float free pulsing. Ali put his hands over his head. Spit on his cock. The other sighs deeply as Ali slides his cock in. The mouths grind together smearing blood. Sharp musty odor of penetrated rectum. Nimun drive in like a wedge, force jism out the other cock in long hot spurts. (The author has observed that Arab cocks tend to be wide and wedge shaped.)

Satyr and naked Greek lad in aqualungs trace a

ballet of pursuit in a monster vase of transparent alabaster. The Satyr catches the boy from in front and whirls him around. They move in fish jerks. The boy releases a silver stream of bubbles from his mouth. White sperm ejaculates into the green water and floats lazily around the twisting bodies.

Negro gently lifts exquisite Chinese boy into a hammock. He pushes the boy's legs up over his head and straddles the hammock. He slides his cock up the boy's slender tight ass. He rocks the hammock gently back and forth. The boy screams, a weird high wail of unendurable delight.

A Javanese dancer in ornate teak swivel chair, set in a socket of limestone buttocks, pulls an American boy—red hair, bright green eyes—down onto his cock with ritual motions. The boy sits impaled facing the dancer who propels himself in circular gyrations, lending fluid substance to the chair. "Weeeeeeeeee!" scream the boy as his sperm spurt up over the dancer's lean brown chest. One gob hit the corner of the dancer's mouth. The boy push it in with his finger and laugh: "Man, that's what I call suction!"

Two Arab women with bestial faces have pulled the shorts off a little blond French boy. They are screwing him with red rubber cocks. The boy snarls, bites, kicks, collapses in tears as his cock rises and ejaculates.

Hassan's face swells, tumescent with blood. His lips turn purple. He strip off his suit of banknotes and throw it into an open vault that closes soundless.

"Freedom Hall here, folks!" he screams in his phoney Texas accent. Ten-gallon hat and cowboy boots still on, he dances the Liquefactionist Jig, ending with a grotesque can-can to the tune of *She Started a Heat Wave*.

"Let it be! And no holes barred!!!"

Couples attached to baroque harnesses with artificial wings copulate in the air, screaming like magpies.

Aerialists ejaculate each other in space with one sure touch.

Equilibrists suck each other off deftly, balanced on perilous poles and chairs tilted over the void. A warm wind brings the smell of rivers and jungle from misty depths.

Boys by the hundred plummet through the roof, quivering and kicking at the end of ropes. The boys hang at different levels, some near the ceiling and others a few inches off the floor. Exquisite Balinese and Malays, Mexican Indians with fierce innocent faces and bright red gums. Negroes (teeth, fingers, toe nails and pubic hair gilded), Japanese boys smooth and white as China, Titian-haired Venetian lads, Americans with blond or black curls falling across the forehead (the guests tenderly shove it back), sulky blond Pollacks with animal brown eyes, Arab and Spanish street boys, Austrian boys pink and delicate with a faint shadow of blond pubic hair, sneering German youths with bright blue eyes scream "Heil Hitler!" as the trap falls under them. Sollubis shit and whimper.

Mr. Rich-and-Vulgar chews his Havana lewd and nasty, sprawled on a Florida beach surrounded by simpering blond catamites:

"This citizen have a Latah he import from Indo-China. He figure to hang the Latah and send a Xmas TV short to his friends. So he fix up two ropes—one gimmicked to stretch, the other the real McCoy. But that Latah get up in feud state and put on his Santa Claus suit and make with the switcheroo. Come the dawning. The citizen put one rope on and the Latah, going along the way Latahs will, put on the other. When the traps are down the citizen hang for real and the Latah stand with the carny-rubber stretch rope. Well, the Latah imitate every twitch and spasm. Come three times.

"Smart young Latah keep his eye on the ball. I got him working in one of my plants as an expeditor."

Aztec priests strip blue feather robe from the Naked Youth. They bend him back over a limestone altar, fit a crystal skull over his head, securing the two hemispheres back and front with crystal screws. A waterfall pour over the skull snapping the boy's neck. He ejaculate in a rainbow against the rising sun.

Sharp protein odor of semen fills the air. The guests run hands over twitching boys, suck their cocks, hang on their backs like vampires.

Naked lifeguards carry in iron-lungs full of paralyzed youths.

Blind boys grope out of huge pies, deteriorated schizophrenics pop from a rubber cunt, boys with horrible skin diseases rise from a black pond (sluggish fish nibble yellow turds on the surface).

A man with white tie and dress shirt, naked from the waist down except for black garters, talks to the Queen Bee in elegant tones. (Queen Bees are old women who surround themselves with fairies to form a "swarm." It is a sinister Mexican practice.)

"But where is the statuary?" He talks out of one side of his face, the other is twisted by the Torture of a Million Mirrors. He masturbates wildly. The Queen Bee continues the conversation, notices nothing.

Couches, chairs, the whole floor begins to vibrate, shaking the guests to blurred grey ghosts shrieking in cock-bound agony.

Two boys jacking off under railroad bridge. The train shakes through their bodies, ejaculate them, fades with distant whistle. Frogs croak. The boys wash semen off lean brown stomachs.

Train compartment: two sick young junkies on their way to Lexington tear their pants down in convulsions of lust. One of them soaps his cock and works it up the other's ass with a corkscrew motion. "Jeeeeeeeeeeeeeee-sus!" Both ejaculate at once standing up. They move away from each other and pull up their pants.

"Old croaker in Marshall writes for tincture and sweet oil."

"The piles of an aged mother shriek out raw and bleeding for the Black Shit. . . . Doc, suppose it was your mother, rimmed by resident leaches, squirming around so nasty. . . . De-active that pelvis, mom, you disgust me already"

"Let's stop over and make him for an RX."

The train tears on through the smoky, neon-lighted June night.

Pictures of men and women, boys and girls, animals, fish, birds, the copulating rhythm of the universe flows through the room, a great blue tide of life. Vibrating, soundless hum of deep forest—sudden quiet of cities when the junky copes. A moment of stillness and wonder. Even the Commuter buzzes clogged lines of cholesterol for contact.

Hassan shrieks out: "This is your doing, A.J.! You poopa my party!"

A.J. looks at him, face remote as limestone: "Uppa your ass, you liquefying gook."

A horde of lust-mad American women rush in. Dripping cunts, from farm and dude ranch, factory, brothel, country club, penthouse and suburb, motel and yacht and cocktail bar, strip off riding clothes, ski togs, evening dresses, levis, tea gowns, print dresses, slacks, bathing suits and kimonos. They scream and yipe and howl, leap on the guests like bitch dogs in heat with rabies. They claw at the hanged boys shrieking: "You fairy! You bastard! Fuck me! Fuck me! Fuck me!" The guests flee screaming, dodge among the hanged boys, overturn iron lungs.

A.J.: "Call out my Sweitzers, God damn it! Guard me from these she-foxes!"

Mr. Hyslop, A. J.'s secretary, looks up from his comic book: "The Sweitzers liquefy already."

(Liquefaction involves protein cleavage and reduction to liquid which is absorbed into someone else's protoplasmic being. Hassan, a notorious liquefactionist, is probably the beneficiary in this case.)

A.J.: "Gold-bricking cocksuckers! Where's a man without his Sweitzers? Our backs are to the wall, gentlemen. Our very cocks at stake. Stand by to resist boarders, Mr. Hyslop, and issue short arms to the men."

A.J. whips out a cutlass and begins decapitating the American Girls. He sings lustily:

Fifteen men on the dead man's chest
Yo Ho Ho and a bottle of rum.
Drink and the devil had done for the rest
Yo Ho Ho and a bottle of rum.

Mr. Hyslop, bored and resigned: "Oh Gawd! He's at it again." He waves the Jolly Roger listlessly.

A.J., surrounded and fighting against overwhelming odds, throws back his head and makes with the hog-call. Immediately a thousand rutting Eskimos pour in grunting and squealing, faces tumescent, eyes hot and red, lips purple, fall on the American women.

(Eskimos have a rutting season when the tribes meet in short Summer to disport themselves in orgies. Their faces swell and lips turn purple.)

A House Dick with cigar two feet long sticks his head in through the wall: "Have you got a menagerie in here?"

Hassan wrings his hands: "A shambles! A filthy shambles! By Allah I never see anything so downright nasty!"

He whirls on A.J. who is sitting on a sea chest, parrot on shoulder, patch over one eye, drinking rum from a tankard. He scans the horizon with a huge brass telescope.

Hassan: "You cheap Factualist bitch! Go and never darken my rumpus room again!"

CAMPUS OF INTERZONE UNIVERSITY

Donkeys, camels, llamas, rickshaws, carts of merchandise pushed by straining boys, eyes protruding like strangled tongues—throbbing red with animal hate. Herds of sheep and goats and long-horned cattle pass between the students and the lecture platform. The students sit around on rusty park benches, limestone blocks, outhouse seats, packing crates, oil drums, stumps, dusty leather hassacks, mouldy gym mats. They wear levis—jellabas . . . hose and doublet—drink corn from mason jars, coffee from tin cans, smoke gage (marijuana) in cigarettes made of wrapping paper and lottery tickets . . . shoot junk with a safety pin and dropper, study racing forms, comic books, Mayan codices. . . .

The Professor arrives on a bicycle carrying a string of bull heads. He mounts the platform holding his back (crane swings a bellowing cow over his head).

PROF: "Fucked by the Sultan's Army last night. I have dislocate the back in the service of my resident queen. . . . Can't evict that old gash. Need a licensed brain electrician disconnect her synapsis by synapsis and a surgical bailiff put her guts out on the sidewalk. When Ma move in on a boy bag and buggage he play Hell dispossess that Gold Star Boarder. . . ."

He looks at the bull heads humming tunes from the 1920s. "The nostalgia fit is on me boys and will out willy silly . . . boys walk down the carny Midway eating pink spun sugar . . . goose each other at the peep show . . . jack off in the Ferris Wheel throw sperm at the moon rising red and smoky over the foundries across the river. A Nigra hangs from a cotton wood in front of The Old Court House . . . whimpering women catch his sperm in vaginal teeth. . . . (Husband looks at the little changeling with narrow eyes the color of a faded grey flannel shirt. . . . 'Doc, I suspect it to be a Nigra.'

The Doctor shrugs: 'It's the Old Army Game, son. Pea under the shell . . . Now you see it now you don't. . . .')

"And Doc Parker in the back room in his drugstore shooting horse heroin three grains a jolt—'Tonic,' he mutters 'It's always Spring.'

" 'Hands' Benson Town Pervert has took up a querencia in the school privy (Querencia is bullfight term. . . . The bull will find a spot in the ring he likes and stay there and the bullfighter has to go in and meet the bull on his bull terms or coax him out—one or the other). Sheriff A.Q. 'Flat' Larsen say 'Some way we gotta lure him outa that querencia.' . . . And Old Ma Lottie sleep ten years with a dead daughter and home cured too, wakes shivering in the East Texas dawn . . . vultures out over the black swamp water and cypress stumps. . . .

"And now gentlemen—I trust there are no transvestites present— he he—and you are all gentlemen by act of Congress it being only remain to establish you *male humans*, positively no Transitionals in either direction will be allowed in this decent hall. Gentlemen, present short arms. Now you have all been briefed on the importance of keeping your weapons well lubricated and ready for any action flank or rear guard."

STUDENTS: "Hear! Hear!" They wearily unbutton their flies. One of them brandishes a huge erection.

PROF: "And now, gentlemen, where was I? Oh yes, Ma Lottie . . . She wake shivering in the gentle pink dawn, pink as the candles on a little girl's birthday cake, pink as spun sugar, pink as a sea-shell, pink as a cock pulsing in a red fucking light. . . . Ma Lottie . . . hurumph . . . if this prolixity be not cut short will succumb to the infirmities of age and join her daughter in formaldehyde.

"The Rime of the Ancient Mariner by Coleridge the poet . . . I should like to call your attention to the symbolism of the Ancient Mariner *himself*."

STUDENTS: "*Himself* the man says."

"Thereby call attention to his own unappetizing person."

"That wasn't a nice thing to do, Teach."

A hundred juvenile delinquents . . . switch blades clicking like teeth move at him.

PROF: "Oh Landsakes!" He tries desperately to disguise himself as an old woman with high black shoes and umbrella. . . . "If it wasn't for my lumbago can't rightly bend over I'd turn them offering my Sugar Bum the way baboons do it. . . . If a weaker baboon be attacked by a stronger baboon the weaker baboon will either (a) present his hrump fanny I believe is the word, gentlemen, heh heh for passive intercourse *or* (b) if he is a different type baboon more extrovert and well-adjusted, lead an attack on an even weaker baboon if he can find one."

Dilapidated Diseuse in 1920 clothes like she sleep in them ever since undulates across dreary neonlighted Chicago street . . . dead weight of the Dear Dead Days hanging in the air like an earth-bound ghost. Diseuse: (canned heat tenor). "Find the weakest baboon."

Frontier saloon: Fag Baboon dressed in little girl blue dress sings in resigned voice to tune of *Alice Blue Gown*: "I'm the weakest baboon of them all."

A freight train separates the Prof. from the juveniles. . . . When the train passes they have fat stomachs and responsible jobs. . . .

STUDENTS: "We want Lottie!"

PROF: "That was in another country, gentlemen. . . . As I was saying before I was so rudely irrupted by one of my multiple personalities . . . troublesome little beasts . . . consider the Ancient Mariner without curare, lasso, bulbocapnine or straitjacket, albeit able to capture and hold a live audience. . . . What is his hurmp gimmick? He he he he . . . He does not, like so-called artists at this time, stop just *anybody* thereby inflicting unsent for boredom and working random hardship. . . . He stops those who cannot choose but hear owing to already existing relation between The Mariner (however ancient) and the uh Wedding Guest. . . .

"What the Mariner actually says is not important. . . . He may be rambling, irrelevant, even crude and rampant senile. But something happens to the Wedding Guest like happens in psychoanalysis when it happens if it happens. If I may be permitted a slight digression . . . an anlyst of my acquaintance does all the talking —patients listen patiently or not. . . . He reminiscences . . . tells dirty jokes (old ones) achieves counterpoints of idiocy undreamed of by The County Clerk. He is illustrating at some length that nothing can ever be accomplished on the verbal level. . . . He arrived at this method through observing that The Listener—The Analyst—was not reading the mind of the patient. . . . The patient—The Talker—was reading *his* mind. . . . That is the patient has ESP awareness of the analyst's dreams and schemes whereas the analyst contacts the patient strictly from front brain. . . . Many agents use this approach—they are notoriously long-winded bores and bad listeners. . . .

"Gentlemen I will slop a pearl: *You can find out more about someone by talking than by listening.*"

Pigs rush up and the Prof. pours buckets of pearls into a trough. . . .

"I am not worthy to eat his feet," says the fattest hog of them all.

"Clay anyhoo."

A.J.'S ANNUAL PARTY

A.J. turns to the guests. "Cunts, pricks, fence straddlers, tonight I give you—that international-known impressario of blue movies and short-wave TV, the one, the only, The Great Slashtubitch!"

He points to a red velvet curtain sixty feet high. Lightning rends the curtain from top to bottom. The Great Slashtubitch stands revealed. His face is immense, immobile like a Chimu funeral urn. He wears full evening dress, blue cape and blue monocle. Huge grey eyes with tiny black pupils that seem to spit needles. (Only the Coordinate Factualist can meet his gaze.) When he is angered the charge of it will blow his monocle across the room. Many an ill-starred actor has felt the icy blast of Slashtubitch's displeasure: "Get out of my studio, you cheap four-flushing ham! Did you think to pass a counterfeit orgasm on me! THE GREAT SLASHTU-BITCH! I could tell if you come by regard the beeg toe. Idiot! Mindless scum!! Insolent baggage!!! Go peddle thy ass and know that it takes sincerity and art, and devotion, to work for Slashtubitch. Not shoddy trickery, dubbed gasps, rubber turds and vials of milk concealed in the ear and shots of Yohimbine sneaked in the wings." (Yohimbine, derived from the bark of a tree growing in Central Africa, is the safest and most efficient aphrodisiac. It operates by dilating the blood vessels on the surface of the skin, particularly in the genital area.)

Slashtubitch ejects his monocle. It sails out of sight, returns like a boomerang into his eye. He pirouettes and disappears in a blue mist, cold as liquid air . . . fadeout. . . .

On Screen. Red-haired, green-eyed boy, white skin with a few freckles . . . kissing a thin brunette girl in slacks. Clothes and hair-do suggest existentialist bars of all the world cities. They are seated on low bed covered in white silk. The girl opens his pants with gentle fingers and pulls out his cock which is small and very hard. A drop of lubricant gleams at its tip like a pearl. She caresses the crown gently: "Strip, Johnny." He takes off his clothes with swift sure movements and stands naked before her, his cock pulsing. She makes a motion for him to turn around and he pirouettes across the floor parodying a model, hand on hip. She takes off her shirt.

Her breasts are high and small with erect nipples. She slips off her underpants. Her pubic hairs are black and shiny. He sits down beside her and reaches for her breast. She stops his hands.

"Darling, I want to rim you," she whispers.

"No. Not now."

"Please, I want to."

"Well, all right. I'll go wash my ass."

"No, I'll wash it."

"Aw shucks now, it ain't dirty."

"Yes it is. Come on now, Johnny boy."

She leads him into the bathroom. "All right, get down." He gets down on his knees and leans forward, with his chin on the bath mat. "Allah," he says. He looks back and grins at her. She washes his ass with soap and hot water sticking her finger up it.

"Does that hurt?"

"Nooooooooooo."

"Come along, baby." She leads the way into the bedroom. He lies down on his back and throws his legs back over his head, clasping elbows behind his knees. She kneel down and caress the backs of his thighs, his balls, running her fingers down the perennial divide. She push his cheeks apart, lean down and begin licking the anus, moving her head in a slow circle. She push at the sides of the asshole, licking deeper and deeper. He close his eyes and squirm. She lick up the perennial divide. His small, tight balls. . . . A great pearl stands out on the tip of his circumcised cock. Her mouth closes over the crown. She sucks rhythmically up and down, pausing on the up stroke and moving her head around in a circle. Her hand plays gently with his balls, slide down and middle finger up his ass. As she suck down toward the root of his cock she tickle his prostate mockingly. He grin and fart. She is sucking his cock now in a frenzy. His body begins to contract, pulling up toward his chin. Each time the contraction is longer. "Wheeeeeeee!" the boy yell, every muscle tense, his whole body strain to empty through his cock. She drinks his jissom which fills her mouth in great hot spurts. He lets his feet flop back onto the bed. He arches his back and yawns.

Mary is strapping on a rubber penis: "Steely Dan III from Yokohama," she says, caressing the shaft. Milk spurts across the room.

"Be sure that milk is pasteurized. Don't go giving me some kinda awful cow disease like anthrax or glanders or aftosa. . . ."

"When I was a transvestite Liz in Chi used to work as an exterminator. Make advances to pretty boys for the thrill of being beaten as a man. Later I catch this one kid, overpower him with supersonic judo I learned from an old Lesbian Zen monk. I tie him up, strip off his clothes with a razor and fuck him with Steely Dan I. He is so relieved I don't castrate him literal he come all over my bedbug spray."

"What happen to Steely Dan I?"

"He was torn in two by a bull dike. Most terrific vaginal grip I ever experienced. She could cave in a lead pipe. It was one of her parlor tricks."

"And Steely Dan II?"

"Chewed to bits by a famished candiru in the Upper Baboonsasshole. And don't say 'Wheeeeeeee!' this time."

"Why not? It's real boyish."

"Barefoot boy, check thy bullheads with the madame"

He looks at the ceiling, hands behind his head, cock pulsing. "So what shall I do? Can't shit with that dingus up me. I wonder is it possible to laugh and come at the same time? I recall, during the war, at the Jockey Club in Cairo, me and my asshole buddy, Lu, both gentlemen by act of Congress . . . nothing else could have done such a thing to either of us. . . . So we got laughing so hard we piss all over ourselves and the waiter say: 'You bloody hash-heads, get out of here!' I mean, if I can laugh the piss out of me I should be able to laugh out jissom. So tell me something real funny when I start coming. You can tell by certain premonitory quiverings of the prostate gland. . . ."

She puts on a record, metallic cocaine be-bop. She greases the dingus, shoves the boy's legs over his head and works it up his ass with a series of corkscrew movements of her fluid hips. She moves in a slow circle, revolving on the axis of the shaft. She rubs her hard nipples across his chest. She kisses him on neck and chin and eyes. He runs his hands down her back to her buttocks, pulling her into his ass. She revolves faster, faster. His body jerks and writhes in convulsive spasms. "Hurry up, please," she says. "The milk is getting cold." He does not hear. She presses her mouth against his. Their faces run together. His sperm hits her breast with light, hot licks.

Mark is standing in the doorway. He wears a turtleneck black sweater. Cold, handsome, narcissistic face. Green eyes and black hair. He looks at Johnny with a slight sneer, his head on one side, hands on his jacket pockets, a graceful hoodlum ballet. He jerk his head and Johnny walk ahead of him into the bedroom. Mary follow. "All right, boys," she say, sitting down naked on a pink silk dais overlooking the bed. "Get with it!"

Mark begin to undress with fluid movements, hip-rolls, squirm out of his turtle-neck sweater revealing his beautiful white torso in a mocking belly dance. Johnny deadpan, face frozen, breath quick, lips dry, remove his clothes and drop them on the floor. Mark lets his shorts fall on one foot. He kick like a chorus-girl, sending the shorts across the room. Now he stand naked, his cock stiff, straining up and out. He run slow eyes over Johnny's body. He smile and lick his lips.

Mark drop on one knee, pulling Johnny across his back by one arm. He stand up and throw him six feet onto the bed. Johnny land on his back and bounce. Mark jump up and grab Johnny's ankles, throw his legs over his head. Mark's lips are drawn back in a tight snarl. "All right, Johnny boy." He contracts his body, slow and steady as an oiled machine, push his cock up Johnny's ass. Johnny give a great sigh, squirming in ecstasy. Mark hitches his hands behind Johnny's shoulders, pulling him down onto his cock which is buried to the hilt in Johnny's ass. Great whistles through his teeth. Johnny screams like a bird. Mark is rubbing his face against Johnny's, snarl gone, face innocent and boyish as his whole liquid being spurt into Johnny's quivering body.

A train roar through him whistle blowing . . . boat whistle, foghorn, sky rocket burst over oily lagoons . . . penny arcade open into a maze of dirty pictures . . . ceremonial cannon boom in the harbor . . . a scream shoots down a white hospital corridor . . . out along a wide dusty street between palm trees, whistles out across the desert like a bullet (vulture wings husk in the dry air), a thousand boys come at once in outhouses, bleak public school toilets, attics, basements, treehouses, Ferris wheels, deserted houses, limestone caves, rowboats, garages, barns, rubbly windy city outskirts behind mud walls (smell of dried excrement) . . . black dust blowing over lean copper bodies . . . ragged pants dropped to cracked bleeding bare feet . . . (place where vultures fight over fish heads) . . . by jungle lagoons, vicious fish snap at white sperm floating on black water, sand flies bite the copper ass, howler monkeys like wind in the trees (a land of great brown rivers where whole trees float, bright colored snakes in the branches, pensive lemurs watch the shore with sad eyes), a red plane traces arabesques in blue substance of sky, a rattlesnake strike, a cobra rear, spread, spit white venom, pearl and opal chips fall in a slow silent rain through air clear as glycerine. Time jump like a broken typewriter, the boys are old men, young hips quivering and twitching in boy-spasms go slack and flabby, draped over an outhouse seat, a park bench, a stone wall in Spanish sunlight, a sagging furnished room bed (outside red brick slum in clear winter sunlight) . . . twitching and shivering in dirty underwear, probing for a vein in the junk-sick morning, in an Arab café muttering and slobbering—the Arabs whisper "Medjoub" and edge away—(a Medjoub is a special sort of religious Moslem lunatic . . . often epileptic among other disorders). "The Moslems must have blood and jissom. . . . See, see where Christ's blood streams in the spermament," howls the Medjoub. . . . He stand up screaming and black blood spurt solid from his last erection, a pale white statue standing there, as if he had stepped whole across the Great Fence, climbed it innocent and calm as a boy climb the fence to fish in the forbidden pond—in a few seconds he catch a huge catfish—The Old Man will rush out of a little black hut cursing, with a pitchfork and the boy run laughing across the Missouri field—he find a beautiful pink arrowhead and snatch it up as he runs with a flowing swoop of young bone and muscle—(his bones blend into the field, he lies dead by the wooden fence a shotgun by his side, blood on frozen red clap seeps into the winter stubble of Georgia). . . . The catfish billows out behind him. . . . He come to the fence and throw the catfish over into blood-streaked grass . . . the fish lies squirming and squawking—vaults the fence. He snatch up the catfish and disappear up a flint-studded red clay road between oaks and persimmons dropping red-brown leaves in a windy fall sunset, green and dripping in Summer dawn, black against a clear winter day . . . the Old Man scream curses after him . . . his teeth fly from his mouth and whistle over the boy's head, he strain forward, his neck-cords tight as steel hoops, black blood spurt in one solid piece over the fence and he fall a fleshless mummy by the fever grass. Thorns grow through his ribs, the windows break in his hut, dusty glass-slivers in black putty—rats run over the floor and boys jack off in the dark musty bedroom on summer afternoons and eat the berries that grow from his body and bones, mouths smeared with purple-red juices. . . .

The old junky has found a vein . . . blood blossoms in

the dropper like a Chinese flower . . . he push home the heroin and the boy who jacked off fifty years ago shine immaculate through the ravaged flesh, fill the outhouse with the sweet nutty smell of young male lust. . . .

How many years threaded on a needle of blood? Hands slack on lap he sit looking out at the winter dawn with the cancelled eyes of junk. The old queer squirm on a limestone bench in Chapultepec Park as Indian adolescents walk by, arms around each other's necks and ribs, straining his dying flesh to occupy young buttocks and thighs, tight balls and spurting cocks.

Mark and Johnny sit facing each other in a vibrating chair, Johnny impaled on Mark's cock.

"All set, Johnny?"

"Turn it on."

Mark flips the switch and the chair vibrate. . . . Mark tilt his head looking up at Johnny, his face remote, eyes cool and mocking on Johnny's face. . . . Johnny scream and whimper. . . . His face disintegrates as if melted from within. . . . Johnny scream like a mandrake, black out as his sperm spurt, slump against Mark's body an angel on the nod. Mark pat Johnny's shoulder absently. . . . Room like gymnasium. . . . The floor is foam rubber, covered in white silk . . . . One wall is glass. . . . The rising sun fills the room with pink light. Johnny is led in, hands tied, between Mary and Mark. Johnny sees the gallows and sags with a great "Ohhhhhhhhhhh!" his chin pulling down towards his cock, his legs bending at the knees. Sperm spurts, arching almost vertical in front of his face. Mark and Mary are suddenly impatient and hot. . . . They push Johnny forward onto the gallows platform covered with moldy jockstraps and sweat shirts. Mark is adjusting the noose.

"Well, here you go." Mark starts to push Johnny off the platform.

Mary: "No, let me." She locks her hands behind Johnny's buttocks, puts her forehead against him, smiling into his eyes she moves back, pulling him off the platform into space. . . . His face swells with blood. . . . Mark reaches up with one lithe movement and snaps Johnny's neck . . . sound like a stick broken in wet towels. A shudder runs down Johnny's body . . . one foot flutters like a trapped bird.   Mark has draped himself over a swing and mimics Johnny's twitches, closes his eyes and sticks his tongue out. . . . Johnny's cock springs up and Mary guides it up her cunt, writhing against him in a fluid belly dance, groaning and shrieking with delight . . . sweat pours down her body, hair hangs over her face in wet strands. "Cut him down, Mark," she screams. Mark reaches over with a snap knife and cuts the rope, catching Johnny as he falls, easing him onto his back with Mary still impaled and writhing. . . . She bites away Johnny's lips and nose and sucks out his eyes with a pop. . . . She tears off great hunks of cheek. . . . Now she lunches on his prick. . . . Mark walks over to her and she looks up from Johnny's half-eaten genitals, her face covered with blood, eyes phosphorescent. . . . Mark puts his foot on her shoulder and kicks her over on her back. . . . He leaps on her, fucking her insanely . . . they roll from one end of the room to the other, pinwheel end-over-end and leap high in the air like great hooked fish.

"Let me hang you, Mark. . . . Let me hang you. . . . Please, Mark, let me hang you!"

"Sure baby." He pulls her brutally to her feet and pins her hands behind her.

"No, Mark!! No! No! No," she screams, shitting and pissing in terror as he drags her to the platform. He leaves her tied on the platform in a pile of old used condoms, while he adjusts the rope across the room . . . and comes back carrying the noose on a silver tray. He jerks her to her feet and tightens the noose. He sticks his cock up her and waltzes around the platform and off into space swinging in a great arc. . . . "Wheeeeee!" he screams, turning into Johnny. Her neck snaps. A great fluid wave undulates through her body. Johnny drops to the floor and stands poised and alert like a young animal.

He leaps about the room. With a scream of longing that shatters the glass wall he leaps out into space. Masturbating end-over-end, three thousand feet down, his sperm floating beside him, he screams all the way against the shattering blue of sky, the rising sun burning over his body like gasoline, down past great oaks and persimmons, swamp cypress and mahogany, to shatter in liquid relief in a ruined square paved with limestone. Weeds and vines grow between the stones, and rusty iron bolts three feet thick penetrate the white stone, stain it shit-brown of rust.

Johnny dowses Mary with gasoline from an obscene Chimu jar of white jade. . . . He anoints his own body. . . . They embrace, fall to the floor and roll under a great magnifying glass set in the roof . . . burst into flame with a cry that shatters the glass wall, roll into space, fucking and screaming through the air, burst in blood and flames and soot on brown rocks under a desert sun. Johnny leaps about the room in agony. With a scream that shatters the glass wall he stands spread-eagle to the rising sun, blood spurting out his cock . . . a white marble god, he plummets through epileptic explosions into the old Medjoub writhe in shit and rubbish by a mud wall under a sun that scar and grab the flesh into goose-pimples. . . . He is a boy sleeping against the mosque wall, ejaculates wet dreaming into a thousand cunts pink and smooth as sea shells, feeling the delight of prickly pubic hairs slide up his cock

John and Mary in hotel room (music of East St. Louis Toodleoo). Warm spring wind blows faded pink curtains in through open window. . . . Frogs croak in vacant lots where corn grows and boys catch little green garter snakes under broken limestone stelae stained with shit and threaded with rusty barbed wire. . . .

Neon—chlorophyll green, purple, orange—flashes on and off.)

Johnny extracts a candiru from Mary's cunt with his calipers. . . . He drops it into a bottle of mescal where it turns into a Maguey worm. . . . He gives her a douche of jungle bone-softener, her vaginal teeth flow out mixed with blood and cysts. . . . Her cunt shines fresh and sweet as spring grass. . . . Johnny licks Mary's cunt, slow at first, with rising excitement parts the lips and licks inside feeling the prickle of pubic hairs on his tumescent tongue. . . . Arms thrown back, breasts poin-

ing straight up, Mary lies transfixed with neon nails.
. . . Johnny moves up her body, his cock with a shining
round opal of lubricant at the open slit, slides through
her pubic hairs and enters her cunt to the hilt, drawn in
by a suction of hungry flesh. . . . His face swells with
blood, green lights burst behind his eyes and he falls
with a scenic railway through screaming girls. . . .

Damp hairs on the back of his balls dry to grass in
the warm spring wind. High jungle valley, vines creep
in the window. Johnny's cock swells, great rank buds
burst out. A long tuber root creeps from Mary's cunt,
feels for the earth. The bodies disintegrate in green
explosions. The hut falls in ruins of broken stone. The
boy is a limestone statue, a plant sprouting from his
cock, lips parted in the half-smile of a junky on the nod.

•
• •

The Beagle has stached the heroin in a lottery ticket.
One more shot—tomorrow the cure.

The way is long. Hard-ons and bring-downs are frequent.

It was a long time over the stony reg to the oasis of
date palms where Arab boys shit in the well and rock
n' roll across the sands of muscle beach eating hot-dogs
and spitting out gold teeth in nuggets.

Toothless and strictly from the long hunger, ribs you
could wash your filthy overalls on, that corrugate, they
quaver down from the outrigger in Easter Island and
stalk ashore on legs stiff and brittle as stilts . . . they nod

in club windows . . . fallen into the fat of lack-need to sell a slim body.

The date palms have died of meet lack, the well filled with dried shit and mosaic of a thousand newspapers: "Russia denies . . . The Home Secretary views with pathic alarm . . . The trap was sprung at 12:02. At 12:30 the doctor went out to eat oysters, returned at 2:00 to clap the hanged man jovially on the back. 'What! Aren't you dead yet? Guess I'll have to pull your leg. Haw Haw! Can't let you choke at this rate—I'd get a warning from the President. And what a disgrace if the dead wagon cart you out alive. My balls would drop off with the shame of it and I apprenticed myself to an experienced ox. One two three pull.' "

The sail plane falls silent as erection, silent as greased glass broken by the young thief with old-woman hands and cancelled eyes of junk. . . . In a noiseless explosion he penetrates the broken house, stepping over the greased crystals, a clock ticks loud in the kitchen, hot air ruffles his hair, his head disintegrates in a heavy duck load. . . . The Old Man flips out a red shell and pirouettes around his shotgun. "Aw, shucks, fellers, tweren't nothing. . . . Fish in the barrel. . . . Money in the bank . . . round-heeled boy, one greased shot brain goose and he flop in an obscene position. . . . Can you hear me from where you are, boy?

"I was young myself once and heard the siren call of easy money and women and tight boy-ass and lands sake don't get my blood up I am subject to tell a tale make your cock stand up and yipe for the pink pearly way of young cunt or the lovely brown mucous-covered palpitating tune of the young boy-ass play your cock like a recorder . . . and when you hit the prostate pearl sharp diamonds gather in the golden lad balls inexorable as a kidney stone. . . . Sorry I had to kill you. . . . The old grey mare aint what she used to be. . . . Cant run down an audience . . . got to *bring* down that house on the wing, run or sit. . . . Like an old lion took bad with cavities he need that amident toothpaste keep a feller biting fresh at all times. . . . Them old lions shit sure turn boyeater. . . . And who can blame them, boys being so sweet so cold so fair in St. James Infirmary?? Now, son, don't you get rigor mortis on me. Show respect for the aging prick. . . . You may be a tedious old fuck yourself some day. . . . Oh, uh; I guess not. . . . You have, like Housman's barefoot shameless catamite The Congealed Shropshire Ingenue set your fleet foot on the silo of change. . . . But you cant kill those Shropshire boys . . . been hanged so often he resist it like a gonococcus half castrate with pencillin rallies to a hideous strength and multiplies geometric. . . . So leave us cast a vote for decent acquittal and put an end to those beastly exhibitions for which the sheriff levy a pound of flesh."

Sheriff: "I'll lower his pants for a pound, folks. Step right up. A serious and scientific exhibit concerning the locality of the Life Center. This character has nine inches, ladies and gentlemen, measure them yourself inside. Only one pound, one queer three dollar bill to see a young boy come three times at least—I never demean myself to process a eunuch—*completely against his will*. When his neck snaps sharp, this character will shit-sure come to rhythmic attention and spurt it out all over you."

The boy stands on the trap shifting his weight from one leg to the other: "Gawd! What a boy hasta put up with in this business. Sure as shit some horrible old character get physical."

Traps falls, rope sings like wind in wire, neck snaps loud and clear as a Chinese gong.

The boy cuts himself down with a switch-blade, chases a screaming fag down the midway. The faggot dives through the glass of a penny arcade peep-show and rims a grinning Negro. Fadeout.

(Mary, Johnny and Mark take a bow with the ropes around their necks. They are not as young as they appear in the Blue Movies. . . . They look tired and petulant.)

MEETING OF INTERNATIONAL CONFERENCE OF TECHNOLOGICAL PSYCHIATRY

Doctor "Fingers" Schafer, the Lobotomy Kid, rises and turns on the Conferents the cold blue blast of his gaze:

"Gentlemen, the human nervous system can be reduced to a compact and abbreviated spinal column. The brain, front, middle and rear must follow the adenoid, the wisdom tooth, the appendix. . . . I give you my Master Work: *The Complete All American Deanxietized Man*. . . ."

Blast of trumpets: The Man is carried in naked by two Negro Bearers who drop him on the platform with bestial, sneering brutality. . . . The Man wriggles. . . . His flesh turns to viscid, transparent jelly that drifts away in green mist, unveiling a monster black centipede. Waves of unknown stench fill the room, searing the lungs, grabbing the stomach. . . .

Schafer wrings his hands sobbing: "Clarence!! How can you do this to me?? Ingrates!! Every one of them ingrates!!"

The Conferents start back muttering in dismay:

"I'm afraid Schafer has gone a bit too far. . . ."

"I sounded a word of warning. . . ."

"Brilliant chap Schafer . . . but . . ."

"Man will do anything for publicity. . . ."

"Gentlemen, this unspeakable and in every sense illegitimate child of Doctor Schafer's perverted brain must not see the light. . . . Our duty to the human race is clear. . . ."

"Man he done seen the light," said one of the Negro Bearers.

"We must stomp out the Un-American crittah," says a fat, frog-faced Southern doctor who has been drinking corn out of a mason jar. He advances drunkenly, then halts, appalled by the formidable size and menacing aspect of the centipede. . . .

"Fetch gasoline!" he bellows. "We gotta burn the son of a bitch like an uppity Nigra!"

"I'm not sticking my neck out, me," says a cool hip young doctor high on LSD25. . . . "Why a smart D.A. could . . ."

Fadeout. "Order in The Court!"

D.A.: "Gentlemen of the jury, these 'learned gentlemen' claim that the innocent human creature they have so wantonly slain suddenly turned himself into a huge black centipede and it was 'their duty to the human race' to destroy this monster before it could, by any means at its disposal, perpetrate its kind. . . .

"Are we to gulp down this tissue of horse shit? Are we to take these glib lies like a greased and nameless asshole? Where *is* this wondrous centipede?

" 'We have destroyed it,' they say smugly. . . . And I would like to remind you, Gentlemen and Hermaphrodites of the Jury, that this Great Beast"—he points to Doctor Schafer—"has, on several previous occasions, appeared in this court charged with the unspeakable crime of brain rape. . . . In plain English"—he pounds the rail of the jury box, his voice rises to a scream—"in plain English, Gentlemen, *forcible lobotomy.* . . ."

The Jury gasps. . . . One dies of a heart attack. . . . Three fall to the floor writhing in orgasms of prurience. . . .

The D.A. points dramatically: "He it is. . . . He and no other who has reduced whole provinces of our fair land to a state bordering on the far side of idiocy. . . . He it is who has filled great warehouses with row on row, tier on tier of helpless creatures who must have their every want attended. . . . 'The Drones' he calls them with a cynical leer of pure educated evil. . . . Gentlemen, I say to you that the wanton murder of Clarence Cowie must not go unavenged: This foul crime shrieks like a wounded faggot for justice at least!"

The centipede is rushing about in agitation.

"Man, that mother fucker's hungry," screams one of the Bearers.

"I'm getting out of here, me."

A wave of electric horror sweeps through the Conferents. . . . They storm the exits screaming and clawing. . . .

THE MARKET

Panorama of the City of Interzone. Opening bars of East St. Louis Toodleoo . . . at times loud and clear then faint and intermittent like music down a windy street. . . .

The room seems to shake and vibrate with motion. The blood and substance of many races, Negro, Polynesian, Mountain Mongol, Desert Nomad, Polyglot Near East, Indian—races as yet unconceived and unborn, combinations not yet realized pass through your body. Migrations, incredible journeys through deserts and jungles and mountains (stasis and death in closed mountain valleys where plants grow out of genitals, vast crustaceans hatch inside and break the shell of body) across the Pacific in an outrigger canoe to Easter Island. The Composite City where all human potentials are spread out in a vast silent market.

Minarets, palms, mountains, jungle . . . A sluggish river jumping with vicious fish, vast weed-grown parks where boys lie in the grass, play cryptic games. Not a locked door in the City. Anyone comes into your room at any time. The Chief of Police is a Chinese who picks his teeth and listens to denunciations presented by a lunatic. Every now and then the Chinese takes the toothpick out of his mouth and looks at the end of it.

Hipsters with smooth copper-colored faces lounge in doorways twisting shrunk heads on gold chains, their faces blank with an insect's unseeing calm.

Behind them, through open doors, tables and booths and bars, and kitchens and baths, copulating couples on rows of brass beds, crisscross of a thousand hammocks, junkies tying up for a shot, opium smokers, hashish smokers, people eating talking bathing back into a haze of smoke and steam.

Gaming tables where the games are played for incredible stakes. From time to time a player leaps up with a despairing cry, having lost his youth to an old man or become Latah to his opponent. But there are higher stakes than youth or Latah, games where only two players in the world know what the stakes are.

All houses in the City are joined. Houses of sod—high mountain Mongols blink in smokey doorways—houses of bamboo and teak, houses of adobe, stone and red brick, South Pacific and Maori houses, houses in trees and river boats, wood houses one hundred feet long sheltering entire tribes, houses of boxes and corrugated iron where old men sit in rotten rags cooking down canned heat, great rusty iron racks rising two hundred foot in the air from swamps and rubbish with perilous partitions built on multi-levelled platforms, and hammocks swinging over the void.

Expeditions leave for unknown places with unknown purposes. Strangers arrive on rafts of old packing crates tied together with rotten rope, they stagger in out of the jungle their eyes swollen shut from insect bites, they come down the mountain trails on cracked bleeding feet through the dusty windy outskirts of the city, where people defecate in rows along adobe walls and vultures fight over fish heads. They drop down into parks in patched parachutes. . . . They are escorted by a drunken cop to register in a vast public lavatory. The data taken down is put on pegs to be used as toilet paper.

Cooking smells of all countries hang over the City, a haze of opium, hashish, the resinous red smoke of Yage, smell of the jungle and salt water and the rotting river and dried excrement and sweat and genitals.

High mountain flutes, jazz and bebop, one-stringed Mongol instruments, gypsy xylophones, African drums, Arab bagpipes . . .

The City is visited by epidemics of violence, and the untended dead are eaten by vultures in the streets. Albinos blink in the sun. Boys sit in trees, languidly masturbate. People eaten by unknown diseases watch the passerby with evil, knowing eyes.

In the City Market is the Meet Café. Followers of obsolete, unthinkable trades doodling in Etruscan, addicts of drugs not yet synthesized, pushers of souped-up Harmaline, junk reduced to pure habit offering precarious vegetable serenity, liquids to induce Latah, Tithonian longevity serums, black marketeers of World War III, excisors of telepathic sensitivity, osteopaths of the spirit, investigators of infractions denounced by bland paranoid chess players, servers of fragmentary warrants taken down in hebephrenic shorthand charging unspeakable mutilations of the spirit, bureaucrats of spectral departments, officials of unconstituted police states, a Lesbian dwarf who has perfected operation Bangutot, the lung erection that strangles a sleeping enemy, sellers of orgone tanks and relaxing machines, brokers of exquisite dreams and memories tested on the sensitized cells of junk sickness and bartered for raw materials of the will, doctors skilled in the treatment of diseases dormant in the black dust of ruined cities, gathering virulence in the white blood of eyeless worms feeling slowly to the surface and the human host, maladies of the ocean floor and the stratosphere, maladies of the laboratory and atomic war. . . . A place where the unknown past and the emergent future meet in a vibrating soundless hum . . . Larval entities waiting for a Live One . . .

(Section describing The City and the Meet Café written in state of Yage intoxication . . . Yage, Ayuahuasca, Pilde, Nateema are Indian names for Bannisteria Caapi, a fast growing vine indigenous to the Amazon region. See discussion of Yage in Appendix.)

Notes from Yage state: Images fall slow and silent like snow. . . . Serenity . . . All defenses fall . . . everything is free to enter or to go out. . . . Fear is simply impossible. . . . A beautiful blue substance flows into me. . . . I see an archaic grinning face like South Pacific mask. . . . The face is blue purple splotched with gold. . . .

The room takes on aspect of Near East whorehouse with blue walls and red tasseled lamps. . . . I feel myself turning into a Negress, the black color silently invading my flesh. . . . Convulsions of lust . . . My legs take on a well rounded Polynesian substance. . . . Everything stirs with a writhing furtive life. . . . The room is Near East, Negro, South Pacific, in some familiar place I cannot locate. . . . Yage is space-time travel. . . . The room seems to shake and vibrate with motion. . . . The blood and substance of many races, Negro, Polynesian, Mountain Mongol, Desert Nomad, Polyglot Near East, Indian, races as yet unconceived and unborn, passes through the body. . . . Migrations, incredible journeys through deserts and jungles and mountains (stasis and death in closed mountain valley where plants grow out of genitals, vast crustaceans hatch inside and break the shell of body) across the Pacific in an outrigger canoe to Easter Island. . . .

(It occurs to me that preliminary Yage nausea is motion sickness of transport to Yage state. . . .)

"All medicine men use it in their practice to foretell the future, locate lost or stolen objects, to diagnose and treat illness, to name the perpetrator of a crime." Since the Indian (straitjacket for Herr Boas—trade joke—nothing so maddens an anthropologist as Primitive Man) does not regard any death as accidental, and they are unacquainted with their own sel-destructive trends referring to them contemptuously as "our naked cousins," or perhaps feeling that these trends above all are subject to the manipulation of alien and hostile wills, any death is murder. The medicine man takes Yage and the identity of the murderer is revealed to him. As you may imagine, the deliberations of the medicine man during one of these jungle inquests give rise to certain feelings of uneasiness among his constituents.

"Let's hope Old Xiuptutol don't wig and name one of the boys."

"Take a curare and relax. We got the fix in . . ."

"But if he *wig*? Picking up on that Nateema all the time he don't touch the ground in twenty years. . . . I tell you, Boss, nobody can hit the stuff like that. . . . It cooks the brains. . . ."

"So we declare him incompetent. . . ."

So Xiuptutol reels out of the jungle and says the boys in the Lower Tzpino territory done it, which surprises no one. . . . Take it from an old Brujo, dearie, they don't like surprises. . . .

A funeral passes through the market. Black coffin— Arabic inscriptions in filigreed silver—carried by four pallbearers. Procession of mourners singing the funeral song . . . Clem and Jody fall in beside them carrying coffin, the corpse of a hog bursts out of it. . . . The hog is dressed in a jellaba, a keif pipe juts from its mouth, one hoof holds a packet of feelthy pictures, a mezuzzoth hangs about its neck. . . . Inscribed on the coffin: "This was the noblest Arab of them all."

They sing hideous parody of the funeral song in false Arabic. Jody can do a fake Chinese spiel that'll just kill you—like a hysterical ventriloquist's dummy. In fact, he precipitated an anti-foreign riot in Shanghai that claimed 3,000 casualties.

"Stand up, Gertie, and show respect for the local gooks."

"I suppose one *should*."

"My dear, I'm working on the most marvelous invention . . . a boy who disappears as soon as you come leaving a smell of burning leaves and a sound effect of distant train whistles."

"Ever make sex in no gravity? Your jism just floats out in the air like lovely ectoplasm, and female guests are subject to immaculate or at least indirect conception. . . . Reminds me of an old friend of mine, one of the handsomest men I have ever known and one of the maddest and absolutely ruined by wealth. He used to go about with a water pistol shooting jism up career women at parties. Won all his paternity suits hands down. Never use his own jism you understand."

Fadeout . . . "Order in the Court." Attorney for A. J., "Conclusive tests have established that my client has no uh personal connection with the uh little accident of the charming plaintiff. . . . Perhaps she is preparing to emulate the Virgin Mary and conceive immaculately naming my client as a hurumph ghostly pander. . . . I am reminded of a case in fifteenth-century Holland where a young woman accused an elderly and respectable sorcerer of conjuring up a succubus who then had uh carnal knowledge of the young person in question with the under the circumstances regrettable result of pregnancy. So the sorcerer was indicted as an accomplice and rampant voyeur before during and after the fact. However, gentlemen of the jury, we no longer credit such uh legends; and a young woman attributing her uh interesting condition to the attentions of a succubus would be accounted, in these enlightened days, a romanticist or in plain English a God damned liar hehe hehe heh. . . ."

And now The Prophet's Hour:

"Millins died in the mud flats. Only one blast free to lungs.

" 'Eye Eye, Captain,' he said, squirting his eyes out on the deck. . . . And who would put on the chains to-night? It is indicate to observe some caution in the up-wind approach, the down wind having failed to turn up anything worth a rusty load. . . . Señoritas are the wear this season in Hell, and I am tired with the long climb to a pulsing Vesuvius of alien pricks."

Need Orient Express out of here to no hide place(r) mines are frequent in the area. . . . Every day dig a little it takes up the time. . . .

Jack off phantoms whisper hot into the bone ear. . . .

Shoot your way to freedom.

"Christ?" sneers the vicious, fruity old Saint applying pancake from an alabaster bowl. . . . "That cheap ham! You think I'd demean myself to commit a miracle? . . . That one should have stood in carny. . . .

" 'Step right up, Marquesses and Marks, and bring the little Marks too. Good for young and old, man and beast. . . . The one and only legit *Son of Man* will cure a young boy's clap with one hand—by contact alone, folks—create marijuana with the other, whilst walking on water and squirting wine out his ass. . . . Now keep your distance, folks, you is subject to be irradiated by the sheer charge of this character.'

"And I knew him when, dearie. . . . I recall we was doing an Impersonation Act—very high class too—in Sodom, and that is one cheap town. . . . Strictly from hunger . . . Well, this citizen, this fucking Philistine wandered in from Podunk Baal or some place, called me a fuckin fruit right on the floor. And I said to him: 'Three thousand years in show business and I always keep my nose clean. Besides I don't hafta take any shit off any uncircumcised cocksucker.' . . . Later he come to my dressing room and made an apology. . . . Turns out he is a big physician. And he was a lovely fellah, too. . . .

"*Buddha*? A notorious metabolic junky . . . Makes his own you dig. In India, where they got no sense of time, The Man is often a month late. . . . 'Now let me see, is that the second or the third monsoon? I got like a meet in Ketchupore about more or less.'

"And all them junkies sitting around in the lotus posture spitting on the ground and waiting on The Man.

"So Buddha says: 'I don't hafta take this sound. I'll by God metabolize my own junk.'

" 'Man, you can't do that. The Revenooers will swarm all over you.'

" 'Over me they won't swarm. I gotta gimmick, see? I'm a fuckin Holy Man as of right now.'

" 'Jeez, boss, what an angle.'

" 'Now some citizens really wig when they make with the New Religion. These frantic individuals do not know how to come on. No class to them . . . Besides, they is subject to be lynched like who wants somebody hanging around being better'n other folks? "What you trying to do, Jack, give people a bad time? . . ." So we gotta play it cool, you dig, cool. . . . We got a take it or leave it proposition here, folks. We don't shove anything up your soul, unlike certain cheap characters who shall be nameless and are nowhere. Clear the cave for action. I'm gonna metabolize a speed ball and make with the Fire Sermon.'

"*Mohammed*? Are you kidding? He was dreamed up by the Mecca Chamber of Commerce. An Egyptian ad man on the skids from the sauce write the continuity.

" 'I'll have one more, Gus. Then, by Allah, I will go home and receive a Surah. . . . Wait'll the morning edition hits the souks. I am blasting Amalgamated Images wide open.'

"The bartender looks up from his racing form. 'Yeah. And theirs will be a painful doom.'

" 'Oh . . . uh . . . quite. Now, Gus, I'll write you a check.'

" 'You are only being the most notorious paper hanger in Greater Mecca. I am not a wall, Mr. Mohammed.'

" 'Well, Gus, I got like two types publicity, favorable and otherwise. You want some otherwise already? I am subject to receive a Surah concerning bartenders who extendeth not credit to those in a needy way.'

" 'And theirs will be a painful doom. Sold Arabia.' He vaults over the bar. 'I'm not taking any more, Ahmed. Pick up thy Surahs and walk. In fact, I'll help you. And *stay out.*'

" 'I'll fix your wagon good, you unbelieving cocksucker. I'll close you up tight and dry as a junky's asshole. I'll by Allah dry up the Peninsula.'

" 'It's a continent already. . . .'

"Leave what Confucius say stand with Little Audrey and the shaggy dogs. Lao-Tze? They scratch him already. . . . And enough of these gooey saints with a look of pathic dismay as if they getting fucked up the ass and try not to pay it any mind. And why should we let some old brokendown ham tell us what wisdom is? 'Three thousand years in show business and I always keep my nose clean. . . .'

"First, every Fact is incarcerate along with the male hustlers and those who desecrate the gods of commerce by playing ball in the streets, and some old whitehaired fuck staggers out to give us the benefits of his ripe idiocy. Are we never to be free of this grey-beard loon lurking on every mountain top in Tibet, subject to drag himself out of a hut in the Amazon, waylay one in the Bowery? 'I've been expecting you, my son,' and he make with a silo full of corn. 'Life is a school where every pupil must learn a different lesson. And now I will unlock my Word Hoard. . . .'

" 'I do fear it much.'

" 'Nay, nothing shall stem the rising tide.'

" 'I can't stem him, boys. *Sauve qui peut.*'

" 'I tell you when I leave the Wise Man I don't even feel like a human. He converting my live orgones into dead bullshit.'

"So I got an exclusive why don't I make with the live word? The word cannot be expressed direct. . . . It can perhaps be indicated by mosaic of juxtaposition like articles abandoned in a hotel drawer, defined by negatives and absence. . . .

"Think I'll have my stomach tucked. . . . I may be old, but I'm still desirable."

(The Stomach Tuck is surgical intervention to remove stomach fat at the same time making a tuck in the abdominal wall, thus creating a flesh corset, which is, however, subject to break and spurt your horrible old guts across the floor. . . . The slim and shapely F.C. models are, of course, the most dangerous. In fact, some extreme models are known as O.N.S.—One Night Stands —in the industry.

Doctor "Doodles" Rindfest states bluntly: "Bed is the most dangerous place for an F.C. man."

The F.C. theme song is "Believe Me If All These

Endearing Young Charms." An F.C. partner is indeed subject to "fleet from your arms like fairy gifts fading away.")

In a white museum room full of sunlight pink nudes sixty feet high. Vast adolescent muttering.

Silver guard rail . . . chasm a thousand feet down into the glittering sunlight. Little green plots of cabbage and lettuce. Brown youths with adzes spied by the old queen across a sewage canal.

"Oh dear, I wonder if they fertilize with human excrement. . . . Maybe they'll do it right now."

He flips out mother of pearl opera glasses—Aztec mosaic in the sun.

Long line of Greek lads march up with alabaster bowls of shit, empty into the limestone marl hole.

Dusty poplars shake across the red brick Plaza de Toros in the afternoon wind.

Wooden cubicles around a hot spring . . . rubble of ruined walls in a grove of cottonwoods . . . the benches worn smooth as metal by a million masturbating boys.

Greek lads white as marble fuck dog style on the portico of a great golden temple . . . naked Mugwump twangs a lute.

Walking down by the tracks in his red sweater met Sammy the Dock Keeper's son with two Mexicans.

"Hey, Skinny," he said, "want to get screwed?"

"Well . . . Yeah."

On a ruined straw mattress the Mexican pulled him up on all fours—Negro boy dance around them beating out the strokes . . . sun through a knot hole pink spotlights his cock.

A waste of raw pink shame to the pastel blue horizon where vast iron mesas crash into the shattered sky.

"It's all right." The God screams through you three thousand year rusty load. . . .

Hail of crystal skulls shattered the greenhouse to slivers in the winter moon. . . .

The American woman has left a whiff of poison behind in the dank St. Louis garden party.

Pool covered with green slime in a ruined French garden. Huge pathic frog rises slowly from the water on a mud platform playing the clavichord.

A Sollubi rushes into the bar and starts polishing The Saint's shoes with the oil on his nose. . . . The Saint kicks him petulantly in the mouth. The Sollubi screams, whirls around and shits on the Saint's pants. Then he dashes into the street. A pimp looks after him speculatively. . . .

The Saint calls the manager: "Jesus, Al, what kinda creep joint you running here? My brand new fishskin Dégagées . . ."

"I'm sorry, Saint. He slipped by me."

(The Sollubi are an untouchable caste in Arabia noted for their abject vileness. De luxe cafés are equipped with Sollubi who rim the guests while they eat—holes in the seating benches being provided for this purpose. Citizens who want to be utterly humiliated and degraded—so many people do, nowadays, hoping to jump the gun—offer themselves up for passive homosexual intercourse to an encampment of Sollubis. . . . Nothing like it, they tell me. . . . In fact, the Sollubi are subject to become wealthy and arrogant and lose their native vileness. What is origin of untouchable? Perhaps a fallen priest caste. In fact, untouchables perform a priestly function in taking on themselves all human vileness.)

A. J. strolls through the Market in black cape with a vulture perched on one shoulder. He stands by a table of agents.

"This you gotta hear. Boy in Los Angeles fifteen year old. Father decide it is time the boy have his first piece of ass. Boy is lying on the lawn reading comic books, father go out and say: 'Son, here's twenty dollars; I want you to go to a good whore and get a piece of ass off her.'

"So they drive to this plush jump joint, and the father say, 'All right, son. You're on your own. So ring the bell and when the woman come give her the twenty dollars and tell her you want a piece of ass.'

" 'Solid, pop.'

"So about fifteen minutes later the boy comes out:

" 'Well, son, did you get a piece of ass?'

" 'Yeah. This gash comes to the door, and I say I want a piece of ass and lay the double sawski on her. We go up to her trap, and she remove the dry goods. So I switch my blade and cut a big hunk off her ass, she raise a beef like I am reduce to pull off one shoe and beat her brains out. Then I hump her for kicks."

Only the laughing bones remain, flesh over the hills and far away with the dawn wind and a train whistle. We are not unaware of the problem, and the needs of our constituents are never out of our mind being their place of residence and who can break a ninety-nine year synapses lease?

Another installment in the adventures of Clem Snide

the Private Ass Hole: "So I walk in the joint, and this female hustler sit at the bar, and I think, 'Oh God you're poule de luxe already.' I mean it's like I see the gash before. So I don't pay her no mind at first, then I dig she is rubbing her legs together and working her feet up behind her head shoves it down to give herself a douche job with a gadget sticks out of her nose the way a body can't help but notice."

Iris—half Chinese and half Negro—addicted to dihydro-oxy-heroin—takes a shot every fifteen minutes to which end she leaves droppers and needles sticking out all over her. The needles rust in her dry flesh, which, here and there, has grown completely over a joint to form a smooth green brown wen. On the table in front of her is a samovar of tea and a twenty-pound hamper of brown sugar. No one has ever seen her eat anything else. It is only just before a shot that she hears what anyone says or talks herself. Then she makes some flat, factual statement relative to her own person.

"My asshole is occluding."

"My cunt got terrible green juices."

Iris is one of Benway's projects. "The human body can run on sugar alone, God damn it. . . . I am aware that certain of my learned colleagues, who are attempting to belittle my genius work, claim that I put vitamins and proteins into Iris's sugar clandestinely. . . . I challenge these nameless assholes to crawl up out of their latrines and run a spot analysis on Iris's sugar and her tea. Iris is a wholesome American cunt. I deny categorically that she nourishes herself on semen. And let me take this opportunity to state that I am a reputable scientist, not a charlatan, a lunatic, or a pretended worker of miracles. . . . I never claimed that Iris could subsist exclusive on photosynthesis. . . . I did not say she could breathe in carbon dioxide and give off oxygen—I confess I have been tempted to experiment being of course restrained by my medical ethics. . . . In short, the vile slanders of my creeping opponents will inevitably fall back onto them and come to roost like a homing stool pigeon."

ORDINARY MEN AND WOMEN

Luncheon of Nationalist Party on balcony overlooking the Market. Cigars, scotch, polite belches. . . . The Party Leader strides about in a jellaba smoking a cigar and drinking scotch. He wears expensive English shoes, loud socks, garters, muscular, hairy legs—overall effect of successful gangster in drag.

P.L. (pointing dramatically): "Look out there. What do you see?"

LIEUTENANT: "Huh? Why, I see the Market."

P.L.: "No you don't. You see men and women. *Ordinary* men and women going about their ordinary everyday tasks. Leading their ordinary lives. That's what we need. . . ."

A street boy climbs over the balcony rail.

LIEUTENANT: "No, we do not want to buy any used condoms! Cut!"

P.L.: "Wait! . . . Come in, my boy. Sit down. . . . Have a cigar. . . . Have a drink."

He paces around the boy like an aroused tom cat.

"What do you think about the French?"

"Huh?"

"The French. The Colonial bastards who is sucking your live corpuscles."

"Look mister. It cost two hundred francs to suck my corpuscule. Haven't lowered my rates since the year of the rindpest when all the tourists died, even the Scandinavians."

P.L.: "You see? This is pure uncut boy in the street."

"You sure can pick 'em, boss."

"M.I. never misses."

P.L.: "Now look, kid, let's put it this way. The French have dispossessed you of your birthright."

"You mean like Friendly Finance? . . . They got this toothless Egyptian eunuch does the job. They figure he arouse less antagonism, you dig, he always take down his pants to show you his condition. 'Now I'm just a poor old eunuch trying to keep up my habit. Lady, I'd like to give you an extension on that artificial kidney, I got a job to do is all. . . . Disconnect her, boys.' He shows his gums in a feeble snarl. . . . 'Not for nothing am I known as Nellie the Repossessor.'

"So they disconnect my own mother, the sainted old gash, and she swell up and turn black and the whole souk stink of piss and the neighbors beef to the Board of Health and my father say: 'It's the will of Allah. She won't piss any more of my loot down the drain.'

"Sick people disgust me already. When some citizen start telling me about his cancer of the prostate or his rotting septum make with that purulent discharge I tell him: 'You think I am innarested to hear about your horrible old condition? I am not innarested at all.' "

P.L.: "All *right*. Cut . . . You hate the French, don't you?"

"Mister, I hate everybody. Doctor Benway says it's metabolic, I got this condition of the blood. . . . Arabs and Americans got it special. . . . Doctor Benway is concocting this serum."

P.L.: "Benway is an infiltrating Western Agent."

L.1: "A rampant French Jew . . ."

L.2: "A hog-balled, black-assed Communist Jew Nigger."

P.L.: "Shut up, you fool!"

L.2: "Sorry, chief. I am after being stationed in Pigeonhole."

P.L.: "Don't go near Benway." (Aside: "I wonder if this will go down. You never know how primitive they are. . . .") "Confidentially he's a black magician."

L.1: "He's got this resident djinn."

"Uhuh . . . Well I got a date with a high-type American client. A real classy fellah."

P.L.: "Don't you know it's shameful to peddle your ass to the alien unbelieving pricks?"

"Well that's a point of view. Have fun."

P.L.: "Likewise." Exit boy. "They're hopeless I tell you. Hopeless."

L.1. "What's with this serum?"

P.L.: "I don't know, but it sounds ominous. We better put a telepathic direction finder on Benway. The man's not to be trusted. Might do almost anything. . . . Turn a massacre into a sex orgy. . . ."

"Or a joke."

"Precisely. Arty type . . . No principles . . ."

AMERICAN HOUSEWIFE (opening a box of Lux): "Why don't it have an electric eye the box flip open when it see me and hand itself to the Automat Handy Man he should put it inna water already. . . . The Handy Man is outa control since Thursday, he been getting physical with me and I didn't put it in his combination at all. . . . And the Garbage Disposal Unit snapping at me, and the nasty old Mixmaster keep trying to get up under my dress. . . . I got the most awful cold, and my intestines is all constipated. . . . I'm gonna put it in the Handy Man's combination he should administer me a high colonic awready."

SALESMAN (he is something between an aggressive Latah and a timid Sender): "Recollect when I am travelling with K. E., hottest idea man in the gadget industry.

"'Think of it!' he snaps. 'A cream seperator in your own kitchen!'

"'K. E., my brain reels at the thought.'

"'It's five, maybe ten, yes, maybe twenty years away. . . . But it's coming.'

"'I'll wait, K. E. No matter how long it is I'll wait. When the priority numbers are called up yonder I'll be there.'

"It was K. E. put out the Octopus Kit for Massage Parlors, Barber Shops and Turkish Baths, with which you can administer a high colonic, an unethical massage, a shampoo, whilst cutting the client's toenails and removing his blackheads. And the M.D.'s Can Do Kit for busy practitioners will take out your appendix, tuck in a hernia, pull a wisdom tooth, ectomize your piles and circumcise you. Well, K. E. is such an atomic salesman if he runs out of Octopus Kits he is subject, by sheer charge, to sell an M.D. Can Do to a barber shop and some citizen wakes up with his piles cut out. . . .

"'Jesus, Homer, what kinda creep joint you running here? I been gang fucked.'

"'Well, landsake, Si, I was just aiming to administer our complimentary high colonic free and gratis on Thanksgiving Day. K. E. musta sold me the wrong kit again. . . .'"

MALE HUSTLER: "What a boy hasta put up with in this business. Gawd! The propositions I get you wouldn't believe it. . . . They wanta play Latah, they wanta merge with my protoplasm, they want a replica cutting, they wanta suck my orgones, they wanta take over my past experience and leave old memories that disgust me. . . .

"I am fucking this citizen so I think, 'A straight John at last'; but he comes to a climax and turns himself into some kinda awful crab. . . . I told him, 'Jack, I don't hafta stand still for such a routine like this. . . . You can take that business to Walgreen's.' Some people got no class to them. Another horrible old character just sits there and telepathizes and creams in his dry goods. So nasty."

The bum boys fall back in utter confusion to the brink of the Soviet network where Cossacks hang partisans to the wild wail of bagpipes and the boys march up Fifth Avenue to be met by Jimmy Walkover with the keys to The Kingdom and no strings attached carry them loose in your pocket. . . .

Why so pale and wan, fair bugger? Smell of dead leeches in a rusty tin can latch onto that live wound, suck out the body and blood and bones of Jeeeeesus, leave him paralyzed from the waist down.

Yield up thy forms, boy, to thy sugar daddy got the exam three years early and know all the answer books fix the World Series.

Slunk traffikers tail a pregnant cow to her labor. The farmer declares a couvade, rolls screaming in bullshit. The veterinarian wrestles with a cow skeleton. The traffikers machinegun each other, dodging through the machinery and silos, storage bins, haylofts and mangers of a vast red barn. The calf is born. The forces of death melt in morning. Farm boy kneels reverently—his throat pulses in the rising sun.

Junkies sitting on the courthouse steps, waiting on The Man. Red Necks in black stetsons and faded Levis tie a Nigra boy to an old iron lamppost and cover him with burning gasoline. . . . The junkies rush over and draw the flesh smoke deep into their aching lungs. . . . They really got relief. . . .

THE COUNTY CLERK: "So there I was sitting in front of Jed's store over in Cunt Lick my peter standing up straight as a jack pine under my Levis just apulsin' in the sun. . . . Weell, old Doc Scranton walks by, a good old boy too, there's not a finer man 'n this valley than Doc Scranton. He's got a prolapsed asshole and when he wants to get screwed he'll pass you his ass on three feet of in-tes-tine. . . . If he's a mind to it he can drop out a piece of gut reaches from his office clear over to Roy's Beer Place, and it go feelin' around lookin' for a peter, just afeelin' around like a blind worm. . . . So old Doc Scranton sees my peter and he stops like a pointin' dog and he says to me, 'Luke, I can take your pulse from here.' "

Browbeck and Young Seward fight with hog castrators through barns and cages and yiping kennels . . . whinnying horses bare great yellow teeth, cows bellow, dogs howl, copulating cats scream like babies, a pen of huge hogs, spines bristling, give a great Bronx cheer. Browbeck the Unsteady has fallen to the sword of Young Seward, clutches at blue intestines spurting from an eight-inch gash. Young Seward cuts off Browbeck's cock and holds it pulsing in the smoky rose sunrise. . . .

Browbeck screams . . . subway brakes spit ozone. . . .

"Stand back, folks. . . . Stand back."

"They say somebody pushed him."

"He was weaving around unsteady like he couldn't see good."

"Too much smoke in the eyes, I guess."

Mary the Lesbian Governess has slipped to the pub floor on a bloody kotex. . . . A three-hundred-pound fag tramples her to death with pathic whinnies. . . .

He sings in hideous falsetto:

He is trampling out the vintage where the grapes of [wrath are stored,
He has loosed the fatal lightning of his terrible swift [sword.

He pulls a gilded wooden sword and chops the air. His corset flies off and whistles into the dart board.

The old bullfighter's sword buckles on bone and whistles into the heart of the Espontaneo, pins his unconsummate valor to the stands.

"So this elegant faggot comes to New York from Cunt Lick, Texas, and he is the most piss elegant fag of them all. He is taken up by old women of the type batten on young fags, toothless old predators too weak and too slow to run down other prey. Old moth-eaten tigress shit sure turn into a fag eater. . . . So this citizen, being an arty and crafty fag, begins making costume jewelry and jewelry sets. Every rich old gash in Greater New York wants he should do her sets, and he is making money, 21, El Morocco, Stork, but no time for sex, and all the time worrying about his rep. . . . He begins playing the horses, supposed to be something manly about gambling God knows why, and he figures it will build him up to be seen at the track. Not many fags play the horses, and those that play lose more than the others, they are lousy gamblers plunge in a losing streak and hedge when they win . . . which being the pattern of their lives. . . . Now every child knows there is one law of gambling: winning and losing come in streaks. Plunge when you win, fold when you lose. (I once knew a fag dip into the till—not the whole two thousand at once on the nose win or Sing Sing. Not our Gertie . . . Oh no a deuce at a time . . .)

"So he loses and loses and lose some more. One day he is about to put a rock in a set when the obvious occur. 'Of course, I'll replace it later.' Famous last words. So all that winter, one after the other, the diamonds, emeralds, pearls, rubies and star sapphires of the haut monde go in hock and replaced by queer replicas. . . .

"So the opening night of the Met this old hag appear as she thinks resplendent in her diamond tiara. So this other old whore approach and say, 'Oh, Miggles, you're so smart . . . to leave the real ones at home. . . . I mean we're simply mad to go around tempting fate.'

" 'You're mistaken, my dear. These *are* real.'

" 'Oh but Miggles dahling, they're *not*. . . . I mean ask your jeweler. . . . Well just ask *anybody*. Haaaaaa.'

"So a Sabbath is hastily called. (Lucy Bradshinkel, look to thy emeralds.) All these old witches examining their rocks like a citizen find leprosy on himself.

" 'My chicken blood ruby!'

" 'My bleck oopalls!' Old bitch marry so many times so many gooks and spics she don't know her accent from her ass. . . .

" 'My stah sahphire!' shriek a *poule de luxe*. 'Oh it's all so awful!'

" 'I mean they are strictly from Woolworth's. . . .'

" 'There's only one thing to do. I'm going to call the police,' says a strong-minded, outspoken old thing; and she clump across the floor on her low heels and calls the fuzz."

"Well, the faggot draws a deuce; and in the box he meets this cat who is some species of cheap hustler, and love sets in or at least a facsimile thereof convince the parties inna first and second parts. As continuity would have it, they are sprung at the same time more or less and take up residence in a flat on the Lower East Side. . . . And cook in and both are working legit modest jobs. . . . So Brad and Jim know happiness for the first time.

"Enter the powers of evil. . . . Lucy Bradshinkel has

come to say all is forgiven She has faith in Brad and wants to set him up in a studio. Of course, he will have to move to the East Sixties. . . . 'This place is impossible, dahling; and your friend . . .' And a safe mob wants Jim back to drive a car. This is a step up, you dig? Offer from citizens hardly see him before.

"Will Jim go back to crime? Will Brad succumb to the blandishments of an aging vampire, a ravening Maw? . . . Needless to say, the forces of evil are routed and exit with ominous snarls and mutterings.

" 'The Boss isn't going to like this.'

" 'I don't know why I ever wasted my time with you, you cheap, vulgar little fairy.'

"The boys stand at the tenement window, their arms around each other, looking at the Brooklyn Bridge. A warm spring wind ruffles Jim's black curls and the fine hennaed hair of Brad.

" 'Well, Brad, what's for supper?'

" 'You just go in the other room and wait.' Playfully he shoos Jim out of the kitchen, and puts on his apron.

"Dinner is Lucy Bradshinkel's cunt saignant cooked in kotex papillon. The boys eat happily looking into each other's eyes. Blood runs down their chins."

Let the dawn blue as a flame cross the city. . . . The backyards are clean of fruit, and the ash pits give up their hooded dead. . . .

"Could you show me the way to Tipperary, lady?"

Over the hills and far away to Blue Grass. . . . Across the bone meal of lawn to the frozen pond where suspended goldfish wait for the spring Squaw Man.

The screaming skull rolls up the back stairs to bite

off the cock of erring husband taking dour advantage of his wife's earache to do that which is inconvenient. The young landlubber dons a southwester, beats his wife to death in the shower. . . .

BENWAY: "Don't take it so hard, kid. . . . 'Jeder macht eine kleine Dummheit.'" (Everyone makes a little dumbness.)

SCHAFER: "I tell you I can't escape a feeling . . . well, of *evil* about this."

BENWAY: "Balderdash, my boy . . . We're scientists. . . . Pure scientists. Disinterested research and damned be him who cries 'Hold, *too much!*' Such people are no better than party poops."

SCHAFER: "Yes, yes, of course . . . and yet . . . I can't get that stench out of my lungs. . . ."

BENWAY (irritably): "None of us can. . . . Never smelled anything remotely like it. . . . Where was I? Oh yes, what would be result of administering curare plus iron lung during acute mania? Possibly the subject, unable to discharge his tensions in motor activity, would succumb on the spot like a jungle rat. Interesting cause of death, what?"

Schafer is not listening. "You know," he says impulsively, "I think I'll go back to plain old-fashioned surgery. The human body is scandalously inefficient. Instead of a mouth and an anus to get out of order why not have one all-purpose hole to eat *and* eliminate? We could seal up nose and mouth, fill in the stomach, make an air hole direct into the lungs where it should have been in the first place. . . ."

BENWAY: "Why not one all-purpose blob? Did I ever

tell you about the man who taught his asshole to talk?
His whole abdomen would move up and down you dig
farting out the words. It was unlike anything I ever
heard.

"This ass talk had a sort of gut frequency. It hit you
right down there like you gotta go. You know when the
old colon gives you the elbow and it feels sorta cold
inside, and you know all you have to do is turn loose?
Well this talking hit you right down there, a bubbly,
thick stagnant sound, a sound you could *smell*.

"This man worked for a carnival you dig, and to
start with it was like a novelty ventriloquist act. Real
funny, too, at first. He had a number he called 'The
Better 'Ole' that was a scream, I tell you. I forget most
of it but it was clever. Like, 'Oh I say, are you still
down there, old thing?'

" 'Nah! I had to go relieve myself.'

"After a while the ass started talking on its own. He
would go in without anything prepared and his ass
would ad-lib and toss the gags back at him every time.

"Then it developed sort of teeth-like little raspy in-
curving hooks and started eating. He thought this was
cute at first and built an act around it, but the asshole
would eat its way through his pants and start talking
on the street, shouting out it wanted equal rights. It
would get drunk, too, and have crying jags nobody
loved it and it wanted to be kissed same as any other
mouth. Finally it talked all the time day and night, you
could hear him for blocks screaming at it to shut up,
and beating it with his fist, and sticking candles up it,
but nothing did any good and the asshole said to him:
'It's you who will shut up in the end. Not me. Because

we don't need you around here any more. I can talk and eat *and* shit.'

"After that he began waking up in the morning with a transparent jelly like a tadpole's tail all over his mouth. This jelly was what the scientists call un-D.T., Undifferentiated Tissue, which can grow into any kind of flesh on the human body. He would tear it off his mouth and the pieces would stick to his hands like burning gasoline jelly and grow there, grow anywhere on him a glob of it fell. So finally his mouth sealed over, and the whole head would have amputated spontaneous—(did you know there is a condition occurs in parts of Africa and only among Negroes where the little toe amputates spontaneously?)—except for the *eyes* you dig. That's one thing the asshole *couldn't* do was see. It needed the eyes. But nerve connections were blocked and infiltrated and atrophied so the brain couldn't give orders any more. It was trapped in the skull, sealed off. For a while you could see the silent, helpless suffering of the brain behind the eyes, then finally the brain must have died, because the eyes *went out*, and there was no more feeling in them than a crab's eye on the end of a stalk.

"That's the sex that passes the censor, squeezes through between bureaus, because there's always a space *between*, in popular songs and Grade B movies, giving away the basic American rottenness, spurting out like breaking boils, throwing out globs of that un-D.T. to fall anywhere and grow into some degenerate cancerous life-form, reproducing a hideous random image. Some would be entirely made of penis-like erectile tissue, others viscera barely covered over with skin, clusters of 3 and 4 eyes together, criss-cross of mouth and assholes, human parts shaken around and poured out any way they fell.

"The end result of complete cellular representation is cancer. Democracy is cancerous, and bureaus are its cancer. A bureau takes root anywhere in the state, turns malignant like the Narcotic Bureau, and grows and grows, always reproducing more of its own kind, until it chokes the host if not controlled or excised. Bureaus cannot live without a host, being true parasitic organisms. (A cooperative on the other hand *can* live without the state. That is the road to follow. The building up of independent units to meet needs of the people who participate in the functioning of the unit. A bureau operates on opposite principle of *inventing needs* to justify its existence.) Bureaucracy is wrong as a cancer, a turning away from the human evolutionary direction of infinite potentials and differentiation and independent spontaneous action, to the complete parasitism of a virus.

"(It is thought that the virus is a degeneration from more complex life form. It may at one time have been capable of independent life. Now has fallen to the borderline between living and dead matter. It can exhibit living qualities only in a host, by using the life of another—the renunciation of life itself, a *falling* towards inorganic, inflexible machine, towards dead matter.)

"Bureaus die when the structure of the state collapses. They are as helpless and unfit for independent existences as a displaced tapeworm, or a virus that has killed the host.

"In Timbuctu I once saw an Arab boy who could

play a flute with his ass, and the fairies told me he was really an individual in bed. He could play a tune up and down the organ hitting the most erogenously sensitive spots, which are different on everyone, of course. Every lover had his special theme song which was perfect for him and rose to his climax. The boy was a great artist when it came to improving new combines and special climaxes, some of them notes in the unknown, tie-ups of seeming discords that would suddenly break through each other and crash together with a stunning, hot sweet impact."

"Fats" Terminal has organized a purple-assed baboon stick from motorcycles.

The Huntsmen have gathered for the Hunt Breakfast in The Swarm Bar, a hang-out for elegant pansies. The Huntsmen strut about with imbecile narcissism in black leather jackets and studded belts, flexing their muscles for the fags to feel. They all wear enormous falsie baskets. Every now and then one of them throws a fag to the floor and pisses on him.

They are drinking Victory Punch, compounded of paregoric, Spanish Fly, heavy black rum, Napoleon brandy and canned heat. The punch is served from a great, hollow, gold baboon, crouched in snarling terror, snapping at a spear in his side. You twist the baboon's balls and punch runs out his cock. From time to time hot hors-d'oeuvres pop out the baboon's ass with a loud farting noise. When this happens the Huntsmen roar with bestial laughter, and the fags shriek and twitch.

Master of the Hunt is Captain Everhard, who was drummed out of the Queen's 69th for palming a jockstrap in a game of strip poker. Motorcycles careening, jumping, overturning. Spitting, shrieking, shitting baboons fighting hand to hand with the Huntsmen. Riderless cycles scrabbling about in the dust like crippled insects, attacking baboon and Huntsman. . . .

The Party Leader rides in triumph through yiping crowds. A dignified old man shits at sight of him and tries to sacrifice himself under the wheels of the car.

PARTY LEADER: "Don't sacrifice your old dried up person under the wheels of my brand new Buick Roadmaster Convertible with white-walled tires, hydraulic windows and all the trimmings. It's a chip Arab trick—look to thy accent, Ivan—save it for fertilizer. . . . We refer you to the conservation department to consummate your swell purpose. . . ."

The washing boards are down, and the sheets are sent to the Laundromat lose those guilty stains—Emmanuel prophesies a Second Coming. . . .

There's a boy across the river with an ass like a peach; alas I was no swimmer and lost my Clementine.

The junky sits with needle poised to the message of blood, and the con man palpates the mark with fingers of rotten ectoplasm. . . .

Dr. Berger's Mental Health Hour. . . . Fadeout.

TECHNICIAN: "Now listen, I'll say it again, and I'll say it slow. 'Yes.'" He nods. "And make with the smile. . . . The *smile*." He shows his false teeth in hideous parody of a toothpaste ad. "'We like apple pie, and we like each other. It's just as simple as that,'—and make it sound *simple*, country simple. . . . Look bovine, whyncha? You want the switchboard again? Or the pail?"

Subject—Cured Criminal Psychopath— "No! . . . No! . . . What's this bovine?"

Technician: "Look like a cow."

Subject—with cow's head— "Moooo Moooo."

Technician (starting back): "Too much!! No! Just look square, you dig, like a nice popcorn John. . . ."

Subject: "A mark?"

Technician: "Well, not exactly a mark. Not enough larceny in this citizen. He is after light concussion. . . . You know the type. Telepathic sender and receiver excised. The Service Man Look . . . Action, camera."

Subject: "Yes, we like apple pie." His stomach rumbles loud and long. Streamers of saliva hang off his chin. . . .

Dr. Berger looks up from some notes. He look like Jewish owl with black glasses, the light hurt his eyes: "I think he is an unsuitable subject. . . . See he reports to Disposal."

Technician: "Well, we could cut that rumble out of the sound track, stick a drain in his mouth and . . ."

Dr. Berger: "No . . . He's *unsuitable*." He looks at the subject with distaste as if he commit some terrible faux-pas like look for crabs in Mrs. Worldly's drawing room.

Technician (resigned and exasperated): "Bring in the cured swish."

The cured homosexual is brought in. . . . He walks through invisible contours of hot metal. He sits in front of the camera and starts arranging his body in a countrified sprawl. Muscles move into place like autonomous parts of a severed insect. Blank stupidity blurs and softens his face: "Yes," he nods and smiles, "we like apple pie and we like each other. It's just as simple as that." He nods and smiles and nods and smiles and—

"Cut! . . ." screams the Technician. The cured homosexual is led out nodding and smiling.

"Play it back."

The Artistic Adviser shakes his head: "It lacks something. To be specific, it lacks health."

BERGER (leaps to his feet): "Preposterous! It's health incarnate! . . ."

ARTISTIC ADVISER (primly): "Well if you have anything to enlighten me on this subject I'll be very glad to hear it, *Doctor* Berger. . . . If you with your brilliant mind can carry the project alone, I don't know why you *need* an Art Adviser at *all*." He exits with hand on hip singing softly: "I'll be around when you're gone."

TECHNICIAN: "Send in the cured writer. . . . He's got *what*? Buddhism? . . . Oh, he can't talk. Say so at first, whyncha?" He turns to Berger: "The writer can't talk. . . . Overliberated, you might say. Of course we can dub him. . . ."

BERGER (sharply): "No, that wouldn't do at all. . . . Send in someone else."

TECHNICIAN: "Those two was my white-haired boys. I put in a hundred hours overtime on those kids for which I am not yet compensate. . . ."

BERGER: "Apply triplicate. . . . Form 6090."

TECHNICIAN: "You telling me how to apply already? Now look, Doc, you say something once. 'To speak of a healthy homosexual it's like how can a citzen be perfectly healthy with terminal cirrhosis.' Remember?"

BERGER: "Oh yes. Very well put, of course," he snarls viciously. "I don't pretend to be a *writer*." He spits the word out with such ugly hate that the Technician reels back appalled. . . .

TECHNICIAN (aside): "I can't bear the smell of him. Like old rotten replica cultures. . . . Like the farts of a maneating plant. . . . Like Schafer's hurumph" (parodies academic manner) "Strange Serpent . . . What I'm getting at, Doc, is how can you expect a body to be healthy with its brains washed out? . . . Or put it another way. Can a subject be healthy *in abstentia* by proxy already?"

BERGER (leaps up): "I got the health! . . . All the health! Enough health for the whole world, the whole fuckin world!! I cure everybody!"

The Technician looks at him sourly. He mixes a bicarbonate of soda and drinks it and belches into his hand. "Twenty years I've been a martyr to dyspepsia."

Lovable Lu your brainwashed poppa say: "I'm strictly for fish, and I luuuuuve it. . . . Confidentially, girls, I use Steely Dan's Yokohama, wouldn't you? Danny Boy never lets you down. Besides it's more hygienic that way and avoids all kinda awful contacts leave a man paralyzed from the waist down. Women have poison juices. . . ."

"So I told him, I said: '*Doctor* Berger, don't think you can pass your tired old brainwashed belles on me. I'm the oldest faggot in the Upper Baboon's Asshole. . . .'"

Switch envelopes in clip clap joint where fraudulent girls put the B on you in favor of the House 666 and there is no health in them clap broads rotten to the apple corer of my unconsummate cock. Who shot Cock Robin? . . . The sparrow falls to my trustful Webley, and a drop of blood gathers at his beak. . . .

Lord Jim has turned bright yellow in the woe withered moon of morning like white smoke against the blue stuff, and shirts whip in a cold spring wind on limestone cliffs across the river, Mary, and the dawn is broken in two pieces like Dillinger on the lamster way to the Biograph. Smell of neon and atrophied gangsters, and the criminal *manqué* nerves himself to crack a pay toilet sniffing ammonia in a bucket. . . . "A caper," he says. "I'll pull this capon I mean caper."

PARTY LEADER (mixing another scotch): "The next riot goes off like a football play. We have imported a thousand bone fed, blue ribbon Latahs from Indochina. . . . All we need is one riot leader for the whole unit." His eyes sweep the table.

LIEUTENANT: "But, chief, can't we get them started and they imitate each other like a chained reaction?"

The Diseuse undulate through the Market: "What's a Latah do when he's alone?"

P.L.: "That a technical point. We'll have to consult Benway. Personally, I think someone should follow through on the whole operation."

"I do not know," he said for lack of the requisite points and ratings to secure the appointment.

"They have no feelings," said Doctor Benway, slashing his patient to shreds. "Just reflexes . . . I urge distraction."

"The age of consent is when they learn to talk."

"May all your troubles be little ones as one child molester say to the other."

"It's really ominous, my dear, when they start trying on your clothes and give you those doppelgänger kicks. . . ."

Frantic queen trying to claw sport jacket off departing boy.

"My two hundred dollar cashmere jacket," she screeches. . . .

"So he has an affair with this Latah, he wants to dominate someone complete the silly old thing. . . . The Latah imitates all his expressions and mannerisms and simply sucks all the persona right out of him like a sinister ventriloquist's dummy. . . . 'You've taught me everything you are. . . . I need a new amigo.' And poor Bubu can't answer for himself, having no self left."

JUNKY: "So there we are in this no-horse town strictly from cough syrup."

PROFESSOR: "Coprophilia . . . gentlemen . . . might be termed the hurumph . . . redundant vice. . . ."

"Twenty years an artist in the blue movies and I never sink so low as fake an orgasm."

"No good junky cunt hang up her unborn child. . . . Women are no good, kid."

"I mean this dead level conscious sex. . . . Might as well take your old clothes to the Laundromat. . . ."

"And right in the heat of passion he says, 'Do you have an extra shoetree?' "

"She tell me how forty Arabs drag her into a mosque and rape her presumably in sequence. . . . Though they're bad to push—all right, end of the line, Ali. Really, my pets, most distasteful routine I ever listen to. I was after being raped myself by a pride of rampant bores."

A group of sour Nationalists sits in front of the Sargasso sneering at the queens and jabbering in Arabic. . . . Clem and Jody sweep in dressed like The Capitalist in a communist mural.

CLEM: "We have come to feed on your backwardness."

JODY: "In the words of the Immortal Bard, to batten on these Moors."

NATIONALIST: "Swine! Filth! Son of dogs! Don't you realize my people are hungry?"

CLEM: "That's the way I like to see them."

The Nationalist drops dead, poisoned by hate. . . . Dr. Benway rushes up: "Stand back everybody, give me air." He takes a blood sample. "Well, that's all I can do. When you gotta go you gotta go."

The travelling queer Christmas tree burns bright on the rubbish heaps of home where boys jack off in the school toilet—how many young spasms on that old oaken seat worn smooth as gold. . . .

Sleep long in the valley of the Red Rver where cobwebs hang black windows and boy bones. . . .

Two Negro fags shriek at each other.

FAG 1: "Shut up, you cheap granuloma gash. . . . You known as Loathsome Lu in the trade."

DISEUSE: "The girl with the innaresting groin."

FAG 2: "Meow. Meow." He slips on leopard skin and iron claws. . . .

FAG 1: "Oh oh. A Society Woman." He flees screaming through the Market, pursued by the grunting, growling transvestite. . . .

Clem trips a spastic cripple and takes his crutches. . . .
He does a hideous parody twitching and drooling. . . .

Riot noises in the distance—a thousand hysterical
Pomeranians.

Shop shutters slam like guillotines. Drinks and trays
hang in the air as the patrons are whisked inside by the
suction of panic.

CHORUS OF FAGS: "We'll all be raped. I know it, I
know it." They rush into a drugstore and buy a case of
KY.

PARTY LEADER (holding up his hand dramatically):
"The voice of the People."

Pearson the Money Changeling comes acropping the
short grass seized by the extortionate commandant of
Karma, hiding in a vacant lot with the garter snakes, to
be sniffed out by the scrutable dog. . . .

The Market is empty except for an old drunkard of
indeterminate nationality passed out with his head in a
pissoir. The rioters erupt into the Market yiping and
screaming "Death to the French" and tear the drunkard
to pieces.

SALVADOR HASSAN (squirming at a keyhole): "Just
look at those expressions, the whole beautiful protoplasmic being *all exactly alike*." He dances the Liquefactionist Jig.

Whimpering queen falls to the floor in an orgasm.
"Oh God it's too exciting. Like a million hot throbbing
cocks."

BENWAY: "Like to run a blood test on those boys."

A portentously inconspicuous man, grey beard and
grey face and shabby brown jellaba, sings in slight un-
placeable accent without opening his lips:

"Oh you dolls, you great big beautiful dolls."

Squads of police with thin lips, big noses and cold grey eyes move into the Market from every entrance street. They club and kick the rioters with cold, methodical brutality.

The rioters have been carted away in trucks. The shutters go up and the citizens of Interzone step out into the square littered with teeth and sandals and slippery with blood.

The sea chest of the dead man is in the Embassy, and the vice consul breaks the news to mother.

There is no . . . Morning . . . Daybreak . . . *n'existe plus.* . . . If I knew I'd be glad to tell you. Either way is a bad move to the East Wing. . . . He is gone through an invisible door. . . . Not here . . . You can look any place. . . . No good . . . No bueno . . . Hustling myself. . . . C'lom Fliday.

(Note: Old time, veteran Schmeckers, faces beaten by grey junk weather, will remember. . . . In 1920s a lot of Chinese pushers around found The West so unreliable, dishonest and wrong, they all packed in, so when an Occidental junky came to score, they say:

"No glot. . . . C'lom Fliday. . . .")

ISLAM INCORPORATED AND THE PARTIES OF INTERZONE

I was working for an outfit known as Islam Inc., financed by A. J., the notorious Merchant of Sex, who scandalized international society when he appeared at the Duc de Ventre's ball as a walking penis covered by a huge condom emblazoned with the A. J. motto "They Shall Not Pass."

"Rather bad taste, old boy," said the Duke.

To which A. J. replied: "Up yours with Interzone K.Y." The reference is to the K.Y. scandal which was still in a larval state at that time. A. J.'s repartee often refers to future events. He is a master of the delayed squelch.

Salvador Hassan O'Leary, the After Birth Tycoon, is also involved. That is, one of his subsidiary companies has made unspecified contributions, and one of his subsidiary personalities is attached to the organization in an advisory capacity without in any way committing himself to, or associating himself with, the policies, actions or objectives of Islam Inc. Mention should also be made of Clem and Jody, the Ergot Brothers, who decimated the Republic of Hassan with poison wheat, Autopsy Ahmed, and Hepatitis Hal, the fruit and vegetable broker.

A rout of Mullahs and Muftis and Musseins and Caids and Glaouis and Sheiks and Sultans and Holy Men and representatives of every conceivable Arab party make up the rank and file and attend the actual meetings from which the higher ups prudently abstain. Though the delegates are carefully searched at the door, these gatherings invariably culminate in riots. Speakers are often doused with gasoline and burned to death, or some uncouth desert Sheik opens up on his opponents with a machine gun he had concealed in the belly of a pet sheep. Nationalist martyrs with grenades up the ass mingle with the assembled conferents and suddenly ex-

plode, occasioning heavy casualties. . . . And there was
the occasion when President Ra threw the British Prime
Minister to the ground and forcibly sodomized him, the
spectacle being televised to the entire Arab World.
Wild yipes of joy were heard in Stockholm. Interzone
has an ordinance forbidding a meeting of Islam Inc.
within five miles of the city limits.

A. J.—he is actually of obscure Near East extraction
—had at one time come on like an English gentleman.
His English accent waned with the British Empire, and
after World War II he became an American by Act of
Congress. A. J. is an agent like me, but for whom or for
what no one has ever been able to discover. It is ru-
mored that he represents a trust of giant insects from
another galaxy. . . . I believe he is on the Factualist side
(which I also represent); of course he could be a Liquefaction Agent (the Liquefaction program involves the
eventual merging of everyone into One Man by a process of protoplasmic absorption). You can never be sure
of anyone in the industry.

A. J.'s cover story? An international playboy and
harmless practical joker. It was A. J. who put the pir-
anha fish in Lady Sutton-Smith's swimming pool, and
dosed the punch with a mixture of Yage, Hashish and
Yohimbine during a Fourth of July reception at the U.S.
Embassy, precipitating an orgy. Ten prominent citizens
—American, of course—subsequently died of shame. Dy-
ing of shame is an accomplishment peculiar to Kwakiutl
Indians and Americans—others simply say "*Zut alors*" or
"*Son cosas de la vida*" or "Allah fucked me, the All
Powerful. . . ."

And when the Cincinnati Anti-Fluoride Society met to toast their victory in pure spring water, all their teeth dropped out on the spot.

"And I say unto you, brothers and sisters of the Anti-Fluoride movement, we have this day struck such a blow for purity as will never call a retreat. . . . Out, I say, with the filthy foreign fluorides! We will sweep this fair land sweet and clean as a young boy's tensed flank. . . . I will now lead you in our theme song *The Old Oaken Bucket*."

A well head is lighted by fluorescent lights that play over it in hideous juke-box colors. The Anti-Fluorides file past the well singing as each dips up a drink from the oaken bucket. . . .

"The old oaken bucket, the gold oaken bucket
The glublthulunnubbeth . . ."

A. J. had tampered with the water, inserting a South American vine that turns the gums to mush.

(I hear about this vine from an old German prospector who is dying of uremia in Pasto, Columbia. Supposed to grow in the Putumayo area. Never located any. Didn't try very hard. . . . The same citizen tells me about a bug like a big grasshopper known as the Xiucutil: "Such a powerful aphrodisiac if one flies on you and you can't get a woman right away you will die. I have seen the Indians running around pulling themselves off from the contact with this animal." Unfortunately I never score for a Xiucutil. . . .)

On opening night of the New York Metropolitan, A. J., protected by bug repellent, released a swarm of Xiucutils.

Mrs. Vanderbligh swatting at a Xiucutil: "Oh! . . .

Oh! . . . OOOOOOOOOOOH!!!" Screams, breaking
glass, ripping cloth. A rising crescendo of grunts and
squeals and moans and whimpers and gasps. . . . Reek
of semen and cunts and sweat and the musty odor of
penetrated rectums. . . . Diamonds and fur pieces, evening dresses, orchids, suits and underwear litter the
floor covered by a writhing, frenzied, heaving mass of
naked bodies.

A. J. once reserved a table a year in advance *Chez
Robert* where a huge, icy gourmet broods over the
greatest cuisine in the world. So baneful and derogatory
is his gaze that many a client, under that withering
blast, has rolled on the floor and pissed all over himself
in convulsive attempts to ingratiate.

So A. J. arrives with six Bolivian Indians who chew
coca leaves between courses. And when Robert, in all
his gourmet majesty, bears down on the table, A. J.
looks up and yells: "Hey, Boy! Bring me some ketchup."

(Alternative: A. J. whips out a bottle of ketchup and
douses the haute cuisine.)

Thirty gourmets stop chewing at once. You could
have heard a *soufflé* drop. As for Robert, he lets out a
bellow of rage like a wounded elephant, runs to the
kitchen and arms himself with a meat cleaver. . . . The
Sommelier snarls hideously, his face turning a strange
iridescent purple. . . . He breaks off a bottle of Brut Champagne . . . '26. . . . Pierre, the Head Waiter, snatches up
a boning knife. All three chase A. J. through the restaurant with mangled inhuman screams of rage. . . .
Tables overturn, vintage wines and matchless food
crash to the floor. . . . Cries of "Lynch him!" ring through

the air. An elderly gourmet with the insane bloodshot eyes of a mandril, is fashioning a hangman's knot with a red velvet curtain cord. . . . Seeing himself cornered and in imminent danger of dismemberment at least, A.J. plays his trump card. . . . He throws back his head and lets out a hog call; and a hundred famished hogs he had stationed nearby rush into the restaurant, slopping the haute cuisine. Like a great tree Robert falls to the floor in a stroke where he is eaten by the hogs: "Poor bastards don't know enough to appreciate him," says A. J.

Robert's brother Paul emerges from retirement in a local nut house and takes over the restaurant to dispense something he calls the "Transcendental Cuisine." . . . Imperceptibly the quality of the food declines until he is serving literal garbage, the clients being too intimidated by the reputation of *Chez Robert* to protest.

Sample Menu:

The Clear Camel Piss Soup with boiled Earth Worms

The Filet of Sun-Ripened Sting Ray
basted with Eau de Cologne and garnished with nettles

The After-Birth Suprême de Boeuf,
cooked in drained crank case oil,
served with a piquant sauce of rotten egg yolks
and crushed bed bugs

The Limburger Cheese sugar cured in diabetic urine
doused in Canned Heat Flamboyant. . . .

So the clients are quietly dying of botulism. . . . Then A. J. returns with an entourage of Arab refugees from the Middle East. He takes one mouthful and screams:

"Garbage God damn it. Cook this wise citizen in his own swill!"

And so the legend of A. J. the laughable, lovable eccentric grew and grew. . . . Fadeout to Venice. . . . Gondoliers singing and pathic cries swell up from San Marco and Harry's.

Charming old Venetian anecdote about this bridge, it seems some Venetian sailors take a trip around the world and all turn into fruits they fuck the cabin boy already, so when they get back to Venice it is necessary women walk over this bridge with their lungs hanging out to arouse the desires of these dubious citizens. So get a battalion of shock troops up to San Marco on the double.

"Girls, this is O.A.O., Operation All Out. If your tits won't stop them bring up your cunts and confound these faggots."

"Oh Gertie it's true. It's all true. They've got a horrid gash instead of a thrilling thing."

"I can't face it."

"Enough to turn a body to stone."

Paul spoke wiser than he know being a really evil old shit when he talk about men lying with men doing that which is inconvenient. Inconvenient is the word. So who want to trip over a cock on the way to a cunt, and when a citizen get the yen to hump a gash, some evil stranger rush in and do that which is inconvenien. to his ass.

A. J. rush across San Marco slashing at pigeons with a cutlass: "Bastards! Sons of bitches!" he screams. . . .

He staggers aboard his barge, a monstrous construction in gilt and pink and blue with sails of purple velvet. He is dressed in a preprosterous naval uniform covered with braid and ribbons and medals, dirty and torn, the coat buttoned in the wrong holes. . . . A. J. walks to a huge reproduction of a Greek urn topped by a gold statue of a boy with an erection. He twists the boy's balls and a jet of champagne spurts into his mouth. He wipes his mouth and looks around.

"Where are my Nubians, God damn it?" he yells.

His secretary looks up from a comic book: "Juicing. . . . Chasing cunt."

"Goldbricking cocksuckers. Where's a man without his Nubians?"

"Take a gondola whyncha?"

"A gondola?" A. J. screams. "I put out for this cocksucker I should ride in a gondola already? Reef the mainsail and ship the oars, Mr. Hyslop. . . . I'm gonna make with the auxiliary." Mr. Hyslop shrugs resignedly. With one finger he begins punching a switchboard. . . . The sails drop, the oars draw into the hull.

"And turn on the perfume whyncha? The canal stinks up a breeze."

"Gardenia? Sandlewood?"

"Naw. Ambrosia." Mr. Hyslop presses another button and a thick cloud of perfume settles over the barge. A. J. is seized with a fit of coughing. . . .

"Make with the fans!" he yells. "I'm suffocatin'!" Mr. Hyslop is coughing into a handkerchief. He presses a button. Fans whir and thin out the ambrosia. A. J. installs himself at the rudder on a raised dais. "Contact!" The barge begins to vibrate. "Avanti, God damn it!"

A. J. yells and the barge takes off across the canal at a tremendous speed overturning gondolas full of tourists, missing the motoscafi by inches, veering from one side of the canal to the other (the wake washes over the sidewalks drenching passersby) shattering a fleet of moored gondolas, and finally piles up against a pier, spins out into the middle of the canal. . . . A column of water spurts six feet in the air from a hole in the hull.

"Man the pumps, Mr. Hyslop. She's shipping water." The barge gives a sudden lurch throwing A. J. into the canal.

"Abandon ship, God damn it! Every man for himself!" Fadeout to Mambo music.

The inauguration of Escuela Amigo, a school for delinquent boys of Latin American origin, endowed by A. J., Faculty Boys and press attending. A. J. staggers out onto a platform draped with American flags.

"In the immortal words of Father Flanagan there is no such thing as a bad boy. . . . Where's the statuary, God damn it?"

TECHNICIAN: "You want it now?"

A. J.: "What you think I'm doing here Furthucrisakes? I should unveil the son of a bitch *in abstentia*?"

TECHNICIAN: "All right . . . All *right*. Coming right up." The statue is towed out by a Graham Hymie tractor and placed in front of the platform. A. J. presses a button. Turbines start under the platform, rising to a deafening whine. Wind blows the red velvet drapes off the statue. They tangle around the Faculty members in the front row. . . . Clouds of dust and debris whip through the spectators. The sirens slowly subside. The

Faculty disengages itself from the drapes. . . . Everyone is looking at the statue in breathless silence.

FATHER GONZALEZ: "Mother of God!"

THE MAN FROM *Time*: "I don't *believe* it."

Daily News: "It's nothing but fruity."

Chorus of whistles from the boys.

A monumental creation in shiny pink stone stands revealed as the dust settles. A naked boy is bending over a sleeping comrade with evident intention to waken him with a flute. One hand is holding the flute, the other reaching for a piece of cloth draped over the sleeper's middle. The cloth bulges suggestively. Both boys wear a flower behind the ear, identical expressions, dreamy and brutal, depraved and innocent. This creations tops a limestone pyramid on which is inscribed in letters of porcelain mosaic—pink and blue and gold—the school motto: *"With it and for it."*

A. J. lurches forward and breaks a champagne bottle across the boy's taut buttocks.

"And remember, boys, that's where champagne comes from."

Manhattan Serenade. A. J. and entourage start into New York night club. A. J. is leading a purple-assed baboon on a gold chain. A. J. is dressed in checked linen plus fours with a cashmere jacket.

MANAGER: *"Wait* a minute. Wait a *minute*. What's that?"

A. J.: "It's an Illyrian poodle. Choicest beast a man can latch onto. It'll raise the tone of your trap."

MANAGER: "I suspect it to be a purple-assed baboon and it stands outside."

STOOGE: "Don't you know who this is? It's A. J., last of the big time spenders."

MANAGER: "Leave him take his purple-assed bastard and big time spend some place else."

A. J. stops in front of another club and looks in. "Elegant fags and old cunts, God damn it! We come to the right place. Avanti, ragazzi!"

He drives a gold stake into the floor and pickets the baboon. He begins talking in elegant tones, his stooges filling in.

"Fantastic!"

"Monstrous!"

"Utter heaven!"

A. J. puts a long cigarette holder in his mouth. The holder is made of some obscenely flexible material. It swings and undulates as if endowed with loathsome reptilian life.

A. J.: "So there I was flat on my stomach at thirty thousand feet."

Several nearby fags raise their heads like animals scenting danger. A. J. leaps to his feet with an inarticulate snarl.

"You purple-assed cocksucker!" he screams. "I'll teach you to shit on the floor!" He pulls a whip from his umbrella and cuts the baboon across the ass. The baboon screams and tears loose the stake. He leaps on the next table and climbs up an old woman who dies of heart failure on the spot.

A. J.: "Sorry, lady. Discipline you know."

In a frenzy he whips the baboon from one end of the bar to the other. The baboon, screaming and snarling and shitting with terror, climbs over the clients, runs up and down on top of the bar, swings from drapes and chandeliers. . . .

A. J.: "You'll straighten up and shit right or you won't be inna condition to shit one way or the other."

STOOGE: "You ought to be ashamed of yourself upsettin' A. J. after all he's done for you."

A. J.: "Ingrates! Every one of them ingrates! Take it from an old queen."

Of course no one believes this cover story. A. J. claims to be an "independent," which is to say: "Mind your own business." There are no independents any more. . . . The Zone swarms with every variety of dupe but there are no neutrals there. A neutral at A. J.'s level is of course unthinkable. . . .

Hassan is a notorious Liquefactionist and suspect to be a secret Sender—"Shucks, boys," he says with a disarming grin, "I'm just a blooming old cancer and I gotta proliferate." He picks up a Texas accent associating with Dry Hole Dutton, the Dallas wildcatter, and he wears cowboy boots and ten gallon hat at all times indoors and out. . . . His eyes are invisible behind black glasses, his face smooth and blank as wax above a well-cut suit made entirely from immature high denomination bank notes. (Bank notes are in fact currency, but they must mature before they can be negotiated. . . . Bank notes run as high as one million clams a note.)

"They keep hatching out all over me," he says shyly. . . . "It's like, gee, I don't know how to say it. It's like I was a Mummy scorpion carrying those little baby notes around on my warm body and feeling them grow. . . . Gosh I hope I don't bore you with all this."

Salvador, known as Sally to his friends—he always keeps a few "friends" around and pays them by the hour—got cured in the slunk business in World War II. (To get cured means to get rich. Expression used by Texas oil men.) The Pure Food and Drug Department have his picture in their files, a heavy faced man with an embalmed look as if paraffin had been injected under the skin which is smooth, shiny and poreless. One eye is dead grey color, round as a marble, with flaws and opaque spots. The other is black and shiny, an old undreaming insect eye.

His eyes are normally invisible behind black glasses. He looks sinister and enigmatic—his gestures and mannerisms are not yet comprehensible—like the secret police of a larval state.

In moments of excitement Salvador is apt to lapse into broken English. His accent at such moments suggests an Italian origin. He reads and speaks Etruscan.

A squad of accountant investigators have made a life work of Sal's international dossier. . . . His operations extend through the world in an inextricable, shifting web of subsidiaries, front companies, and aliases. He has held 23 passports and been deported 49 times—deportation proceedings pending in Cuba, Pakistan, Hongkong and Yokohama.

Salvador Hassan O'Leary, alias The Shoe Store Kid, alias Wrong Way Marv, alias After Birth Leary, alias Slunky Pete, alias Placenta Juan, alias K. Y. Ahmed, alias El Chinche, alias El Culito, etc., etc. for fifteen solid pages of dossier, first tangled with the law in NYC where he was traveling with a character known to the Brooklyn police as Blubber Wilson, who hustled his goof ball money shaking down fetishists in shoe stores. Hassan was charged some third degree extortion and conspiracy to impersonate a police officer. He had learnt the shakeman's Number One rule: D.T.—Ditch Tin—which corresponds to the pilot's KFS—Keep Flying Speed. . . . As The Vigilante puts it: "If you get a rumble, kid, ditch your piece of tin if you have to swallow it." So they didn't bust him with a queer badge. Hassan testified against Wilson, who drew Pen Indef. (longest term possible under New York law for a misdemeanor conviction. Nominally an indefinite sentence, it means three years in Riker's Island). Hassan's case was nolle prossed. "I'd have drawn a nickel," Hassan said, "if I hadn't met a decent cop." Hassan met a decent cop every time he took a fall. His dossier contains three pages of monikers indicating his proclivity for cooperating with the law, "playing ball" the cops call it. Others call it something else: Ab the Fuzz Lover, Finky Marv, The Crooning Hebe, Ali the Stool, Wrongo Sal, The Wailing Spic, The Sheeny Soprano, The Bronx Opera House, The Copper's Djinn, The Answering Service, The Squeaking Syrian, The Cooing Cocksucker, The Musical Fruit, The Wrong Ass Hole, The Fairy Fink, Leary the Nark, The Lilting Leprechaun . . . Grassy Gert.

He opened a sex shop in Yokohama, pushed junk in Beirut, pimpd in Panama. During World War II he shifted into high, took over a dairy in Holland and cut the butter with used axle grease, cornered the K.Y. market in North Africa, and finally hit the jackpot with slunks. He prospered and proliferated, flooding the world with cut medicines and cheap counterfeit goods of every variety. Adulterated shark repellent, cut antibiotics, condemned parachutes, stale anti-venom, inactive serums and vaccines, leaking lifeboats.

Clem and Jody, two oldtime vaudeville hoofers, cope out as Russian agents whose sole function is to represent the U.S. in an unpopular light. When arrested for sodomy in Indonesia, Clem said to the examining magistrate:

" 'Tain't as if it was being queer. After all they's only Gooks."

They appeared in Liberia dressed in black Stetsons and red galluses:

"So I shoot that old nigger and he flop on his side one leg up in the air just akicking."

"Yeah, but you ever burn a nigger?"

They are always pacing round Bidonvilles smoking huge cigars:

"Haveta get some bulldozers in here Jody. Clean out all this crap."

Morbid crowds follow them about hoping to witness some superlative American outrage.

"Thirty years in show business and I never handle such a routine like this. I gotta dispossess a Bidonville, give myself a bang of H, piss on the Black Stone, make with the Prayer Call whilst dressed in my hog suit, cancel Lend Lease and get fucked up the ass simultaneous. . . . What, am I an octopus already?" Clem complains.

They are conspiring to kidnap the Black Stone with a helicopter and substitute a hog pen, the hogs trained to give the Bronx cheer when the pilgrims show. "We try to train them squealing bastards to sing: 'Three cheers for the Red White and Blue,' but it can't be done. . . ."

"We connect for that wheat with Ali Wong Chapultepec in Panama. He tells us it is a high grade of shit this Finnish skipper die inna local jump joint and leave this cargo to the madame. . . . 'She was like a mother to me,' he says and those were his last words. . . . So we buy it in good faith off the old gash. Laid ten pieces of H on her."

"Good H too. Good Aleppo H."

"Just enough milk sugar to keep her strength up."

"We should look a gift horse in the ass already?"

"Isn't it true than when you got to Hassan you gave a banquet for the Caid and served couscous made from the wheat?"

"We sure did. And you know those citizens were so loaded on that marijuana they all wig inna middle of the banquet. . . . Me, I just had bread and milk . . . ulcers you know."

"Likewise."

"So they all run around screaming they is on fire and the bulk of them die the following morning."

"And the rest the morning after that."

"What they expect already when they rot theirselves with Eastern vices?"

"Funny thing those citizens turn all black and their legs drop off."

"Horrible result of marijuana addiction."

"The very same thing occurred to me."

"So we deal directly with the old Sultan who is being a well-known Latah. After that everything is plain sailing you might say."

"But you wouldn't believe it, certain disgruntled elements chased us right down to our launch."

"Handicapped somewhat by lack of legs."

"And a condition in the head."

(Ergot is a fungus disease grows on bad wheat. During the Middle Ages Europe was periodically decimated by outbreaks of Ergotism, which was called St. Anthony's fire. Gangrene frequently supervenes, the legs turn black and drop off.)

They unload a shipment of condemned parachutes on the Ecuadorian Air Force. Manoeuvres: Boys plummet streaming 'chutes like broken condoms splash young blood over pot-bellied generals . . . shattering wake of sound as Clem and Jody disappear over the Andes in jet getaway. . . .

The exact objectives of Islam Inc. are obscure. Needless to say everyone involved has a different angle, and they all intend to cross each other up somewhere along the line.

A. J. is agitating for the destruction of Israel: "With all this feeling against the West a chap has a spot of bother scoring for the young Arab amenities. . . . The situation is little short of intolerable. . . . Israel constitutes a downright inconvenience." Typical A. J. cover story.

Clem and Jody give out they are interested in the destruction of Near East oil fields to boost the value of their Venezuelan holdings.

Clem writes a number to the tune of "Crawdad" (Big Bill Broonzy).

> *What you gonna do when the oil goes dry?*
> *Gonna sit right there and watch those Arabs die.*

Salvador emits a thick screen of international finance to cloak, at least from the rank and file, his Liquefactionist activities. . . . But over a few stiff yages he lets his hair down among friends.

"Islam is jellied consommé already," he says, dancing the Liquefactionist Jig. . . . And then, unable to contain himself, he bursts into a hideous falsetto:

> *It's trembling on the brink*
> *One push and down it sink*
> *Hey, Maw, get ready my veil.*

"Well, these citizens have engaged the services of a Brooklyn Jew who passes hmself off as the second coming of Mohammed. . . . In fact Doctor Benway delivered him by Caesarian section from a Holy Man in Mecca. . . .

"If Ahmed won't come out . . . We'll go in and get him."

This shameless plant is accepted without question by the gullible Arabs.

"Nice folk, these Arabs . . . Nice ignorant folk," Clem says.

So this phony gives out with daily Surahs on the radio: "Now friends of the radio audience, this is Ahmed your friendly prophet. . . . Today I'd like to talk about the importance of being dainty and kissin' fresh at all times. . . . Friends, use Jody's chlorophyll tablets and be sure."

Now a word about the parties of Interzone. . . .

It will be immediately clear that the Liquefaction Party is, except for one man, entirely composed of dupes, it not being clear until the final absorption who is whose dupe. . . . The Liquefactionists are much given to every form of perversion, especially sado-masochistic practices. . . .

Liquefactionists in general know what the score is. The Senders, on the other hand, are notorious for their ignorance of the nature and terminal state of sending, for barbarous and self-righteous manners, and for rabid fear of any *fact*—. It was only the intervention of the Factualists that prevented the Senders from putting Einstein in an institution and destroying his theory. It may be said that only a very few Senders know what they are doing and these top Senders are the most dangerous and evil men in the world. . . . Techniques of Sending were crude at first. Fadeout to the National Electronic Conference in Chicago.

The Conferents are putting on their overcoats. . . . The speaker talks in a flat shopgirl voice:

"In closing I want to sound a word of warning. . . . The logical extension of encephalographic research is bicontrol; that is control of physical movement, mental processes, emotional reactions and *apparent* sensory impressions by means of bioelectric signals injected into the nervous system of the subject."

"Louder and funnier!" The Conferents are trouping out in clouds of dust.

"Shortly after birth a surgeon could install connections in the brain. A miniature radio receiver could be plugged in and the subject controlled from State-controlled transmitters."

Dust settles through the windless air of a vast empty hall—smell of hot iron and steam; a radiator sings in the distance. . . . The Speaker shuffles his notes and blows dust off them. . . .

"The biocontrol apparatus is prototype of one-way telepathic control. The subject could be rendered susceptible to the transmitter by drugs or other processing without installing any apparatus. Ultimately the Senders will use telepathic transmitting exclusively. . . . Ever dig the Mayan codices? I figure it like this: the priests —about one per cent of population—made with one-way telepathic broadcasts instructing the workers what to feel and when. . . . A telepathic sender has to send all the time. He can never receive, because if he receives that means someone else has feelings of his own could louse up his continuity. The sender has to send all the time, but he can't ever recharge himself by contact. Sooner or later he's got no feelings to send. You can't have feelings alone. Not alone like the Sender is alone—and you dig there can only be one Sender at one place-time. . . . Finally the screen goes dead. . . . The Sender has turned into a huge centipede. . . . So the workers come in on the beam and burn the centipede and elect a new Sender by consensus of the general will. . . . The Mayans were limited by isolation. . . . Now one Sender could control

the planet. . . . *You see control can never be a means
to any practical end. . . . It can never be a means to
anything but more control. . . . Like junk . . ."*

The Divisionists occupy a mid-way position, could
in fact be termed moderates. . . . They are called Divisionists because they literally divide. They cut off tiny
bits of their flesh and grow exact replicas of themselves
in embryo jelly. It seems probable, unless the process
of division is halted, that eventually there will be only
one replica of one sex on the planet: that is one person in
the world with millions of separate bodies. . . . Are
these bodies actually independent, and could they in
time develop varied characteristics? I doubt it. Replicas
must periodically recharge with the Mother Cell. This is
an article of faith with the Divisionists, who live in fear
of a replica revolution. . . . Some Divisionists think that
the process can be halted short of the eventual monopoly of one replica. They say: "Just let me plant a few
more replicas all over so I won't be lonely when I
travel. . . . And we must strictly control the division of
Undesirables. . . ." Every replica but your own is eventually an "Undesirable." Of course if someone starts
inundating an area with Identical Replicas, everyone
knows what is going on. The other citizens are subject
to declare a "Schluppit" (wholesale massacre of all
identifiable replicas). To avoid extermination of their
replicas, citizens dye, distort, and alter them with face
and body molds. Only the most abandoned and shameless characters venture to manufacture I.R.s—Identical
Replicas.

A cretinous albino Caid, product of a long line of recessive genes (tiny toothless mouth lined with black hairs, body of a huge crab, claws instead of arms, eyes projected on stalks) accumulated 20,000 I.R.s.

"As far as the eye can see, nothing but replicas," he says, crawling around on his terrace and speaking in strange insect chirps. "I don't have to skulk around like a nameless asshole growing replicas in my cesspool and sneaking them out disguised as plumbers and delivery men. . . . My replicas don't have their dazzling beauty marred by plastic surgery and barbarous dye and bleach processes. They stand forth naked in the sun for all to see, in their incandescent loveliness of body, face and soul. I have made them in my image and enjoined them to increase and multiply geometric for they shall inherit the earth."

A professional witch was called in to make Sheik Aracknid's replica cultures forever sterile. . . . As the witch was preparing to loose a blast of anti-orgones, Benway told him: "Don't knock yourself out. Frederick's ataxia will clean out that replica nest. I studied neurology under Professor Fingerbottom in Vienna . . . and he knew every nerve in your body. Magnificent old thing . . . Came to a sticky end. . . . His falling piles blew out the Duc de Ventre's Hispano Suiza and wrapped around the rear wheel. He was completely gutted, leaving an empty shell sitting there on the giraffe skin upholstery. . . . Even the eyes and brain went with a horrible schlupping sound. The Duc de Ventre says he will carry that ghastly schlup to his mausoleum."

Since there is no sure way to detect a disguised replica (though every Divisionist has some method he considers infallible) the Divisionists are hysterically paranoid. If some citizen ventures to express a liberal opinion, another citizen invariably snarls: "What are you? Some stinking Nigger's bleached-out replica?"

The casualties in barroom fights are staggering. In fact the fear of Negro replicas—which may be blond and blue-eyed—has depopulated whole regions. The Divisionists are all latent or overt homosexuals. Evil old queens tell the young boys: "If you go with a woman your replicas won't grow." And citizens are forever putting the hex on someone else's replica cultures. Cries of: "Hex my culture will you, Biddy Blair!" followed by sound effects of mayhem, continually ring through the quarter. . . . The Divisionists are much given to the practice of black magic in general, and they have innumerable formulas of varying efficacy for destroying the Mother Cell, also known as the Protoplasm Daddy, by torturing or killing a captured replica. . . . The authorities have finally given up the attempt to control, among the Divisionists, the crimes of murder and unlicensed production of replicas. But they do stage preelection raids and destroy vast replica cultures in the mountainous regions of the Zone where replica moonshiners hole up.

Sex with a replica is strictly forbidden and almost universally practised. There are queer bars where shameless citizens openly consort with their replicas. House detectives stick their heads into hotel rooms saying: "Have you got a replica in here?"

Bars subject to be inundated by low class replica lovers put up signs in ditto marks: " " " "s Will Not Be Served Here. . . . It may be said that the average Divisionist lives in a continual crisis of fear and rage, unable to achieve either the self-righteous complacency of the Senders or the relaxed depravity of the Liquefactionists. . . . However the parties are not in practice separate but blend in all combinations.

The Factualists are Anti-Liquefactionist, Anti-Divisionist, and above all Anti-Sender.

Bulletin of the Coordinate Factualist on the subject of replicas: "We must reject the facile solution of flooding the planet with 'desirable replicas.' It is highly doubtful if there are any desirable replicas, such creatures constituting an attempt to circumvent process and change. Even the most intelligent and genetically perfect replicas would in all probability constitute an unspeakable menace to life on this planet. . . ."

T.B.—Tentative Bulletin-Liquefaction: "We must not reject or deny our protoplasmic core, striving at all time to maintain a maximum of flexibility without falling into the morass of liquefaction. . . ." Tentative and Incomplete Bulletin: "Emphatically we do not oppose telepathic research. In fact, telepathy properly used and understood could be the ultimate defense against any form of organized coercion or tyranny on the part of of pressure groups or individual control addicts. We oppose, as we oppose atomic war, the use of such knowledge to control, coerce, debase, exploit or annihilate the individuality of another living creature. Telepathy is not, by its nature, a one-way process. To attempt to set up a one-way telepathic broadcast must be regarded as an unqualified evil. . . ."

D.B.—Definitive Bulletin: "The Sender will be defined by negatives. A low pressure area, a sucking emptiness. He will be portentously anonymous, faceless, colorless. He will—probably—be born with smooth disks of skin instead of eyes. He always knows where he is going like a virus knows. He doesn't need eyes."

"Couldn't there be more than one Sender?"

"Oh yes, many of them at first. But not for long. Some maudlin citizens will think they can send something edifying, not realizing that sending *is* evil. Scientists will say: 'Sending is like atomic power. . . . If properly harnessed.' At this point an anal technician mixes a bicarbonate of soda and pulls the switch that reduces the earth to cosmic dust. ('Belch . . . They'll hear this fart on Jupiter.') . . . Artists will confuse sending with creation. They will camp around screeching 'A new medium' until their rating drops off. . . . Philosophers will bat around the ends and means hassle not knowing that *sending can never be a means to anything but more sending, Like Junk.* Try using junk as a means to something else. . . . Some citizens with 'Coca Cola and aspirin' control habits will be talking about the evil glamor of sending. But no one will talk about anything very long. *The Sender*, he don't like talking."

The Sender is not a human individual. . . . It is The Human Virus. (All virus are deteriorated cells leading a parasitic existence. . . . They have specific affinity for the Mother Cell; thus deteriorated liver cells seek the home place of hepatitis, etc. So every species has a Master Virus: Deteriorated Image of that species.)

The broken image of Man moves in minute by minute and cell by cell. . . . Poverty, hatred, war, police-criminals, bureaucracy, insanity, all symptoms of The Human Virus.

The Human Virus can now be isolated and treated.

THE COUNTY CLERK

The County Clerk has his office in a huge red brick building known as the Old Court House. Civil cases are, in fact, tried there, the proceeding inexorably dragging out until the contestants die or abandon litigation. This is due to the vast number of records pertaining to absolutely everything, all filed in the wrong place so that no one but the County Clerk and his staff of assistants can find them, and he often spends years in the search. In fact, he is still looking for material relative to a damage suit that was settled out of court in 1910. Large sections of the Old Court House have fallen in ruins, and others are highly dangerous owing to frequent cave-ins. The County Clerk assigns the more dangerous missions to his assistants, many of whom have lost their lives in the service. In 1912 two hundred and seven assistants were trapped in a collapse of the North-by-North-East wing.

When suit is brought against anyone in the Zone, his lawyers connive to have the case transferred to the Old Court House. Once this is done, the plaintiff has lost the case, so the only cases that actually go to trial in the Old Court House are those instigated by eccentrics and paranoids who want "a public hearing," which they rarely get since only the most desperate famine of news will bring a reporter to the Old Court House.

The Old Court House is located in the town of Pigeon Hole outside the urban zone. The inhabitants of this town and the surrounding area of swamps and heavy timber are people of such great stupidity and such barbarous practices that the Administration has seen fit to quarantine them in a reservation surrounded by a radioactive wall of iron bricks. In retaliation the citizens of Pigeon Hole plaster their town with signs: *"Urbanite Don't Let The Sun Set On You Here,"* an unnecessary injunction, since nothing but urgent business would take any urbanite to Pigeon Hole.

Lee's case is urgent. He has to file an immediate affidavit that he is suffering from bubonic plague to avoid eviction from the house he has occupied ten years without paying the rent. He exists in perpetual quarantine. So he packs his suitcase of affidavits and petitions and injunctions and certificates and takes a bus to the Frontier. The Urbanite customs inspector waves him through: "I hope you've got an atom bomb in that suitcase."

Lee swallows a handful of tranquilizing pills and steps into the Pigeon Hole customs shed. The inspectors spend three hours pawing through his papers, consulting dusty books of regulations and duties from which they read incomprehensible and ominous excerpts ending with: "And as such is subject to fine and penalty under act 666." They look at him significantly.

They go through his papers with a magnifying glass. "Sometimes they slip dirty limericks between the lines."

"Maybe he figures to sell them for toilet paper. Is this crap for your own personal use?"

"Yes."

"He says yes."

"And how do we know that?"

"I gotta affidavit."

"Wise guy. Take off your clothes."

"Yeah. Maybe he got dirty tattoos."

They paw over his body probing his ass for contraband and examine it for evidence of sodomy. They dunk his hair and send the water out to be analyzed. "Maybe he's got dope in his hair."

Finally, they impound his suitcase; and he staggers out of the shed with a fifty pound bale of documents.

A dozen or so Recordites sit on the Old Court House steps of rotten wood. They watch his approach with pale blue eyes, turning their heads slow on wrinkled necks (the wrinkles full of dust) to follow his body up the steps and through the door. Inside, dust hangs in the air like fog, sifting down from the ceiling, rising in clouds from the floor as he walks. He mounts a perilous staircase—condemned in 1929. Once his foot goes through, and the dry splinters tear into the flesh of his leg. The stairscase ends in a painter's scaffold, attached with frayed rope and pullies to a beam almost invisible in dusty distance. He pulls himself up cautiously to a ferris wheel cabin. His weight sets in motion hydraulic machinery (sound of running water). The wheel moves smooth and silent to stop by a rusty iron balcony, worn through here and there like an old shoe sole. He walks down a long corridor lined with doors, most of them nailed or boarded shut. In one office, *Near East Exqui-sitries* on a green brass plaque, the Mugwump is catch-ing termites with his long black tongue. The door of the County Clerk's office is open. The County Clerk sits in-side gumming snuff, surrounded by six assistants. Lee stands in the doorway. The County Clerk goes on talk-ing without looking up.

"I run into Ted Spigot the other day . . . a good old boy, too. Not a finer man in the Zone than Ted Spigot. . . . Now it was a Friday I happen to remember because the Old Lady was down with the menstral cramps and I went to Doc Parker's drugstore on Dalton Street, just opposite Ma Green's Ethical Massage Parlor, where Jed's old livery stable used to be. . . . Now, Jed, I'll remember his second name directly, had a cast in the left eye and his wife came from some place out East, Algiers I believe it was, and after Jed died she married up again, and she married one of the Hoot boys, Clem Hoot if my memory serves, a good old boy too, now Hoot was around fifty-four fifty-five year old at the time. . . . So I says to Doc Parker: 'My old lady is down bad with the menstral cramps. Sell me two ounces of paregoric.'

"So Doc says, 'Well, Arch, you gotta sign the book. Name, address and date of purchase. It's the law.'

"So I asked Doc what the day was, and he said, 'Fri-day the 13th.'

"So I said, ' I guess I already had mine.'

"'Well,' Doc says, 'there was a feller in here this morning. City feller. Dressed kinda flashy. So he's got him a RX for a mason jar of morphine. . . . Kinda funny looking prescription writ out on toilet paper. . . . And I told him straight out: "Mister, I suspect you to be a dope fiend." '

" ' "I got the ingrowing toe nails, Pop. I'm in agony." ' he says.

" ' "Well," I says, "I gotta be careful. But so long as you got a legitimate condition and an RX from a certified bona feedy M.D., I'm honored to serve you." '

" ' "That croaker's really certified," he say. . . . Well, I guess one hand didn't know what the other was doing when I give him a jar of Saniflush by error. . . . So I reckon he's had his too.'

" 'Just the thing to clean a man's blood.'

" 'You know, that very thing occurred to me. Should be a sight better than sulphur and molasses. . . . Now, Arch, don't think I'm nosey; but a man don't have no secrets from God and his druggist I always say. . . . Is you still humping the Old Gray Mare?'

" 'Why, Doc Parker . . . I'll have you know I'm a family man and an Elder in the First Denominational Non-sextarian Church and I ain't had a piecea hoss ass since we was kids together.'

" 'Them was the days, Arch. Remember the time I got the goose grease mixed up with the mustard? Always was a one to grab the wrong jar, feller say. They could have heard you squealing over in Cunt Lick County, just a squealing like a stoat with his stones cut off.'

" 'You're in the wrong hole, Doc. It was you took the mustard and me as had to wait till you cooled off.'

" 'Wistful thinking, Arch. I read about it one time inna magazin settin' in that green outhouse behind the station. . . . Now what I meant awhile back, Arch, you didn't rightly understand me. . . . I was referring to your wife as the Old Gray Mare. . . . I mean she ain't what she used to be what with all them carbuncles and cataracts and chilblains and haemorrhoids and aftosa.'

" 'Yas, Doc, Liz is right sickly. Never was the same after her eleventh miscarriaging. . . . There was something right strange about that. Doc Ferris he told me straight, he said: "Arch, 'tain't fitting you should see that critter." And he gives me a long look made my flesh crawl. . . . Well, you sure said it right, Doc. She ain't what she used to be. And your medicines don't seem to ease her none. In fact, she ain't been able to tell night from day since using them eye drops you sold her last month. . . . But, Doc, you oughtta know I wouldn't be humping Liz, the old cow, meaning no disrespect to the mother of my dead monsters. Not when I got that sweet little ol' fifteen year old thing. . . . You know that yaller girl used to work in Marylou's Hair Straightening and Skin Bleach Parlor over in Nigga town.'

" 'Getting that dark chicken meat, Arch? Gettin' that coon pone?'

" 'Gettin' it steady, Doc. Gettin' it steady. Well, feller say duty is goosing me. Gotta get back to the old crank case.'

" 'I'll bet she needs a grease job worst way.'

" 'Doc, she sure is a dry hole. . . . Well, thanks for the paregoric.'

" 'And thanks for the trade, Arch. . . . He he he . . . Say, Archy boy, some night when you get caught short with a rusty load drop around and have a drink of Yohimbiny with me.'

"'I'll do that, Doc, I sure will. It'll be just like old times.'

"So I went on back to my place and heated up some water and mixed up some paregoric and cloves and cinnamon and sassyfrass and give it to Liz, and it eased her some I reckon. Leastwise she let up aggravatin' me. . . . Well, later on I went down to Doc Parker's again to get me a rubber . . . and just as I was leaving I run into Roy Bane, a good ol' boy too. There's not a finer man in this Zone than Roy Bane. . . . So he said to me he says, 'Arch, you see that ol' nigger over there in that vacant lot? Well, sure as shit and taxes, he comes there every night just as regular you can set your watch by him. See him behind them nettles? Every night round about eight thirty he goes over into that lot yonder and pulls himself off with steel wool. . . . Preachin' Nigger, they tell me.'

"So that's how I come to know the hour more or less on Friday the 13th and it couldn't have been more than twenty minutes half an hour after that, I'd took some Spanish Fly in Doc's store and it was jest beginning to work on me down by Grennel Bog on my way to Nigger town. . . . Well the bog makes a bend, used to be nigger shack there. . . . They burned that ol' nigger over in Cunt Lick. Nigger had the aftosa and it left him stone blind. . . . So this white girl down from Texarkana screeches out:

"'Roy, that ol' nigger is looking at me so nasty. Land's sake I feel just dirty all over.'

"'Now, Sweet Thing, don't you fret yourself. Me an' the boys will burn him.'

" 'Do it slow, Honey Face. Do it slow. He's give me a sick headache.'

"So they burned the nigger and that ol' boy took his wife and went back up to Texarkana without paying for the gasoline and old Whispering Lou runs the service station couldn't talk about nothing else all Fall: 'These city fellers come down here and burn a nigger and don't even settle up for the gasoline.'

"Well, Chester Hoot tore that nigger shack down and rebuilt it just back of his house up in Bled Valley. Covered up all the windows with black cloth, and what goes on in there ain't fittin' to speak of. . . . Now Chester he's got some right strange ways. . . . Well it was just where the nigger shack used to be, right across from the Old Brooks place floods out every Spring, only it wasn't the Brooks place then . . . belonged to a feller name of Scranton. Now that piece of land was surveyed back in 1919. . . . I reckon you know the man did the job too. . . . Feller name of Hump Clarence used to witch out wells on the side. . . . Good ol' boy too, not a finer man in this Zone than Hump Clarence. . . . Well it was just around about in there I come on Ted Spigot ascrewin a mud puppy."

Lee cleared his throat. The Clerk looked up over his glasses. "Now if you'll take care, young feller, till I finish what I'm asaying, I'll tend to your business."

And he plunged into an anecdote about a nigra got the hydrophobia from a cow.

"So my pappy says to me: 'Finish up your chores, son, and let's go see the mad nigger. . . .' They had that nigger chained to the bed, and he was bawling like a cow. . . . I soon got enough of that ol' nigger. Well, if you all will excuse me I got business in the Privy Council. He he he!"

Lee listened in horror. The County Clerk often spent weeks in the privy living on scorpions and Montgomery Ward catalogues. On several occasions his assistants had forced the door and carried him out in an advanced state of malnutrition. Lee decided to play his last card.

"Mr. Anker," he said, "I'm appealing to you as one Razor Back to another," and he pulled out his Razor Back card, a memo of his lush-rolling youth.

The Clerk looked at the card suspiciously: "You don't look like a bone feed mast-fed Razor Back to me. . . . What you think about the Jeeeeews. . . ?"

"Well, Mr. Anker, you know yourself all a Jew wants to do is doodle a Christian girl. . . . One of these days we'll cut the rest of it off."

"Well, you talk right sensible for a city feller. . . . Find out what he wants and take care of him. . . . He's a good ol' boy."

INTERZONE

The only native in Interzone who is neither queer nor available is Andrew Keif's chauffeur, which is not affectation or perversity on Keif's part, but a useful pretext to break off relations with anyone he doesn't want to see: "You made a pass at Aracknid list night. I can't have you to the house again." People are always blacking out in the Zone, whether they drink or not, and no one can say for sure he didn't make a pass at Aracknid's unappetizing person.

Aracknid is a worthless chauffeur, barely able to drive. On one occasion he ran down a pregnant woman in from the mountains with a load of charcoal on her back, and she miscarriaged a bloody, dead baby in the street, and Keif got out and sat on the curb stirring the blood with a stick while the police questioned Aracknid and finally arrested the woman for a violation of the Sanitary Code.

Aracknid is a grimly unattractive young man with a long face of a strange, slate-blue color. He has a big nose and great yellow teeth like a horse. Anybody can find an attractive chauffeur, but only Andrew Keif could have found Aracknid; Keif the brilliant, decadent young novelist who lives in a remodeled pissoir in the red light district of the Native Quarter.

The Zone is a single, vast building. The rooms are made of a plastic cement that bulges to accommodate people, but when too many crowd into one room there is a soft plop and someone squeezes through the wall right into the next house, the next bed that is, since the rooms are mostly bed where the business of the Zone is transacted. A hum of sex and commerce shakes the Zone like a vast hive:

"Two thirds of one percent. I won't budge from that figure; not even for my bumpkins."

"But where are the bills of lading, lover?"

"Not where you're looking, pet. That's too obvious."

"A bale of levies with built-in falsie baskets. Made in Hollywood."

"Hollywood, Siam."

"Well American *style*."

"What's the commission? . . . The commission. . . .
The Commission."

"Yes, nugget, a shipload of K.Y. made of genuine
whale dreck in the South Atlantic at present quarantined by the Board of Health in Tierra del Fuego. The
commission, my dear! If we can pull this off we'll be in
clover." (Whale dreck is reject material that accumu-
lates in the process of cutting up a whale and cooking
it down. A horrible, fishy mess you can smell for miles.
No one has found any use for it.)

Interzone Imports Unlimited, which consists of Marvie and Leif The Unlucky, had latched onto the K.Y.
deal. In fact they specialize in pharmaceuticals and
run a 24-hour Pro station, six ways coverage fore and
aft, as a side line. (Six separate venereal diseases have
been identified to date.)

They plunge into the deal. They form unmentionable
services for a spastic Greek shipping agent, and one
entire shift of Customs inspectors. The two partners fall
out and finally denounce each other in the Embassy
where they are referred to the We Don't Want To Hear
About It Department, and eased out a back door into
a shit-strewn vacant lot, where vultures fight over fish
heads. They flail at each other hysterically.

"You're trying to fuck me out of my commission!"

"*Your* commission! Who smelled out this good thing
in the first place?"

"But I have the bill of lading."

"Monster! But the check will be made out in my
name."

"Bawstard! You'll never see the bill of lading until my cut is deposited in escrow."

"Well, might as well kiss and make up. There's nothing mean or petty about me."

They shake hands without enthusiasm and peck each other on the cheek. The deal drags on for months. They engage the services of an Expeditor. Finally Marvie emerges with a check for 42 Turkestan kurds drawn on an anonymous bank in South America, to clear through Amsterdam, a procedure that will take eleven months more or less.

Now he can relax in the cafés of The Plaza. He shows a photostatic copy of the check. He would never show the original of course, lest some envious citizen spit ink eradicator on the signature or otherwise mutilate the check.

Everyone asks him to buy drinks and celebrate, but he laughs jovially and says, "Fact is I can't afford to buy myself a drink. I already spent every kurd of it buying Penstrep for Ali's clap. He's down with it fore and aft again. I came near kicking the little bastard right through the wall into the next bed. But you all know what a sentimental old thing I am."

Marvie does buy himself a shot glass of beer, squeezing a blackened coin out of his fly onto the table. "Keep the change." The waiter sweeps the coin into a dust pan, he spits on the table and walks away.

"Sore head! He's envious of my check."

Marvie had been in Interzone since "the year before one" as he put it. He had been retired from some unspecified position in the State Dept. "for the good of the service." Obviously he had once been very good looking in a crew-cut, college boy way, but his face had sagged and formed lumps under the chin like melting paraffin. He was getting heavy around the hips.

Leif The Unlucky was a tall, thin Norwegian, with a patch over one eye, his face congealed in a permanent, ingratiating smirk. Behind him lay an epic saga of unsuccessful enterprises. He had failed at raising frogs, chinchilla, Siamese fighting fish, rami and culture pearls. He had attempted, variously and without success, to promote a Love Bird Two-in-a-Coffin Cemetery, to corner the condom market during the rubber shortage, to run a mail order whore house, to issue penicillin as a patent medicine. He had followed disastrous betting systems in the casinos of Europe and the race tracks of the U.S. His reverses in business were matched by the incredible mischances of his personal life. His front teeth had been stomped out by bestial American sailors in Brooklyn. Vultures had eaten out an eye when he drank a pint of paregoric and passed out in a Panama City park. He had been trapped between floors in an elevator for five days with an oil-burning junk habit and sustained an attack of D.T.s while stowing away in a foot locker. Then there was the time he collapsed with strangulated intestines, perforated ulcers and peritonitis in Cairo and the hospital was so crowded they bedded him in the latrine, and the Greek surgeon goofed and sewed up a live monkey in him, and he was gang-fucked by the Arab attendants, and one of the orderlies stole the penicillin substituting Saniflush; and the time he got clap in his ass and a self-righteous English doctor cured him with an enema of hot, sulphuric acid, and the German practitioner of Technological Medicine who removed his appendix with a rusty can opener and a pair of tin snips (he considered the germ theory "a nonsense.") Flushed with success he then began snipping and cutting out everything in sight: "The human body is filled up vit unnecessitated parts. You can get by vit one kidney. Vy have two? Yes dot is a kidney. . . . The inside parts should not be so close in together crowded. They need lebensraum like the Vaterland."

The Expeditor had not yet been paid, and Marvie was faced by the prospect of stalling him for eleven months until the check cleared. The Expeditor was said to have been born on the Ferry between the Zone and the Island. His profession was to expedite the delivery of merchandise. No one knew for sure whether his services were of any use or not, and to mention his name always precipitated an argument. Cases were cited to prove his miraculous efficiency and utter worthlessness.

The Island was a British Military and Naval station directly opposite the Zone. England holds the Island on yearly rent-free lease, and every year the lease and permit of residence is formally renewed. The entire population turns out, attendance is compulsory, and gathers at the municipal dump. The President of the Island is required by custom to crawl across the garbage on his stomach and deliver the Permit of Residence and Renewal of the Lease, signed by every citizen of the Island, to The Resident Governor who stands resplendent in dress uniform. The Governor takes the permit and shoves it into his coat pocket:

"Well," he says with a tight smile, "so you've decided to let us stay another year have you? Very good of you.

And everyone is happy about it? . . . Is there anyone who isn't happy about it?"

Soldiers in jeeps sweep mounted machine-guns back and forth across the crowd with a slow, searching movement.

"Everybody happy. Well that's fine." He turns jovially to the prostrate President. "I'll keep your papers in case I get caught short. Haw Haw Haw." His loud, metallic laugh rings out across the dump, and the crowd laughs with him under the searching guns.

The forms of democracy are scrupulously enforced on the Island. There is a Senate and a Congress who carry on endless sessions discussing garbage disposal and outhouse inspection, the only two questions over which they have jurisdiction. For a brief period in the mid-nineteenth century, they had been allowed to control the dept. of Baboon Maintenance but this privilege had been withdrawn owing to absenteeism in the Senate.

The purple-assed Tripoli baboons had been brought to the Island by pirates in the 17th century. There was a legend that when the baboons left the Island it would fall. To whom or in what way is not specified, and it is a capital offense to kill a baboon, though the noxious behaviour of these animals harries the citizens almost beyond endurance. Occasionally someone goes berserk, kills several baboons and himself.

The post of President is always forced on some particularly noxious and unpopular citizen. To be elected President is the greatest misfortune and disgrace that can befall an Islander. The humiliations and ignominy are such that few Presidents live out their full term of office, usually dying of a broken spirit after a year or two. The Expeditor had once been President and served the full five years of his term. Subsequently he changed his name and underwent plastic surgery, to blot out, as far as possible, the memory of his disgrace.

"Yes of course . . . we'll pay you," Marvie was saying to the Expeditor.

"But take it easy. It may be a little while yet. . . ."

"Take it easy! A little while! . . . Listen."

"Yes I know it all. The finance company is repossessing your wife's artificial kidney. . . . They are evicting your grandmother from her iron lung."

"That's in rather bad taste, old boy. . . . Frankly I wish I had never involved myself in this uh matter. That bloody grease has too much carbolic in it. I was down to customs one day last week. Stuck a broom handle into a drum of it, and the grease ate the end off straight away. Besides, the stink is enough to knock a man on his bloody ass. You should take a walk down by the port."

"I'll do no such thing," Marvie screeched. It is a mark of caste in the Zone never to touch or even go near what you are selling. To do so gives rise to suspicion of retailing, that is of being a common peddler. A good part of the merchandise in the Zone is sold through street peddlers.

"Why do you tell me all this? It's too sordid! Let the retailers worry about it."

"Oh it's all very well for you chaps, you can scud out from under. But I have a reputation to maintain. . . . There'll be a spot of bother about this."

"Do you suggest there is something *illegitimate* in this operation?"

"Not *illegitimate* exactly. But shoddy. Definitely shoddy."

"Oh go back to your Island before it falls! We knew you when you were peddling your purple ass in the Plaza pissoirs for five pesetas."

"And not many takers either," Leif put in. He pronounced it ither. This reference to his Island origin was more than the Expeditor could stand. . . . He was drawing himself up, mobilizing his most frigid impersonation of an English aristocrat, preparing to deliver an icy, clipped "crusher," but instead, a whining, whimpering, kicked dog snarl broke from his mouth. His presurgery face emerged in an arc-light of incandescent hate. . . . He began to spit curses in the hideous, strangled gutturals of the Island dialect.

The Islanders all profess ignorance of the dialect or flatly deny its existence. "We are Breetish," they say. "We don't got no bloody dealect."

Froth gathered at the corners of the Expeditor's mouth. He was spitting little balls of saliva like pieces of cotton. The stench of spiritual vileness hung in the airs about him like a green cloud. Marvie and Leif fell back twittering in alarm.

'He's gone *mad*," Marvie gasped. "Let's get *out* of here." Hand in hand they skip away into the mist that covers the Zone in the winter months like a cold Turkish Bath.

THE EXAMINATION

Carl Peterson found a postcard in his box requesting him to report for a ten o'clock appointment with Doctor Benway in the Ministry of Mental Hygiene and Prophylaxis. . . .

"What on earth could they want with me?" he thought irritably. . . . "A mistake most likely." But he knew they didn't make mistakes. . . . Certainly not mistakes of identity. . . .

It would not have occurred to Carl to disregard the appointment even though failure to appear entailed no penalty. . . . Freeland was a welfare state. If a citizen wanted anything from a load of bone meal to a sexual partner some department was ready to offer effective aid. The threat implicit in this enveloping benevolence stifled the concept of rebellion. . . .

Carl walked through the Town Hall Square. . . . Nickel nudes sixty feet high with brass genitals soaped themselves under gleaming showers. . . . The Town Hall cupola, of glass brick and copper crashed into the sky.

Carl stared back at a homosexual American tourist who dropped his eyes and fumbled with the light filters of his Leica. . . .

Carl entered the steel enamel labyrinth of the Ministry, strode to the information desk . . . and presented his card.

"Fifth floor . . . Room twenty-six . . ."

In room twenty-six a nurse looked at him with cold undersea eyes.

"Doctor Benway is expecting you," she said smiling. "Go right in."

"As if he had nothing to do but wait for me," thought Carl. . . .

The office was completely silent, and filled with milky light. The doctor shook Carl's hand, keeping his eyes on the young man's chest. . . .

"I've seen this man before," Carl thought. . . . "But where?"

He sat down and crossed his legs. He glanced at an ashtray on the desk and lit a cigarette. . . . He turned to the doctor a steady inquiring gaze in which there was more than a touch of insolence.

The doctor seemed embarrassed. . . . He fidgeted and coughed . . . and fumbled with papers. . . .

"Hurumph," he said finally. . . . "Your name is Carl Peterson I believe. . . ." His glasses slid down into his nose in parody of the academic manner. . . . Carl nodded silently. . . . The doctor did not look at him but seemed none the less to register the acknowledgement. . . . He pushed his glasses back into place with one finger and opened a file on the white enamelled desk.

"Mmmmmmmmm. Carl Peterson," he repeated the name caressingly, pursed his lips and nodded several times. He spoke again abruptly: "You know of course that we are trying. We are all trying. Sometimes of course we don't succeed." His voice trailed off thin and tenuous. He put a hand to his forehead. "To adjust the state—simply a tool—to the needs of each individual citizen." His voice boomed out so unexpectedly deep and loud that Carl started. "That is the only function of the state as we see it. Our knowledge . . . incomplete, of course," he made a slight gesture of depreciation. . . . "For example . . . *for example* . . . take the matter of uh sexual deviation." The doctor rocked back and forth in his chair. His glasses slid down onto his nose. Carl felt suddenly uncomfortable.

"We regard it as a misfortune . . . a sickness . . . certainly nothing to be censored or uh sanctioned any more than say . . . tuberculosis. . . . Yes," he repeated firmly as if Carl had raised an objection. . . . "Tuberculosis. On the other hand you can readily see that any illness imposes certain, should we say obligations, certain necessities of a prophylactic nature on the authorities concerned with public health, such necessities to be imposed, needless to say, with a minimum of inconvenience and hardship to the unfortunate individual who has, through no fault of his own, become uh infected. . . . That is to say, of course, the minimum hardship compatible with adequate protection of other individuals who are not so infected. . . . We do not find obligatory vaccination for smallpox an unreasonable measure. . . . Nor isolation for certain contagious diseases. . . . I am sure you will agree that individuals infected with hurumph what the French call 'Les Maladies galantes' heh heh heh should be compelled to undergo treatment if they do not report voluntarily." The doctor went on chuckling and rocking in his chair like a mechanical toy. . . . Carl realized that he was expected to say something.

"That seems reasonable," he said.

The doctor stopped chuckling. He was suddenly motionless. "Now to get back to this uh matter of sexual deviation. Frankly we don't pretend to understand—at least not completely—why some men and women prefer the uh sexual company of their own sex. We do know that the uh phenomena is common enough, and, under certain circumstances a matter of uh concern to this department."

For the first time the doctor's eyes flickered across Carl's face. Eyes without a trace of warmth or hate or any emotion that Carl had ever experienced in himsef or seen in another, at once cold and intense, predatory and impersonal. Carl suddenly felt trapped in this silent underwater cave of a room, cut off from all sources of warmth and certainty. His picture of himself sitting there calm, alert with a trace of well mannered contempt went dim, as if vitality were draining out of him to mix with the milky grey medium of the room.

"Treatment of these disorders is, at the present time, hurmph symptomatic." The doctor suddenly threw himself back in his chair and burst into peals of metallic laughter. Carl watched him appalled. . . . "The man is insane," he thought. The doctor's face went blank as a gambler's. Carl felt an odd sensation in his stomach like the sudden stopping of an elevator.

The doctor was studying the file in front of him. He spoke in a tone of slightly condescending amusement:

"Don't look so frightened, young man. Just a professional joke. To say treatment is symptomatic means there is none, except to make the patient feel as comfortable as possible. And that is precisely what we attempt to do in these cases." Once again Carl felt the impact of that cold interest on his face. "That is to say reassurance when reassurance is necessary . . . and, of course, suitable outlets with other individuals of similar tendencies. No isolation is indicated . . . the condition is no more directly contagious than cancer. Cancer, my first love," the doctor's voice receded. He seemed actually to have gone away through an invisible door leaving his empty body sitting there at the desk.

Suddenly he spoke again in a crisp voice. "And so you may well wonder why we concern ourselves with the matter at all?" He flashed a smile bright and cold as snow in sunlight.

Carl shrugged: "That is not my business . . . what I am wondering is why you have asked me to come here and why you tell me all this . . . this . . ."

"Nonsense?"

Carl was annoyed to find himself blushing.

The doctor leaned back and placed the ends of his fingers together:

"The young," he said indulgently. "Always they are in a hurry. One day perhaps you will learn the meaning of patience. No, Carl. . . . I may call you Carl? I am not evading your question. In cases of suspected tuberculosis we—that is the appropriate department—may ask, even *request*, someone to appear for a fluoroscopic examination. This is routine, you understand. Most of such examinations turn up negative. So you have been asked to report here for, should I say a psychic fluoroscope???? I may add that after talking with you I feel *relatively* sure that the result will be, for practical purposes, negative. . . ."

"But the whole thing is ridiculous. I have always interested myself only in girls. I have a steady girl now and we plan to marry."

"Yes Carl, I know. And that is why you are here. A blood test prior to marriage, this is reasonable, no?"

"Please doctor, speak directly."

The doctor did not seem to hear. He drifted out of his chair and began walking around behind Carl, his voice languid and intermittent like music down a windy street.

"I may tell you in strictest confidence that there is definite evidence of a hereditary factor. Social pressure. Many homosexuals latent and overt do, unfortunately, marry. Such marriages often result in . . . Factor of infantile environment." The doctor's voice went on and on. He was talking about schizophrenia, cancer, hereditary disfunction of the hypothalamus.

Carl dozed off. He was opening a green door. A horrible smell grabbed his lungs and he woke up with a shock. The doctor's voice was strangely flat and lifeless, a whispering junky voice:

"The Kleiberg-Stanislouski semen floculation test . . . a diagnostic tool . . . indicative at least in a negative sense. In certain cases useful—taken as part of the whole picture. . . . Perhaps under the uh *circumstances*." The doctor's voice shot up to a pathic scream. "The nurse will take your uh *specimen*."

"This way please. . . ." The nurse opened the door into a bare white walled cubicle. She handed him a jar.

"Use this please. Just yell when you're ready."

There was a jar of K.Y. on a glass shelf. Carl felt ashamed as if his mother had laid out a handkerchief for him. Some coy little message stitched on like: "If I was a cunt we could open a dry goods store."

Ignoring the K.Y., he ejaculated into the jar, a cold brutal fuck of the nurse standing her up against a glass brick wall. "Old Glass Cunt," he sneered, and saw a cunt full of colored glass splinters under the Northern Lights.

He washed his penis and buttoned up his pants.

Something was watching his every thought and movement with cold, sneering hate, the shifting of his testes, the contractions of his rectum. He was in a room filled with green light. There was a stained wood double bed, a black wardrobe with full length mirror. Carl could not see his face. Someone was sitting in a black hotel chair. He was wearing a stiff bosomed white shirt and a dirty paper tie. The face swollen, skull-less, eyes like burning pus.

"Something wrong?" said the nurse indifferently. She was holding a glass of water out to him. She watched him drink with aloof contempt. She turned and picked up the jar with obvious distaste.

The nurse turned to him: "Are you waiting for something special?" she snapped. Carl had never been spoken to like that in his adult life. "Why no. . . ." "You can go then," she turned back to the jar. With a little exclamation of disgust she wiped a gob of semen off her hand. Carl crossed the room and stood at the door.

"Do I have another appointment?"

She looked at him in disapproving surprise: "You'll be notified *of course*." She stood in the doorway of the cubicle and watched him walk through the outer office and open the door. He turned and attempted a jaunty wave. The nurse did not move or change her expression. As he walked down the stairs the broken, false grin burned his face with shame. A homosexual tourist looked at him and raised a knowing eyebrow. "Something *wrong*?"

Carl ran into a park and found an empty bench beside a bronze faun with cymbals.

"Let your hair down, chicken. You'll feel better." The tourist was leaning over him, his camera swinging in Carl's face like a great dangling tit.

"Fuck off you!"

Carl saw something ignoble and hideous reflected back in the queen's spayed animal brown eyes.

"Oh! I wouldn't be calling any names if I were you, chicken. You're hooked too. I saw you coming out of The Institute."

"What do you mean by that?" Carl demanded.

"Oh nothing. Nothing at all."

"Well, Carl," the doctor began smiling and keeping his eyes on a level with Carl's mouth. "I have some good news for you." He picked up a slip of blue paper off the desk and went through an elaborate pantomime of focussing his eyes on it. "Your uh test . . . the Robinson-Kleiberg floculation test . . ."

"I thought it was a Blomberg-Stanlouski test."

The doctor tittered. "Oh dear no. . . . You are getting ahead of me young man. You might have misunderstood. The Blomberg-Stanlouski, weeell that's a different sort of test altogether. I *do hope* . . . not necessary. . . ." He tittered again: "But as I was saying before I was so charmingly interrupted . . . by my hurumph learned young colleague. Your KS seems to be . . ." He held the slip at arm's length. ". . . completely uh negative. So perhaps we won't be troubling you any further. And so . . ." He folded the slip carefully into a file. He leafed through the file. Finally he stopped and frowned and pursed his lips. He closed the file and put his hand flat on it and leaned forward.

"Carl, when you were doing your military service . . . There must have been . . . in fact there *were* long periods when you found yourself deprived of the uh consolations and uh *facilities* of the fair sex. During these no doubt trying and difficult periods you had perhaps a pin up girl?? Or more likely a pin up harem?? Heh heh heh . . ."

Carl looked at the doctor with overt distaste. "Yes, of course," he said. "We all did."

"And now, Carl, I would like to show you some pin up girls." He pulled an envelope out of a drawer. "And ask you to please pick out the one you would most like to uh make heh heh heh. . . ." He suddenly leaned forward fanning the photographs in front of Carl's face. "Pick a girl, any girl!"

Carl reached out with numb fingers and touched one of the photographs. The doctor put the photo back into the pack and shuffled and cut and he placed the pack on Carl's file and slapped it smartly. He spread the photos face up in front of Carl. "Is she there?"

Carl shook his head.

"Of course not. She is in here where she belongs. A woman's place what???" He opened the file and held out the girl's photo attached to a Rorshach plate.

"Is that her?"

Carl nodded silently.

"You have good taste, my boy. I may tell you in strictest confidence that some of these girls . . ." with gambler fingers he shifts the photos in Three Card Monte Passes—"are really *boys*. In uh *drag* I believe is the word???" His eyebrows shot up and down with incredible speed. Carl could not be sure he had seen anything unusual. The doctor's face opposite him was absolutely immobile and expressionless. Once again Carl experienced the floating sensation in his stomach and genitals of a sudden elevator stop.

"Yes, Carl, you seem to be running our little obstacle course with flying colors. . . . I guess you think this is all pretty silly don't you now . . . ???"

"Well, to tell the truth . . . Yes . . ."

"You are frank, Carl. . . . This is good. . . . And now . . . Carl . . ." He dragged the name out caressingly like a sweet con dick about to offer you an Old Gold—(just like a cop to smoke Old Golds somehow) and go into his act. . . .

The con dick does a little dance step.

"Why don't you make The Man a proposition?" he jerks a head towards his glowering super-ego who is always referred to in the third person as "The Man" or "The Lieutenant."

"That's the way the Lieutenant is, you play fair with him and he'll play fair with you. . . . We'd like to go light on you. . . . If you could help us in some way." His words open out into a desolate waste of cafeterias and street corners and lunch rooms. Junkies look the other way munching pound cake.

"The Fag is wrong."

The Fag slumps in a hotel chair knocked out on goof balls with his tongue lolling out.

He gets up in a goof ball trance, hangs himself without altering his expression or pulling his tongue in.

The dick is diddling on a pad.

"Know Marty Steel?" Diddle.

"Yes."

"Can you score off him?" Diddle? Diddle?

"He's skeptical."

"But you can score." Diddle diddle "You scored off him last week didn't you?" Diddle???

"Yes."

"Well you can score off him this week." Diddle . . . Diddle . . . Diddle . . . "You can score off him today." No diddle.

"No! No! Not that!!"

"Now look are you going to cooperate"—three vicious diddles—"or does the . . . does the Man cornhole you???" He raises a fay eyebrow.

"And so Carl you will please oblige to tell me how many times and under what circumstances you have uh indulged in homosexual acts???" His voice drifts away. "If you have never done so I shall be inclined to think of you as a somewhat atypical young man." The doctor raises a coy admonishing finger. "In any case..." He tapped the file and flashed a hideous leer. Carl noticed that the file was six inches thick. In fact it seemed to have thickened enormously since he entered the room.

"Well, when I was doing my military service . . . These queers used to proposition me and sometimes . . . when I was blank . . ."

"Yes, of course, Carl," the doctor brayed heartily. "In your position I would have done the same I don't mind telling you heh heh heh. . . . Well, I guess we can uh *dismiss as irrelevent* these uh understandable means of replenishing the uh *exchequer.* And now, Carl, there were perhaps"—one finger tapped the file which gave out a faint effluvia of moldy jock straps and chlorine— "occasions. When no uh economic factors were involved."

A green flare exploded in Carl's brain. He saw Hans' lean brown body—twisting towards him, quick breath on his shoulder. The flare went out. Some huge insect was squirming in his hand.

His whole being jerked away in an electric spasm of revulsion.

Carl got to his feet shaking with rage.

"What are you writing there?" he demanded.

"Do you often doze off like that??? in the middle of a conversation. . . ?"

"I wasn't asleep that is."

"You weren't?"

"It's just that the *whole thing* is unreal. . . . I'm going now. I don't care. You can't force me to stay."

He was walking across the room towards the door. He had been walking a long time. A creeping numbness dragged his legs. The door seemed to recede.

"Where can you go, Carl?" The doctor's voice reached him from a great distance.

"Out . . . Away . . . Through the door . . ."

"The Green Door, Carl?"

The doctor's voice was barely audible. The whole room was exploding out into space.

HAVE YOU SEEN PANTOPON ROSE

Stay away from Queens Plaza, son. . . . Evil spot haunted by dicks scream for dope fiend lover. . . . Too many levels. . . . Heat flares out from the broom closet high on ammonia . . . like burning lions . . . fall on poor old lush worker scare her veins right down to the bone. . . . Her skin-pop a week or do that five-twenty-nine kick handed out free and gratis by NYC to jostling junkies. . . .

So Fag, Beagle, Irish, Sailor beware. . . . Look down, look down along that line before you travail there. . . .

The subway sweeps by with a black blast of iron. . . .

—Queens Plaza is a bad spot for lush workers. . . . Too many levels and lurking places for subway heat, and impossible to cover when you put the hand out. . . .

Five months and twenty-nine days: sentence given for "jostling," that is, touching a flop with obvious intent. . . . Innocent people may be convicted of murder but not of jostling.

Fag, Beagle, Irish, Sailor, old time, junkies and lush-workers of my acquaintaince. . . . The old 103rd street klatch. . . . Sailor and Irish hanged themselves in the Tombs. . . . The Beagle is dead of an overdose and the Fag went wrong. . . .

"Have you seen Pantopon Rose?" said the old junky. . . . "Time to cosq," put on a black overcoat and made the square. . . . Down skid road to Market Street Museum shows all kinds masturbation and self-abuse. Young boys need it special. . . .

The gangster in concrete rolls down the river channel. . . . They cowboyed him in the steam room. . . . Is this Cherry Ass Gio the Towel Boy or Mother Gillig, Old Auntie of Westminster Place?? Only dead fingers talk in Braille. . . .

The Mississippi rolls great limestone boulders down the silent alley. . . .

"Clutter the glind!" screamed the Captain of Moving Land. . . .

Distant rumble of stomachs. . . . Poisoned pigeons rain from the Northern Lights. . . . The reservoirs are empty. . . . Brass statues crash through the hungry squares and alleys of the gaping city. . . .

Probing for a vein in the junk-sick morning. . . .

Strictly from cough syrup . . .

A thousand junkies storm the crystal spine clinics, cook down the Grey Ladies. . . .

In the limestone cave met a man with Medusa's head in a hat box and said, "Be Careful," to the Customs Inspector. . . . Freezed forever hand an inch from the false bottom. . . .

Window dressers scream through the station, beat the cashiers with the fairy hype. . . . (The Hype is a short change con. . . . Also known as The Bill. . . .)

"Multiple fracture," said the big physician. . . . "I'm very technical. . . ."

Conspicuous consumption is rampant in the porticos slippery with Koch spit. . . .

The centipede nuzzles the iron door rusted to thin black paper by the urine of a million fairies. . . .

This is no rich mother load, but vitiate dust, second run cottons trace the bones of a fix. . . .

COKE BUGS

The Sailor's grey felt hat and black overcoat hung twisted in atrophied yen-wait. Morning sun outlined The Sailor in the orange-yellow flame of junk. He had a paper napkin under his coffee cup—mark of those who do a lot of sitting over coffee in the plazas, restaurants, terminals and waiting rooms of the world. A junky, even at the Sailor's level, runs on junk Time and when he makes his importunate irruption into the Time of others, like all petitioners, he must wait. (How many coffees in an hour?)

A boy came in and sat at the counter in broken lines of long, sick junk-wait. The Sailor shivered. His face fuzzed out of focus in a shuddering brown mist. His hands moved on the table, reading the boy's Braille. His eyes traced little dips and circles, following whorls of brown hair on the boy's neck in a slow, searching movement.

The boy stirred and scratched the back of his neck: "Something bit me, Joe. What kinda creep joint you run here?"

"Coke bugs, kid," Joe said, holding eggs up to the light. "I was travelling with Irene Kelly and her was a sporting woman. In Butte, state of Montany, her got the coke horrors and run through the hotel screaming Chinese coppers chase her with meat cleavers. I knew this cop in Chi sniff coke used to come in form of crystals, blue crystals. So her go nuts and start screaming the Federals is after him and run down this alley and stick his head in the garbage can. And I said, 'What you think you are doing?' and her say, 'Get away or I shoot you! I got myself hid good!' When the roll is called up yonder we'll be there, right?"

Joe looked at the Sailor and spread his hands in the junky shrug.

The Sailor spoke in his feeling voice that reassembles in your head, spelling out the words with cold fingers: "Your connection is broken, kid."

The boy shied. His street-boy face, torn with black scars of junk, retained a wild, broken innocence; shy animals peering out through grey arabesques of terror.

"I don't dig you, Jack."

The Sailor leapt into sharp, junky focus. He turned back his coat lapel, showing a brass hypo needle covered with mold and verdigris. "Retired for the good of the service. . . . Sit down and have a blueberry crumb pie on the expense account. Your monkey loves it. . . . Make his coat glossy."

The boy felt a touch on his arm across eight feet of morning lunch room. He was suddenly siphoned into the booth, landing with an inaudible shlup. He looked into the Sailor's eyes, a green universe stirred by cold black currents.

"You are agent, mister?"

"I prefer the word . . . vector." His sounding laughter vibrated through the boy's substance.

"You holding, man? I got the bread. . . ."

"I don't want your money, Honey: I want your Time."

"I don't dig."

"You want fix? You want straight? You wanta, nooood?"

The Sailor cradled something pink and vibrated out of focus.

"Yeah."

"We'll take the Independent. Got their own special heat, don't carry guns only saps. I recall, me and the Fag fell once in Queen's Plaza. Stay away from Queen's Plaza, son . . . evil spot . . . fuzz haunted. Too many levels. Heat flares out from the broom closet high on ammonia like burning lions . . . fall on poor old lush worker, scare her veins right down to the bone. Her skin pop a week or do that five-twenty-nine kick handed out free and gratis by NYC to jostling junkies. . . . So Fag, Beagle, Irish, Sailor beware! Look down, look down along that line before you travel there. . . ."

The subway sweeps by with a black blast of iron.

THE EXTERMINATOR DOES A GOOD JOB

The Sailor touched the door gently, following patterns of painted oak in a slow twist, leaving faint, iridescent whorls of slime. His arm went through to the elbow. He pulled back an inside bolt and stood aside for the boy to enter.

Heavy, colorless smell of death filled the empty room.

"The trap hasn't been aired since the Exterminator fumigated for coke bugs," said the Sailor apologetically.

The boy's peeled senses darted about in frenzied exploration. Tenement flat, railroad flat vibrating with silent motion. Along one wall of the kitchen a metal trough—or was it metal, exactly?—ran into a sort of aquarium or tank half-filled with translucent green fluid. Moldy objects, worn out in unknown service, littered the floor: a jock-strap designed to protect some delicate organ of flat, fan-shape; multi-levelled trusses, supports and bandages; a large U-shaped yoke of porous pink stone; little lead tubes cut open at one end.

Currents of movement from the two bodies stirred stagnant odor pools; atrophied boy-smell of dusty locker rooms, swimming pool chlorine, dried semen. Other smells curled through pink convolutions, touching unknown doors.

The Sailor reached under the wash-stand and extracted a package in wrapping paper that shredded and fell from his fingers in yellow dust. He laid out dropper, needle and spoon on a table covered with dirty dishes. But no roach antennae felt for the crumbs of darkness.

"The Exterminator does a good job," said the Sailor. "Almost too good, sometimes."

He dipped into a square tin of yellow pyretheum powder and pulled out a flat package covered in red and gold Chinese paper.

"Like a firecracker package," the boy thought. At fourteen lost two fingers. . . . Fourth of July fireworks accident . . . later, in the hospital, first silent proprietary touch of junk.

"They go off, here, kid." The Sailor put a hand to the back of his head. He camped obscenely as he opened the package, a complex arrangement of slots and overlays.

"Pure, one hundred per cent H. Scarcely a man is now alive . . . and it's all yours."

"So what you want off me?"

"Time."

"I don't dig."

"I have something you want," his hand touched the package. He drifted away into the front room, his voice remote and blurred. "You have something I want . . . five minutes here . . . an hour someplace else . . . two . . . four . . . eight . . . Maybe I'm getting ahead of myself. . . . Every day die a little. . . . It takes up The Time. . . ."

He moved back into the kitchen, his voice loud and clear: "Five years a piece. Nobody gives a better deal on the street." He put a finger on the dividing line below the boy's nose. "Right down the middle."

"Mister, I don't know what you're talking about."

"You will, baby . . . in time."

"OK. So what do I do?"

"You accept?"

"Yeah, like . . ." He glanced at the package. "Whatever . . . I accept."

The boy felt a silent black clunk fall through his flesh. The Sailor put a hand to the boy's eyes and pulled out a pink scrotal egg with one closed, pulsing eye. Black fur boiled inside translucent flesh of the egg.

The Sailor caressed the egg with nakedly inhuman hands—black-pink, thick, fibrous, long white tendrils sprouting from abbreviated finger tips. Death fear and Death weakness hit the boy, shutting off his breath, stopping his blood. IIe leaned against a wall that seemed to give slightly. He clicked back into junk focus.

The Sailor was cooking a shot. "When the roll is called up yonder we'll be there, right?" he said, feeling along the boy's vein, erasing goose-pimples with a gentle old woman finger. He slid the needle in. A red orchid bloomed at the bottom of the dropper. The Sailor pressed the bulb, watching the solution rush into the boy-vein, sucked by silent thirst of blood.

"Jesus!" said the boy. "I never been hit like that before!"

He lit a cigarette and looked around the kitchen, twitching in sugar need. "Aren't you taking off?" he asked.

"With that milk sugar shit? Junk is a one-way street. No U-turn. You can't go back no more."

They call me the Exterminator. At one brief point of intersection I did exercise that function and witnessed the belly dance of roaches suffocating in yellow pyretheum powder ("Hard to get now, lady . . . war on. Let you have a little. . . . Two dollars.") Sluiced fat bedbugs from rose wall paper in shabby theatrical hotels on North Clark and poisoned the purposeful Rat, occasional eater of human babies. Wouldn't you?

My present assignment: Find the live ones and *exterminate*. Not the bodies but the "molds," you understand—but I forget that you cannot understand. We have all but a very few. But even one could upset our food tray. The danger, as always, comes from defecting agents: A. J., the Vigilante, the Black Armadillo (carrier of Chagas vectors, hasn't taken a bath since the Argentine epidemic of '35, remember?), and Lee and the Sailor and Benway. And I know some agent is out there in the darkness looking for me. Because all Agents defect and all Resisters sell out. . . .

THE ALGEBRA OF NEED

"Fats" Terminal came from The City Pressure Tanks where open life jets spurt a million forms, immediately eaten, the eaters cancelled by black time fuzz. . . .

Few reach the Plaza, a point where The Tanks empty a tidal river, carrying forms of survival armed with defences of poison slime, black, flesh rotting, fungus, and green odors that sear the lungs and grab the stomach in twisted knots. . . .

Because "Fats'" nerves were raw and peeled to feel the death spasms of a million cold kicks. . . . "Fats" learned The Agebra of Need and survived. . . .

One Friday "Fats" siphoned himself into The Plaza, a translucent-grey, foetal monkey, suckers on his little soft, purple-grey hands, and a lamphrey disk mouth of cold, grey gristle lined with hollow, black, erectile teeth, feeling for the scar patterns of junk. . . .

And a rich man passed and stared at the monster and "Fats" rolled pissing and shitting in terror and ate his shit and the man was moved by this tribute to his potent gaze and clicked a coin out of his Friday cane (Friday is Moslem Sunday when the rich are supposed to distribute alms).

So "Fats" learned to serve The Black Meat and grew a fat aquarium of body. . . .

And his blank, periscope eyes swept the world's surface. . . . In his wake of addicts, translucent-grey monkeys flashed like fish spears to the junk Mark, and hung there sucking and it all drained back into "Fats" so his substance grew and grew filling plazas, restaurants and waiting rooms of the world with grey junk ooze.

Bulletins from Party Headquarters are spelled out in obscene charades by hebephrenics and Latahs and apes, Sollubis fart code, Negroes open and shut mouth to flash messages on gold teeth, Arab rioters send smoke signals by throwing great buttery eunuchs—they make the best smoke, hangs black and shit-solid in the air—onto gasoline fires in a rubbish heap, mosaic of melodies, sad Panpipes of humpbacked beggar, cold wind sweeps down from post card of Chimborazzi, flutes of Ramadan, piano music down a windy street, mutilated police calls, advertising leaflet synchronize with street fight spell SOS.

Two agents have identified themselves each to each by choice of sex practices foiling alien microphones, fuck atomic secrets back and forth in code so complex only two physicists in the world pretend to understand it and each categorically denies the other. Later the receiving agent will be hanged, convict of the guilty possession of a nervous syste m,and play back the message in orgasmal spasms transmitted from electrodes attached to the penis.

Breathing rhythm of old cardiac, bumps of a belly dancer, put put put of a motorboat across oily water. The waiter lets fall a drop of martini of the Man in the Grey Flannel Suit, who lams for the 6:12 knowing that he has been *spotted*. Junkies climb out the lavatory window of the chop suey joint as the El *rumbles* past. The Gimp, cowboyed in the Waldorf, gives birth to a *litter of rats*. (Cowboy: New York hood talk means kill the mother fucker wherever you find him. A rat is a rat is a rat is a rat. Is an informer.) Foolish virgins heed the English colonel who rides by brandishing a screaming *peccary* on his lance. The elegant fag patronizes his neighborhood bar to receive a bulletin from Dead Mother lives on in synapses and will evoke the exciting Nanny Beater. Boys jacking off in the school toilet know each other as agents from Galaxy X, adjourn to a second-run night spot where they sit shabby and portentous drinking wine vinegar and eating lemons to confound the tenor sax, a hip Arab in blue glasses suspect to be Enemy Sender. The world network of junkies, tuned on a cord of rancid jissom . . . tying up in furnished rooms . . . shivering in the sick morning . . . (Old Pete men suck the Black Smoke in a Chink laundry back room. Melancholy Baby dies from an overdose of Time or cold turkey withdrawal of breath—in Arabia —Paris—Mexico City—New York—New Orleans—) The living and the dead . . . in sickness or on the nod . . . hooked or kicked or hooked again . . . come in on the junk beam and The Connection is eating Chop Suey on Dolores Street . . . dunking pound cake in Bickfords . . . chased up Exchange Place by a baying pack of people. Malarials of the world bundle in shivering protoplasm. Fear seals the turd message with a cuneiform account. Giggling rioters copulate to the screams of a burning Nigra. Lonely librarians unite in soul kiss of halitosis. That grippy feeling, brother? Sore throat persistent and disquieting as the hot afternoon wind? Welcome to the International Syphilis Lodge—"Methodith Epithcopal God damn ith" (phrase used to test for speech impairment typical of paresis) or the first silent touch of chancre makes you a member in good standing. The vibrating soundless hum of deep forest and orgone accumulators, the sudden silence of cities when the junky cops and even the Commuter buzzes clogged lines of cholesterol for contact. Signal flares of orgasm burst over the world. A tea head leaps up screaming "I got the fear!" and runs into Mexican night bringing down backbrains of the world. The Executioner shits in terror at sight of the condemned man. The Torturer screams in the ear of his implacable victim. Knife fighters embrace in adrenalin. Cancer is at the door with a Singing Telegram. . . .

HAUSER AND O'BRIEN

When they walked in on me that morning at 8 o'clock, I knew it was my last chance, my only chance. But they didn't know. How could they? Just a routine pick-up. But not quite routine.

Hauser had been eating breakfast when the Lieutenant called: "I want you and your partner to pick up a man named Lee, William Lee, on your way downtown. He's in the Hotel Lamprey. 103 just off B way."

"Yeah I know where it is. I remember him too."

"Good. Room 606. Just pick him up. Don't take time to shake the place down. Except bring in all books, letters, manuscripts. *Anything* printed, typed or written. Ketch?"

"Ketch. But what's the angle. . . . Books . . . "

"Just do it." The Lieutenant hung up.

Hauser and O'Brien. They had been on the City Narcotic Squad for 20 years. Oldtimers like me. I been on the junk for 16 years. They weren't bad as laws go. At least O'Brien wasn't. O'Brien was the con man, and Hauser the tough guy. A vaudeville team. Hauser had a way of hitting you before he said anything just to break the ice. Then O'Brien gives you an Old Gold— just like a cop to smoke Old Golds somehow . . . and starts putting down a cop con that was really bottled in bond. Not a bad guy, and I didn't want to do it. But it was my only chance.

I was just tying up for my morning shot when they walked in with a pass key. It was a special kind you can use even when the door is locked from the inside with a key in the lock. On the table in front of me was a packet of junk, spike, syringe—I got the habit of using a regular syringe in Mexico and never went back to using a dropper—alcohol, cotton and a glass of water.

"Well well," says O'Brien. . . . "Long time no see eh?"

"Put on your coat, Lee," says Hauser. He had his gun out. He always has it out when he makes a pinch for the psychological effect and to forestall a rush for toilet, sink or window.

"Can I take a bang first, boys?" I asked. . . . "There's plenty here for evidence. . . ."

I was wondering how I could get to my suitcase if they said no. The case wasn't locked, but Hauser had the gun in his hand.

"He wants a shot," said Hauser.

"Now you know we can't do that, Bill," said O'Brien in his sweet con voice, dragging out the name with an oily, insinuating familiarity, brutal and obscene.

He meant, of course, "What can you do for *us*, Bill?" He looked at me and smiled. The smile stayed there too long, hideous and naked, the smile of an old painted pervert, gathering all the negative evil of O'Brien's ambiguous function.

"I might could set up Marty Steel for you," I said.

I knew they wanted Marty bad. He'd been pushing for five years, and they couldn't hang one on him. Marty was an oldtimer, and very careful about who he served. He had to know a man and know him well before he would pick up his money. No one can say they ever did time because of me. My rep is perfect, but still Marty wouldn't serve me because he didn't know me long enough. That's how skeptical Marty was.

"Marty!" said O'Brien. "Can you score from him?"

"Sure I can."

They were suspicious. A man can't be a cop all his life without developing a special set of intuitions.

"O.K.," said Hauser finally. "But you'd better deliver, Lee."

"I'll deliver all right. Believe me I appreciate this."

I tied up for a shot, my hands trembling with eagerness, an archetype dope fiend.

"Just an old junky, boys, a harmless old shaking wreck of a junky." That's the way I put it down. As I had hoped, Hauser looked away when I started probing for a vein. It's a wildly unpretty spectacle.

O'Brien was sitting on the arm of a chair smoking an Old Gold, looking out the window with that dreamy what I'll do when I get my pension look.

I hit a vein right away. A column of blood shot up into the syringe for an instant sharp and solid as a red cord. I pressed the plunger down with my thumb, feeling the junk pound through my veins to feed a million junk-hungry cells, to bring strength and alertness to every nerve and muscle. They were not watching me. I filled the syringe with alcohol.

Hauser was juggling his snub-nosed detective special, a Colt, and looking around the room. He could smell danger like an animal. With his left hand he pushed the closet door open and glanced inside. My stomach contracted. I thought, "If he looks in the suitcase now I'm done."

Hauser turned to me abruptly. "You through yet?" he snarled. "You'd better not try to shit us on Marty." The words came out so ugly he surprised and shocked himself.

I picked up the syringe full of alcohol, twisting the needle to make sure it was tight.

"Just two seconds," I said.

I squirted a thin jet of alcohol, whipping it across his eyes with a sideways shake of the syringe. He let out a bellow of pain. I could see him pawing at his eyes with the left hand like he was tearing off an invisible bandage as I dropped to the floor on one knee, reaching for my suitcase. I pushed the suitcase open, and my left hand closed over the gun butt—I am righthanded but I shoot with my left hand. I felt the concussion of Hauser's shot before I heard it. His slug slammed into the wall behind me. Shooting from the floor, I snapped two quick shots into Hauser's belly where his vest had pulled up showing an inch of white shirt. He grunted in a way I could feel and doubled forward. Stiff with panic, O'Brien's hand was tearing at the gun in his shoulder holster. I clamped my other hand around my gun wrist to steady it for the long pull—this gun has the hammer filed off round so you can only use it double

action—and shot him in the middle of his red forehead
about two inches below the silver hairline. His hair had
been grey the last time I saw him. That was about 15
years ago. My first arrest. His eyes went out. He fell off
the chair onto his face. My hands were already reaching
for what I needed, sweeping my notebooks into a brief-
case with my works, junk, and a box of shells. I stuck
the gun into my belt, and stepped out into the corridor
putting on my coat.

I could hear the desk clerk and the bell boy pound-
ing up the stairs. I took the self-service elevator down,
walked through the empty lobby into the street.

It was a beautiful Indian Summer day. I knew I
didn't have much chance, but any chance is better than
none, better than being a subject for experiments with
ST (6) or whatever the initials are.

I had to stock up on junk fast. Along with airports,
R.R. stations and bus terminals, they would cover all
junk areas and connections. I took a taxi to Washington
Square, got out and walked along 4th Street till I
spotted Nick on a corner. You can always find the
pusher. Your need conjures him up like a ghost. "Listen,
Nick," I said, "I'm leaving town. I want to pick up a
piece of H. Can you make it right now?"

We were walking along 4th Street. Nick's voice
seemed to drift into my consciousness from no particular place. An eerie, disembodied voice. "Yes, I think I
can make it. I'll have to make a run uptown."

"We can take a cab."

"O.K., but I can't take you in to the guy, you understand."

"I understand. Let's go."

We were in the cab heading North. Nick was talking in his flat, dead voice.

"Some funny stuff we're getting lately. It's not weak exactly. . . . I don't know. . . . It's different. Maybe they're putting some synthetic shit in it. . . . Dollies or something. . . ."

"What!!!? Already?"

"Huh? . . . But this I'm taking you to now is O.K. In fact it's about the best deal around that I know of. . . . Stop here."

"Please make it fast," I said.

"It should be a matter of ten minutes unless he's out of stuff and has to make a run. . . . Better sit down over there and have a cup of coffee. . . . This is a hot neighborhood."

I sat down at a counter and ordered coffee, and pointed to a piece of Danish pastry under a plastic cover. I washed down the stale rubbery cake with coffee, praying that just this once, please God, let him make it now, and not come back to say the man is all out and has to make a run to East Orange or Greenpoint.

Well here he was back, standing behind me. I looked at him, afraid to ask. Funny, I thought, here I sit with perhaps one chance in a hundred to live out the next 24 hours—I had made up my mind not to surrender and spend the next three or four months in death's waiting room. And here I was worrying about a junk score. But I only had about five shots left, and without junk I would be immobilized. . . . Nick nodded his head.

"Don't give it to me here," I said. "Let's take a cab."

We took a cab and started downtown. I held out my

hand and copped the package, then I slipped a fifty-dollar bill into Nick's palm. He glanced at it and showed his gums in a toothless smile: "Thanks a lot. . . . This will put me in the clear. . . ."

I sat back letting my mind work without pushing it. Push your mind too hard, and it will fuck up like an overloaded switch-board, or turn on you with sabotage. . . . And I had no margin for error. Americans have a special horror of giving up control, of letting things happen in their own way without interference. They would like to jump down into their stomachs and digest the food and shovel the shit out.

Your mind will answer most questions if you learn to relax and wait for the answer. Like one of those thinking machines, you feed in your question, sit back, and wait. . . .

I was looking for a name. My mind was sorting through names, discarding at once F.L.—Fuzz Lover, B.W.—Born Wrong, N.C.B.C.—Nice Cat But Chicken; putting aside to reconsider, narrowing, sifting, feeling for the name, the answer.

"Sometimes, you know, he'll keep me waiting three hours. Sometimes I make it right away like this." Nick had a deprecating little laugh that he used for punctuation. Sort of an apology for talking at all in the telepathizing world of the addict where only the quantity factor—How much $? How much junk?—requires verbal expression. He knew and I knew all about waiting. At all levels the drug trade operates without schedule. Nobody delivers on time except by accident. The addict runs on junk time. His body is his clock, and junk runs through it like an hour-glass. Time has meaning for him only with reference to his need. Then he makes his abrupt intrusion into the time of others, and, like all Outsiders, all Petitioners, he must wait, unless he happens to mesh with non-junk time.

"What can I say to him? He knows I'll wait," Nick laughed.

I spent the night in the Ever Hard Baths—(homosexuality is the best all-around cover story an agent can use)—where a snarling Italian attendant creates such an unnerving atmosphere sweeping the dormitory with infra red see in the dark fieldglasses.

("All right in the North East corner! I see you!" switching on floodlights, sticking his head through trapdoors in the floor and wall of the private rooms, that many a queen has been carried out in a straitjacket. . . .)

I lay there in my open top cubicle room looking at the ceiling . . . listened to the grunts and squeals and snarls in the nightmare halflight of random, broken lust. . . .

"Fuck off you!"

"Put on two pairs of glasses and maybe you can see something!"

Walked out in the precise morning and bought a paper. . . . Nothing. . . . I called from a drugstore phone booth . . . and asked for Narcotics:

"Lieutenant Gonzales . . . who's calling?"

"I want to speak to O'Brien." A moment of static, dangling wires, broken connections . . .

"Nobody of that name in this department. . . . Who are *you*?"

"Well let me speak to Hauser."

"Look, Mister, no O'Brien no Hauser in this bureau. Now what do you want?"

"Look, this is important. . . . I've got info on a big shipment of H coming in. . . . I want to talk to Hauser or O'Brien. . . . I don't do business with anybody else. . . ."

"Hold on. . . . I'll connect you with Alcibiades."

I began to wonder if there was an Anglo-Saxon name left in the Department. . . .

"I want to speak to Hauser or O'Brien."

"How many times I have to tell you no Hauser no O'Brien in this department. . . . Now who is this calling?"

I hung up and took a taxi out of the area. . . . In the cab I realized what had happened. . . . I had been occluded from space-time like an eel's ass occludes when he stops eating on the way to Sargasso. . . . Locked out. . . . Never again would I have a Key, a Point of Intersection. . . . The Heat was off me from here on out . . . relegated with Hauser and O'Brien to a landlocked junk past where heroin is always twenty-eight dollars an ounce and you can score for yen pox in the Chink Laundry of Sioux Falls. . . . Far side of the world's mirror, moving into the past with Hauser and O'Brien . . . clawing at a not-yet of Telepathic Bureaucracies, Time Monopolies, Control Drugs, Heavy Fluid Addicts:

"I thought of that three hundred years ago."

"Your plan was unworkable then and useless now. . . . Like Da Vinci's flying machine plans. . . ."

ATROPHIED PREFACE

WOULDN'T YOU?

Why all this waste paper getting The People from one place to another? Perhaps to spare The Reader stress of sudden space shifts and keep him Gentle? And so a ticket is bought, a taxi called, a plane boarded. We are allowed a glimpse into the warm peach-lined cave as She (the airline hostess, of course) leans over us to murmur of chewing gum, dramamine, even nembutal.

"Talk paregoric, Sweet Thing, and I will hear."

I am not American Express. . . . If one of my people is seen in New York walking around in citizen clothes and next sentence Timbuktu putting down lad talk on a gazelle-eyed youth, we may assume that he (the party non-resident of Timbuktu) transported himself there by the usual methods of communication. . . .

Lee The Agent (a double-four-eight-sixteen) is taking the junk cure . . . space time trip portentously familiar as junk meet corners to the addict . . . cures past and future shuttle pictures through his spectral substance vibrating in silent winds of accelerated Time. . . . Pick a shot. . . . Any Shot. . . .

Formal knuckle biting, floor rolling shots in a precinct cell. . . . "Feel like a shot of *Heroin*, Bill? Haw Haw Haw."

Tentative half impressions that dissolve in light . . . pockets of rotten ectoplasm swept out by an old junky coughing and spitting in the sick morning. . . .

Old violet brown photos that curl and crack like mud

in the sun: Panama City . . . Bill Gains putting down the paregoric con on a Chinese druggist.

"I've got these racing dogs . . . pedigree greyhounds. . . . All sick with the dysentery . . . tropical climate . . . the shits . . . you sabe shit? . . . *My Whippets Are Dying.* . . ." He screamed. . . . His eyes lit up with blue fire. . . . The flame went out . . . smell of burning metal. . . . "Administer with an eye dropper. . . . Wouldn't you? . . . Menstral cramps . . . my wife . . . Kotex . . . Aged mother . . . Piles . . . raw . . . bleeding . . ." He nodded out against the counter. . . . The druggist took a tooth-pick out of his mouth and looked at the end of it and shook his head. . . .

Gains and Lee burned down the Republic of Panama from David to Darien on paregoric. . . . They flew apart with a shlupping sound. . . . Junkies tend to run together into one body. . . . You have to be careful especially in hot places. . . . Gains back to Mexico City. . . . Desperate skeleton grin of chronic junk lack glazed over with codeine and goof balls . . . cigarette holes in his bathrobe . . . coffee stains on the floor . . . smoky kerosene stove . . . rusty orange flame . . .

The Embassy would give no details other than place of burial in the American Cemetery. . . .

And Lee back to sex and pain and time and Yage, bitter Soul Vine of the Amazon. . . .

I recall once after an overdose of Majoun (this is Cannabis dried and finely powdered to consistency of green powdered sugar and mixed with some confection or other usually tasting like gritty plum pudding, but

the choice of confection is arbitrary . . .). I am returning from The Lulu or Johny or Little Boy's Room
(stink of atrophied infancy and toilet training) look
across the living room of that villa outside Tanger and
suddenly don't know where I am. Perhaps I have opened
the wrong door and at any moment The Man In Possession, The Owner Who Got There First will rush in
and scream:

"*What Are You Doing Here? Who Are You?*"

And I don't know what I am doing there nor who I
am. I decide to play it cool and maybe I will get the
orientation before the Owner shows. . . . So instead
of yelling "Where Am I?" cool it and look around and
you will find out approximately. . . . You were not
there for *The Beginning.* You will not be there for *The
End . . . .* Your knowledge of what is going on can only
be superficial and relative. . . . What do I know of this
yellow blighted young junky face subsisting on raw
opium? I tried to tell him: "Some morning you will
wake up with your liver in your lap" and how to process
raw opium so it is not plain poison. But his eyes glaze
over and he don't want to know. Junkies are like that
most of them they don't want to know . . . and you
can't tell them anything. . . . A smoker doesn't want
to know anythng but smoke. . . . And a heroin junky
same way. . . . Strictly the spike and any other route
is Farina. . . .

So I guess he is still sitting there in his 1920 Spanish
villa outside Tanger eating that raw opium full of shit
and stones and straw . . . the whole lot for fear he might
lose something. . . .

There is only one thing a writer can write about: *what is in front of his senses at the moment of writing.* . . . I am a recording instrument. . . . I do not presume to impose "story" "plot" "continuity." . . . In sofaras I succeed in *Direct* recording of certain areas of psychic process I may have limited function. . . . I am not an entertainer. . . .

"Possession" they call it. . . . Sometimes an entity jumps in the body—outlines waver in yellow orange jelly—and hands move to disembowel the passing whore or strangle the nabor child in hope of alleviating a chronic housing shortage. As if I was usually there but subject to goof now and again. . . . *Wrong! I am never here.* . . . Never that is *fully* in possession, but somehow in a position to forestall ill-advised moves. . . . Patrolling is, in fact, my principle occupation. . . . No matter how tight Security, I am always somewhere *Outside* giving orders and *Inside* this straight jacket of jelly that gives and stretches but always reforms ahead of every movement, thought, impulse, stamped with the seal of alien inspection. . . .

Writers talk about the sweet-sick smell of death whereas any junky can tell you that death has no smell . . . at the same time a smell that shuts off breath and stops blood . . . colorless no-smell of death . . . no one can breathe and smell it through pink convolutions and black blood filters of flesh . . . the death smell is unmistakably a smell and complete absence of smell . . . smell absence hits the nose first because all organic life has smell . . . stopping of smell is felt like darkness to the eyes, silence to the ears, stress and weightlessness to the balance and location sense. . . .

You always smell it and give it out for others to smell during junk withdrawal. . . . A kicking junky can make a whole apartment unlivable with his death smell . . . but a good airing will stink the place up again so a body can breathe. . . . You also smell it during one of those oil burner habits that suddenly starts jumping geometric like a topping forest fire. . . .

Cure is always: *Let go! Jump!*

A friend of mine found himself naked in a Marrakech hotel room second floor. . . . (He is after processing by a Texas mother who dressed him in girl's clothes as a child. . . . Crude but effective against infant protoplasm. . . .) The other occupants are Arabs, three Arabs . . . knives in hand . . . watching him . . . glint of metal and points of light in dark eyes . . . pieces of murder falling slow as opal chips through glycerine . . . Slower animal reactions allow him a full second to decide: Straight through the window and down into the crowded street like a falling star his wake of glass glittering in the sun . . . sustained a broken ankle and a chipped shoulder . . . clad in a diaphanous pink curtain, with a curtain-rod staff, hobbled away to the Commissariat de Police. . . .

Sooner or later The Vigilante, The Rube, Lee The Agent, A. J., Clem and Jody The Ergot Twins, Hassan O'Leary the After Birth Tycoon, The Sailor, The Exterminator, Andrew Keif, "Fats" Terminal, Doc Benway, "Fingers" Schafer are subject to say the same thing in the same words to occupy, at that intersection point, the same position in space-time. Using a common vocal apparatus complete with all metabolic appliances that is to be the same person—a most inaccurate way of expressing *Recognition*: The junky naked in sunlight . . .

The writer sees himself reading to the mirror as always. . . . He must check now and again to reassure himself that The Crime Of Separate Action has not, is not, cannot occur. . . .

Anyone who has ever looked into a mirror knows what this crime is and what it means in terms of lost control when the reflection no longer obeys. . . . Too late to dial *P o l i c e.* . . .

I personally wish to terminate my services as of now in that I cannot continue to sell the raw materials of death. . . . Yours, sir, is a hopeless case and a noisome one. . . .

"Defense is meaningless in the present state of our knowledge, said The Defense looking up from an electron microscope. . . .

Take your business to Walgreen's

We are not responsible

Steal anything in sight

I don't know how to return it to the white reader

You can write or yell or croon about it . . . paint about it . . . act about it . . . shit it out in mobiles. . . . *So long as you don't go and do it.* . . .

Senators leap up and bray for the Death Penalty with inflexible authority of virus yen. . . . Death for dope fiends, death for sex queens (I mean fiends) death for the psychopath who offends the cowed and graceless flesh with broken animal innocence of lithe movement. . . .

The black wind sock of death undulates over the

land, feeling, smelling for the crime of separate life, movers of the fear-frozen flesh shivering under a vast probability curve. . . .

Population blocks disappear in a checker game of genocide. . . . Any number can play. . . .

The Liberal Press and The Press Not So Liberal and The Press Reactionary Scream approval: "Above all the myth of other-level experience must be eradicated. . . ." And speak darkly of certain harsh realities . . . cows with the aftosa . . . prophylaxis. . . .

Power groups of the world frantically cut lines of connection. . . .

The Planet drifts to random insect doom. . . .

Thermodynamics has won at a crawl. . . . Orgone balked at the post. . . . Christ bled. . . . Time ran out. . . .

You can cut into *Naked Lunch* at any intersection point. . . . I have written many prefaces. They atrophy and amputate spontaneous like the little toe amputates in a West African disease confined to the Negro race and the passing blonde shows her brass ankle as a manicured toe bounces across the club terrace, retrieved and laid at her feet by her Afghan Hound. . . .

Naked Lunch is a blueprint, a How-To Book. . . . Black insect lusts open into vast, other planet landscapes. . . . Abstract concepts, bare as algebra, narrow down to a black turd or a pair of aging cajones. . . .

How-To extend levels of experience by opening the door at the end of a long hall. . . . Doors that only open in *Silence*. . . . *Naked Lunch* demands Silence from The Reader. Otherwise he is taking his own pulse. . . .

Robert Christie knew The Answering Service. . . .
Kill the old cunts . . . keep pubic hairs in his locket
. . . wouldn't You?

Robert Christie, mass strangler of women—sounds
like a daisy chain—hanged in 1953.

Jack The Ripper, Literal Swordsman of the 1890s
and never caught with his pants down . . . wrote a
letter to The Press.

"Next time I'll send along an ear just for jolly. . . .
Wouldn't you?"

"Oh be careful! There they go again!" said the old
queen as his string broke spilling his balls over the
floor . . . 'Stop them will you, James, you worthless
old shit! Don't just stand there and let the master's balls
roll into the coal-bin!"

Window dressers scream through the station, beat
the cashiers with the Fairy Hyp.

Delaudid deliver poor me (Delaudid is souped up,
dehydrate morphine).

The sheriff in black vest types out a death warrant:
"Gotta make it legal and exempt narcotic. . . ."

Violation Public Health Law 334 . . . Procuring an
orgasm by the use of fraud. . . .

Johnny on all fours and Mary sucking him and running her fingers down the thigh backs and light over
the outfields of the ball park. . . .

Over the broken chair and out through the tool-house
window whitewash whipping in a cold Spring wind on
a limestone cliff over the river . . . piece of moon smoke
hangs in China blue sky . . . out on a long line of jissom
across the dusty floor. . . .

Motel . . . Motel . . . Motel . . . broken neon

arabesque . . . loneliness moans across the continent like fog horns over still oily water of tidal rivers. . . .

Ball squeezed dry lemon rind pest rims the ass with a knife cut off a piece of hash for the water pipe—bubble bubble—indicate what used to be me. . . .

"The river is served, sir."

Dead leaves fill the fountain and geraniums run wild with mint, spill a vending machine route across the lawn. . . .

The aging playboy dons his 1920 autograph slicker, feeds his screaming wife down the garbage-disposal unit. . . . Hair, shit and blood spurt out 1963 on the wall. . . . "Yes sir, boys, the shit really hit the fan in '63," said the tiresome old prophet can bore the piss out of you in any space-time direction. . . .

"Now I happen to remember because it was just two year before that a strain of human aftosa developed in a Bolivian lavatory got loose through the medium of a Chinchilla coat fixed an income tax case in Kansas City. . . . And a Liz claimed Immaculate Conception and give birth to a six-ounce spider monkey through the navel. . . . They say the croaker was party to that caper had the monkey on his back all the time. . . ."

I, William Seward, captain of this lushed up hash-head subway, will quell the Lock Ness monster with rotenone and cowboy the white whale. I will reduce Satan to Automatic Obedience, and sublimate subsidiary fiends. I will banish the candiru from your swimming pools.—I will issue a bull on Immaculate Birth Control. . . .

"The oftener a thing happens the more uniquely

wonderful it is," said the pretentious young Nordic on the trapeze studying his Masonic home work.

"The Jews don't believe in Christ, Clem. . . . All they want to do is doodle a Christian girl. . . ."

Adolescent angels sing on shithouse walls of the world.

"Come and jack off . . ." 1929.

"Gimpy push milk sugar shit . . ." Johnny Hung Lately 1952

(Decayed corseted tenor sings Danny Deever in drag. . . .)

Mules don't foal in this decent county and on hooded dead gibber in the ash pits. . . . Violation Public Health Law 334.

So where is the statuary and the percentage? Who can say? I don't have The Word. . . . Home in my douche bag . . . The King is loose with a flame thrower and the king killer, tortured in effigy of a thousand bums, slides down skid row to shit in the limestone ball court.

Young Dillinger walked straight out of the house and never looked back. . . .

"Don't ever look back, kid. . . . You turn into some old cow's salt lick."

Police bullet in the alley . . . Broken wings of Icarus, screams of a burning boy inhaled by the old junky . . . eyes empty as a vast plain . . . (vulture wings husk in the dry air).

The Crab, aged Dean Of Lush Workers, puts on his crustacean suit to prowl the graveyard shift . . . with steel claws pulls the gold teeth and crowns of any flop sleep with his mouth open. . . . If the flop comes up on him The Crab rears back claws snapping to offer dubious battle on the plains of Queens.

The Boy Burglar, fucked in the long jail term, ousted from the cemetery for the non-payment, comes gibbering into the queer bar with a moldy pawn ticket to pick up the back balls of Tent City where castrate salesmen sing the IBM song.

Crabs frolicked through his forest . . . wrestling with the angel hard-on all night, thrown in the homo fall of valor, take a back road to the rusty limestone cave.

Black Yen ejaculates over the salt marshes where nothing grows not even a mandrake. . . .

Law of averages . . . A few chickens . . . Only way to live. . . .

"Hello, Cash."

"You sure it's here?"

"Of course I'm sure. . . . Go in with you."

Night train to Chi . . . Meet a girl in the hall and I see she is on and ask where is a score?

"Come in sonny."

I mean not a young chick but built . . . "How about a fix first?"

"Ixnay, You wouldn't be inna condition."

Three times around . . . wake up shivering sick in warm Spring wind through the window, water burns the eyes like acid . . . .

She gets out of bed naked. . . . Stach in the Cobra lamp. . . . Cooks up. . . .

"Turn over. . . . I'll give it to you in the ass."

She slides the needle in deep, pulls it out and massages the cheek. . . .

She licks a drop of blood off her finger.

He rolls over with a hard-on dissolving in the grey ooze of junk.

In a vale of cocaine and innocence sad-eyed youths yodel for a lost Danny Boy. . . .

We sniffed all night and made it four times . . . fingers down the black board . . . scrape the white bone. Home is the heroin home from the sea and the hustler home from The Bill. . . .

The Pitchman stirs uneasily: "Take over here will you, kid? Gotta see a man about a monkey."

The Word is divided into units which be all in one piece and should be so taken, but the pieces can be had in any order being tied up back and forth, in and out fore and aft like an innaresting sex arrangement. This book spill off the page in all directions, kaleidoscope of vistas, medley of tunes and street noises, farts and riot yipes and the slamming steel shutters of commerce, screams of pain and pathos and screams plain pathic, copulating cats and outraged squawk of the displaced bull head, prophetic mutterings of brujo in nutmeg trances, snapping necks and screaming mandrakes, sigh of orgasm, heroin silent as dawn in the thirsty cells, Radio Cairo screaming like a berserk tobacco auction, and flutes of Ramadan fanning the sick junky like a gentle lush worker in the grey subway dawn feeling with delicate fingers for the green folding crackle. . . .

This is Revelation and Prophecy of what I can pick up without FM on my 1920 crystal set with antennae of jissom. . . . Gentle reader, we see God through our assholes in the flash bulb of orgasm. . . . Through these orifices transmute your body. . . . The way OUT is the way IN. . . .

Now I, William Seward, will unlock my word horde.
. . . My Viking heart fares over the great brown river
where motors put put put in jungle twilight and whole
trees float with huge snakes in the branches and sad-
eyed lemurs watch the shore, across the Missouri field
(The Boy finds a pink arrowhead) out along distant
train whistles, comes back to me hungry as a street boy
don't know to peddle the ass God gave him. . . .
Gentle Reader, The Word will leap on you with leopard
man iron claws, it will cut off fingers and toes like an
opportunist land crab, it will hang you and catch your
jissom like a scrutable dog, it will coil round your thighs
like a bushmaster and inject a shot glass of rancid ectoplasm. . . . And why a *scrutable* dog?

The other day I am returning from the long lunch
thread from mouth to ass all the days of our years, when
I see an Arab boy have this little black and white dog
know how to walk on his hind legs. . . . And a big
yaller dog come on the boy for affection and the boy
shove it away, and the yaller dog growl and snap at the
little toddler, snarling if he had but human gift of
tongues: "A crime against nature right there."

So I dub the yaller dog Scrutable. . . . And let me
say in passing, and I am always passing like a sincere
Spade, that the Inscrutable East need a heap of salt to
get it down. . . . Your Reporter bang thirty grains of
M a day and sit eight hours inscrutable as a turd.

"What are you *thinking*?" says the squirming American Tourist. . . .

To which I reply: "Morphine have depressed my
hypothalamus, seat of libido and emotion, and since the
front brain acts only at second hand with back-brain

titillation, being a vicarious type citizen can only get his kicks from behind, I must report virtual absence of cerebral event. I am aware of your presence, but since it has for me no affective connotation, my affect having been disconnect by the junk man for the non-payment, I am not innarested in your doings. . . . Go or come, shit or fuck yourself with a rasp or an asp—tis well done and fitting for a queen—but The Dead and The Junky don't care. . . ." They are *Inscrutable*.

"Which is the way down the aisle to the water closet?" I asked the blonde usherette.

"Right through here, sir. . . . Room for one more inside."

"Have you seen Pantopon Rose?" said the old junky in the black overcoat.

The Texas sheriff has killed his complicit Vet., Browbeck The Unsteady, involved in horse heroin racket. . . . A horse down with the aftosa need a sight of heroin to ease his pain and maybe some of that heroin take off across the lonesome prairie and whinny in Washington Square. . . . Junkies rush up yelling: "Heigh oOO Silver."

"But where is the *statuary*?" This arch type bit of pathos screeched out in tea-room cocktail lounge with bamboo decorations, Calle Juarez, Mexico, DF. . . . Lost back there with a meatball rape rap . . . a cunt claw your pants down and you up for rape that's statutory, brother. . . .

Chicago calling . . . come in please . . . Chicago calling . . . come in please. . . . What you think I got the rubber on for goulashes in Puyo? A mighty wet place, reader. . . .

"Take it off! Take it off!"

The old queen meets himself coming round the other way in burlesque of adolescence, gets the knee from his phantom of the Old Old Howard . . . down skid row to Market Street Museum shows all kinds masturbation and self-abuse . . . young boys need it special. . . .

They was ripe for the plucking forgot way back yonder in the corn hole . . . lost in little scraps of delight and burning scrolls. . . .

Read the metastasis with blind fingers.

Fossil message of arthritis . . .

"Selling is more of a habit than using."—Lola La Chata, Mexico, DF.

Sucking terror from needle scars, underwater scream mouthing numb nerve warnings of the yen to come, throbbing bite site of rabies . . .

"If God made anything better he kept it for himself," the Sailor used to say, his transmission slowed down with twenty goof balls.

(Pieces of murder fall slow as opal chips through glycerine.)

Watching you and humming over and over "Johnny's So Long At The Fair."

Pushing in a small way to keep up our habit. . . .

"And *use* that alcohol," I say slamming a spirit lamp down on the table.

"You fucking can't—wait—hungry junkies all the time black up my spoons with matches. . . . That's all I need for pen Indef. the heat rumbles a black spoon in the trap. . . .

"I thought you was quitting. . . . Wouldn't feel right fucking up your cure.

"Takes a lot of guts to kick a habit, kid."

Looking for veins in the thawing flesh. Hour-Glass of junk spills its last black grains into the kidneys. . . .

"Heavily infected area," he muttered, shifting the tie up.

"Death was their Culture Hero," said my Old Lady looking up from the Mayan Codices. . . . "They got fire and speech and the corn seed from death. . . . Death turns into a maize seed."

The Ouab Days are upon us
    raw pealed winds of hate and mischance
        blew the shot.

"Get those fucking dirty pictures out of here," I told her. The Old Time Schmecker supported himself on a chair back, juiced and goof-balled . . . a disgrace to his blood.

"What are you one of these goof-ball artists?"

Yellow smells of skid row sherry and occluding liver drifted out of his clothes when he made the junky gesture throwing the hand out palm up to cope . . .

    smell of chili houses and dank overcoats and atro-
    phied testicles. . . .

He looked at me through the tentative, ectoplasmic flesh of cure . . . thirty pounds materialized in a month when you kick . . . soft pink putty that fades at the first silent touch of junk. . . . I saw it happen . . . ten pounds lost in ten minutes . . . standing there with the syringe in one hand . . . holding his pants up with the other

    sharp reek of diseased metal.

Walking in a rubbish heap to the sky . . . scattered gasoline fires . . . smoke hangs black and solid as excrement in the motionless air . . . smudging the white film of noon heat . . . D.L. walks beside me . . . a reflection of my toothless gums and hairless skull . . . flesh smeared over the rotting phosphorescent bones consumed by slow cold fires. . . . He carries an open can of gasoline and the smell of gasoline envelopes him. . . . Coming over a hill of rusty iron we meet a group of Natives . . . flat two-dimension faces of scavenger fish. . . .

"Throw the gasoline on them and light it. . . .

QUICK . . .

white flash . . . mangled insect screams . . .
I woke up with the taste of metal in my mouth back from the dead
trailing the colorless death smell
afterbirth of a withered grey monkey
phantom twinges of amputation . . .
"Taxi boys waiting for a pickup," Eduardo said and died of an overdose in Madrid. . . .
Powder trains burn back through pink convolutions of tumescent flesh . . . set off flash bulbs of orgasm . . . pin-point photos of arrested motion . . . smooth brown side twisted to light a cigarette. . . .
He stood there in a 1920 straw hat somebody gave him . . . soft mendicant words fallings like dead birds in the dark street. . . .
"No . . . No more . . . No mas . . ."

A heaving sea of air hammers in the purple brown dusk tainted with rotten metal smell of sewer gas . . . young worker faces vibrating out of focus in yellow halos of carbide lanterns . . . broken pipes exposed. . . .

"They are rebuilding the City."

Lee nodded absently. . . . "Yes . . . Always . . ."

Either way is a bad move to The East Wing. . . .

If I knew I'd be glad to tell you. . . .

"No good . . . no bueno . . . hustling myself. . . ."

"No glot . . . C'lom Fliday"

Tangier, 1959.

APPENDIX

The British Journal of Addiction   Vol. 53, No. 2

LETTER FROM A MASTER ADDICT TO
DANGEROUS DRUGS

August 3rd, 1956.
Venice.

DEAR DOCTOR,

Thanks for your letter. I enclose that article on the effects of various drugs I have used. I do not know if it is suitable for your publication. I have no objection to my name being used.

No difficulty with drinking. No desire to use any drug. General health excellent. Please give my regards to Mr.——. I use his system of exercises daily with excellent results.

I have been thinking of writing a book on narcotic drugs if I could find a suitable collaborator to handle the technical end.

Yours,
WILLIAM BURROUGHS.

The use of opium and opium derivatives leads to a state that defines limits and describes "addiction"—(The term is loosely used to indicate anything one is used to or wants. We speak of addiction to candy, coffee, tobacco, warm weather, television, detective stories, crossword puzzles). So misapplied the term loses any useful precision of meaning. The use of morphine leads to a metabolic dependence on morphine. Morphine becomes a biologic need like water and the user may die if he is suddenly deprived of it. The diabetic will die without insulin, but he is not addicted to insulin. His need for insulin was not brought about by the use of insulin. He needs insulin to maintain a normal metabolism. The addict needs morphine to maintain a morphine metabolism, and so avoid the excruciatingly painful return to a normal metabolism.

I have used a number of "narcotic" drugs over a period of twenty years. Some of these drugs are addicting in the above sense. Most are not:

Opiates.—Over a period of twelve years I have used opium, smoked and taken orally (injection in the skin causes abscesses. Injection in the vein is unpleasant and perhaps dangerous), heroin injected in skin, vein, muscle, sniffed (when no needle was available), morphine, dilaudid, pantopon, eukodol, paracodine, dionine, codeine, demerol, methodone. They are all habit forming in varying degree. Nor does it make much difference how the drug is administered, smoked, sniffed, injected, taken orally, inserted in rectal suppositories, the end result will be the same: addiction. And a smoking habit is as difficult to break as an intravenous injection habit. The concept that injection habits are particularly injurious derives from an irrational fear of needles—("Injections poison the blood stream"—as though the blood stream were any less poisoned by substances absorbed from the stomach, the lungs or the mucous membrane). Demerol is probably less addicting than morphine. It is also less satisfying to the addict, and less effective as a pain killer. While a demerol habit is easier to break than a morphine habit, demerol is certainly more injurious to the health and specifically to the nervous system. I once used demerol for three months and developed a number of distressing symptoms: trembling hands (with morphine my hands are always steady), progressive loss of coordination, muscular contractions, paranoid obsessions, fear of insanity. Finally I contracted an opportune intolerance for demerol—no doubt a measure of self preservation—and switched to methodone. Immediately all my symptoms disappeared. I may add that demerol is quite as constipating as morphine, that it exerts an even more depressing effect on the appetite and the sexual functions, does not, however, contract the pupils. I have given myself thousands of injections over a period of years with unsterilized, in fact dirty, needles and never sustained an infection until I used demerol. Then I came down with a series of abscesses one of which had to be lanced and drained. In short demerol seems to me a more dangerous drug than morphine. Methodone is completely satisfying to the addict, an excellent pain killer, at least as addicting as morphine.

I have taken morphine for acute pain. Any opiate that effectively relieves pain to an equal degree relieves withdrawal symptoms. The conclusion is obvious: Any opiate that relieves pain is habit forming, and the more effectively it relieves pain the more habit forming it is. The habit forming molecule, and the pain killing molecule of morphine are probably identical, and the process by which morphine relieves pain is the same process that leads to tolerance and addiction. Non habit forming morphine appears to be a latter day Philosopher's Stone. On the other hand variations of apomorphine may prove extremely effective in controlling the withdrawal syndrome. But we should not expect this drug to be a pain killer as well.

The phenomena of morphine addiction are well known and there is no reason to go ever them here. A few points, it seems to me, have received insufficient attention: The metabolic incompatibility between morphine and alcohol has been observed, but no one, so far as I know, has advanced an explanation. If a morphine addict drinks alcohol he experiences no agreeable or euphoric sensations. There

is a feeling of slowly mounting discomfort, and the need
for another injection. The alcohol seems to be short-cir-
cuited perhaps by the liver. I once attempted to drink in a
state of incomplete recovery from an attack of jaundice (I
was not using morphine at this time). The metabolic sensation was identical. In one case the liver was partly out of
action from jaundice, in the other preoccupied, literally, by
a morphine metabolism. In neither case could it metabolize
alcohol. If an alcoholic becomes addicted to morphine,
morphine invariably and completely displaces alcohol. I
have known several alcoholics who began using morphine.
They were able to tolerate large doses of morphine immediately (1 grain to a shot) without ill effects, and in a matter
of days stopped taking alcohol. The reverse never occurs.
The morphine addict can not tolerate alcohol when he is
using morphine or suffering from morphine withdrawal.
The ability to tolerate alcohol is a sure sign of disintoxication. In consequence alcohol can never be substituted
for morphine directly. Of course a disintoxicated addict
may start drinking and become an alcoholic.

During withdrawal the addict is acutely aware of his
surroundings. Sense impressions are sharpened to the point
of hallucination. Familiar objects seem to stir with a writhing furtive life. The addict is subject to a barrage of sensations external and visceral. He may experience flashes of
beauty and nostalgia, but the overall impression is extremely painful—(Possibly his sensations are painful because
of their intensity. A pleasurable sensation may become intolerable after a certain intensity is reached.)

I have noticed two special reactions of early withdrawal:
(1) Everything looks threatening; (2) mild paranoia. The
doctors and nurses appear as monsters of evil. In the course
of several cures, I have felt myself surrounded by dangerous lunatics. I talked with one of Dr. Dent's patients who
had just undergone disintoxication for a pethidine habit. He

reported an identical experience, told me that for 24 hours the nurses and the doctor "seemed brutal and repugnant." And everything looked blue. And I have talked with other addicts who experienced the same reactions. Now the psychological basis for paranoid notions during withdrawal is obvious. The specific similarity of these reactions indicates a common metabolic origin. The similarity between withdrawal phenomena and certain states of drug intoxication, is striking. Hashish, Bannisteria Caapi (Harmaline), Peyote (Mescaline) produce states of acute sensitivity, with hallucinatory viewpoint. Everything looks alive. Paranoid ideas are frequent. Bannisteria Caapi intoxication specifically reproduces the state of withdrawal. Everything looks threatening. Paranoid ideas are marked, especially with overdose. After taking Bannisteria Caapi, I was convinced that the Medicine Man and his apprentice were conspiring to murder me. It seems that metabolic states of the body can reproduce the effects of various drugs.

In the U.S.A. heroin addicts are receiving an involuntary reduction cure from the pushers who progressively dilute their wares with milk sugar and barbiturates. As a result many of the addicts who seek treatment are lightly addicted so they can be completely disintoxicated in a short time (7 to 8 days). They recover rapidly without medication. Meanwhile any tranquillizing, anti-allergic, or sedative drug, will afford some relief, especially if injected. The addict feels better if he knows that some alien substance is coursing through his blood stream. Tolserol, Thorazine and related "tranquillizers," every variety of barbiturate, Chloral and Paraldehyde, anti-histamines, cortisone, reserpine, even shock (can lobotomy be far behind?) have all been used with results usually described as "encouraging." My own experience suggests that these results be accepted with some reserve. Of course, symptomatic treatment is indicated, and all these drugs (with possible exception of the drug most commonly used: barbiturates) have a place in the treatment of the withdrawal syndrome. But none of these drugs is in itself the answer to withdrawal. Withdrawal symptoms vary with individual metabolism and physical type. Pigeon chested, hay fever and asthma liable individuals suffer greatly from allergic symptoms during withdrawal: running nose, sneezing, smarting, watering eyes, difficulty in breathing. In such cases cortisone, and anti-histamine drugs may afford definite relief. Vomiting could probably be controlled with anti-nausea drugs like thorazine.

I have undergone ten "cures" in the course of which all these drugs were used. I have taken quick reductions, slow reductions, prolonged sleep, apomorphine, antihistamines, a French system involving a worthless product known as "amorphine," everything but shock. (I would be interested to hear results of further experiments with shock treatment on somebody else.) The success of any treatment depends on the degree and duration of addiction, the stage of withdrawal (drugs which are effective in late or light withdrawal can be disastrous in the acute phase) individual symptoms, health, age, etc. A method of treatment might be completely ineffective at one time, but give excellent results at another. Or a treatment that does me no good may help someone else. I do not presume to pass any final judgements, only to report my own reactions to various drugs and methods of treatment.

Reduction Cures.—This is the commonest form of treatment, and no method yet discovered can entirely replace it in cases of severe addiction. The patient must have some morphine. If there is one rule that applies to all cases of addiction this is it. But the morphine should be withdrawn as quickly as possible. I have taken slow reduction cures and in every case the result was discouragement and eventual relapse. Imperceptible reduction is likely to be endless reduction. When the addict seeks cure, he has, in most cases, already experienced withdrawal symptoms many times. He expects an unpleasant ordeal and he is prepared to endure it. But if the pain of withdrawal is spread over two months instead of ten days he may not be able to endure it. It is not the intensity but the duration of pain that breaks the will to resist. If the addict habitually takes any quantity, however small, of any opiate to alleviate the weakness, insomnia, boredom, restlessness, of late withdrawal, the withdrawal symptoms will be prolonged indefinitely and complete relapse is almost certain.

Prolonged Sleep.—The theory sounds good. You go to sleep and wake up cured. Industrial doses of chloral hydrate, barbiturates, thorazine, only produced a nightmare state of semi-consciousness. Withdrawal of sedation, after 5 days, occasioned a severe shock. Symptoms of acute morphine deprivation supervened. The end result was a combined syndrome of unparalleled horror. No cure I ever took was as painful as this allegedly painless method. The cycle of sleep and wakefulness is always deeply disturbed during withdrawal. To further disturb it with massive sedation seems contraindicated to say the least. Withdrawal of morphine is sufficiently traumatic without adding to it withdrawal of barbiturates. After two weeks in the hospital (five days sedation, ten days "rest") I was still so weak that I fainted when I tried to walk up a slight incline. I consider prolonged sleep the worst possible method of treating withdrawal.

Anti-histamines.—The use of anti-histamines is based on the allergic theory of withdrawal. Sudden withdrawal of morphine precipitates an overproduction of histamine with consequent allergic symptoms. (In shock resulting from traumatic injury with acute pain large quantities of histamine are released in the blood. In acute pain as in addiction toxic doses of morphine are readily tolerated. Rabbits,

who have a high histamine content in the blood, are extremely resistant to morphine.) My own experience with
anti-histamines has not been conclusive. I once took a cure
in which only anti-histamines were used, and the results
were good. But I was lightly addicted at that time, and had
been without morphine for 72 hours when the cure started.
I have frequently used anti-histamines since then for withdrawal symptoms with disappointing results. In fact they
seem to increase my depression and irritability (I do not
suffer from typical allergic symptoms).

Apomorphine.—Apomorphine is certainly the best method of treating withdrawal that I have experienced. It does
not completely eliminate the withdrawal symptoms, but
reduces them to an endurable level. The acute symptoms
such as stomach and leg cramps, convulsive or manic states
are completely controlled. In fact apomorphine treatment
involves less discomfort than a reduction cure. Recovery
is more rapid and more complete. I feel that I was never
completely cured of the craving for morphine until I took
apomorphine treatment. Perhaps the "psychological" craving for morphine that persists after a cure is not psychological at all, but metabolic. More potent variations of the
apomorphine formula might prove qualitatively more effective in treating all forms of addiction.

Cortisone.—Cortisone seems to give some relief especially
when injected intravenously.

Thorazine.—Provides some relief from withdrawal symptoms, but not much. Side effects of depression, disturbances
of vision, indigestion offset dubious benefits.

Reserpine.—I never noticed any effect whatever from this
drug except a slight depression.

Tolserol.—Negligible results.

Barbiturates.— It is common practice to prescribe barbiturates for the insomnia of withdrawal. Actually the use of
barbiturates delays the return of normal sleep, prolongs

the whole period of withdrawal, and may lead to relapse. (The addict is tempted to take a little codeine or paregoric with his nembutal. Very small quantities of opiates, that would be quite innocuous for a normal person, immediately re-establish addiction in a cured addict.) My experience certainly confirms Dr. Dent's statement that barbiturates are contraindicated.

Chloral and paraldehyde.—Probably preferable to barbiturates if a sedative is necessary, but most addicts will vomit up paraldehyde at once. I have also tried, on my own initiative, the following drugs during withdrawal:

Alcohol.—Absolutely contraindicated at any stage of withdrawal. The use of alcohol invariably exacerbates the withdrawal symptoms and leads to relapse. Alcohol can only be tolerated after metabolism returns to normal. This usually takes one month in cases of severe addiction.

Benzedrine.—May relieve temporarily the depression of late withdrawal, disastrous during acute withdrawal, contraindicated at any stage because it produces a state of nervousness for which morphine is the physiological answer.

Cocaine.—The above goes double for cocaine.

Cannabis indica (marijuana).—In late or light withdrawal relieves depression and increases the appetite, in acute withdrawal an unmitigated disaster. (I once smoked marijuana during early withdrawal with nightmarish results.) Cannabis is a sensitizer. If you feel bad already it will make you feel worse. Contraindicated.

Peyote, Bannisteria caapi.—I have not ventured to experiment. The thought of Bannisteria intoxication superimposed on acute withdrawal makes the brain reel. I know of a man who substituted peyote during late withdrawal, claimed to lose all desire for morphine, ultimately died of peyote poisoning.

In cases of severe addiction, definite, physical, withdrawal symptoms persist for one month at least.

I have never seen or heard of a psychotic morphine addict, I mean anyone who showed psychotic symptoms while addicted to an opiate. In fact addicts are drearily sane. Perhaps there is a metabolic incompatibility between schizophrenia and opiate addiction. On the other hand the withdrawal of morphine often precipitates psychotic reactions—usually mild paranoia. Interesting that drugs and methods of treatment that give results in schizophrenia, are also of some use in withdrawal: anti-histamines, tranquillizers, apomorphine, shock.

Sir Charles Sherington definies pain as "the psychic adjunct of an imperative protective reflex."

The vegetative nervous system expands and contracts in response to visceral rhythms and external stimuli, expanding to stimuli which are experienced as pleasurable—sex, food, agreeable social contacts, etc.—contracting from pain, anxiety, fear, discomfort, boredom. Morphine alters the whole cycle of expansion and contraction, release and tension. The sexual function is deactivated, peristalsis inhibited, the pupils cease to react in response to light and darkness. The organism neither contracts from pain nor expands to normal sources of pleasure. It adjusts to a morphine cycle. The addict is immune to boredom. He can look at his shoe for hours or simply stay in bed. He needs no sexual outlet, no social contacts, no work, no diversion, no exercise, nothing but morphine. Morphine may relieve pain by imparting to the organism some of the qualities of a plant. (Pain could have no function for plants which are, for the most part, stationary, incapable of protective reflexes.)

Scientists look for a non-habit forming morphine that will kill pain without giving pleasure, addicts want—or think they want—euphoria without addiction. I do not see how the functions of morphine can be separated, I think that any effective pain killer will depress the sexual function, induce euphoria and cause addiction. The perfect pain killer would probably be immediately habit forming. (If anyone is interested to develop such a drug, dehydro-oxy-heroin might be a good place to start.)

The addict exists in a painless, sexless, timeless state. Transition back to the rhythms of animal life involves the withdrawal syndrome. I doubt if this transition can ever be made in comfort. Painless withdrawal can only be approached.

Cocaine.—Cocaine is the most exhilarating drug I have ever used. The euphoria centres in the head. Perhaps the drug activates pleasure connections directly in the brain. I suspect that an electric current in the right place would produce the same effect. The full exhilaration of cocaine can only be realised by an intravenous injection. The pleasurable effects do not last more than five or ten minutes. If the drug is injected in the skin, rapid elimination vitiates the effects. This goes doubly for sniffing.

It is standard practice for cocaine users to sit up all night shooting cocaine at one minute intervals, alternating with shots of heroin, or cocaine and heroin mixed in the same injection to form a "speed ball." (I have never known an habitual cocaine user who was not a morphine addict.)

The desire for cocaine can be intense. I have spent whole days walking from one drug store to another to fill a cocaine prescription. You may want cocaine intensely, but you don't have any metabolic need for it. If you can't get cocaine you eat, you go to sleep and forget it. I have talked with people who used cocaine for years, then were suddenly cut off from their supply. None of them experienced any withdrawal symptoms. Indeed it is difficult to see how a front brain stimulant could be addicting. Addiction seems to be a monopoly of sedatives.

Continued use of cocaine leads to nervousness, depression, sometimes drug psychosis with paranoid hallucinations. The nervousness and depression resulting from cocaine use are not alleviated by more cocaine. They are effectively relieved by morphine. The use of cocaine by a morphine addict, always leads to larger and more frequent injections of morphine.

Cannabis Indica (hashish, marijuana).—The effects of this drug have been frequently and luridly described: disturbance of space-time perception, acute sensitivity to impressions, flight of ideas, laughing jags, silliness. Marijuana is a sensitiser, and the results are not always pleasant. It makes a bad situation worse. Depression becomes despair, anxiety panic. I have already mentioned my horrible experience with marijuana during acute morphine withdrawal. I once gave marijuana to a guest who was mildly anxious about something ("On bum kicks" as he put it). After smoking half a cigarette he suddenly leapt to his feet screaming "I got the fear!" and rushed out of the house.

An especially unnerving feature of marijuana intoxication is a disturbance of the affective orientation. You do not know whether you like something or not, whether a sensation is pleasant or unpleasant.

The use of marijuana varies greatly with the individual. Some smoke it constantly, some occasionally, not a few dislike it intensely. It seems to be especially unpopular with confirmed morphine addicts, many of whom take a puritanical view of marijuana smoking.

The ill effects of marijuana have been grossly exaggerated in the U.S. Our national drug is alcohol. We tend to regard the use of any other drug with special horror. Anyone given over to these alien vices deserves the complete ruin of his mind and body. People believe what they want to believe without regard for the facts. Marijuana is not habit forming. I have never seen evidence of any ill effects from moderate use. Drug psychosis may result from prolonged and excessive use.

Barbiturates.—The barbiturates are definitely addicting if taken in large quantities over any period of time (about a gramme a day will cause addiction). Withdrawal syndrome is more dangerous than morphine withdrawal, consisting of hallucinations with epilepsy type convulsions. Addicts often injure themselves flopping about on concrete floors (concrete floors being a usual corollary of abrupt withdrawal). Morphine addicts often take barbiturates to potentiate inadequate morphine rations. Some of them become barbiturate addicts as well.

I once took two nembutal capsules (one and a half grain each) every night for four months and suffered no withdrawal symptoms. Barbiturate addiction is a question of quantity. It is probably not a metabolc addiction like morphine, but a mechanical reaction from excessive front brain sedation.

The barbiturate addict presents a shocking spectacle. He can not coordinate, he staggers, falls off bar stools, goes to sleep in the middle of a sentence, drops food out of his mouth. He is confused, quarrelsome and stupid. And he almost always uses other drugs, anything he can lay hands on: alcohol, benzedrene, opiates, marijuana. Barbiturate users are looked down on in addict society: "Goof ball bums. They got no class to them." The next step down is coal gas and milk, or sniffing ammonia in a bucket—"The scrub woman's kick."

It seems to me that barbiturates cause the worst possible form of addiction, unsightly, deteriorating, difficult to treat.

Benzedrene.—This is a cerebral stimulant like cocaine. Large doses cause prolonged sleeplessness with feelings of exhilaration. The period of euphoria is followed by a horrible depression. The drug tends to increase anxiety. It causes indigestion and loss of appetite.

I know of only one case where definite symptoms followed the withdrawal of benzedrene. This was a woman of my acquaintance who used incredible quantities of benzedrene for six months. During this period she developed a drug psychosis and was hospitalized for ten days. She continued the use of benzedrene, but was suddenly cut off. She suffered an asthma type seizure. She could not get her breath and turned blue. I gave her a dose of anti-histamine (thepherene) which afforded immediate relief. The symptoms did not return.

Peyote (mescaline).—This is undoubtedly a stimulant. It dilates the pupils, keeps one awake. Peyote is extremely nauseating. Users experience difficulty keeping it down long enough to realize the effect, which is similar, in some respects, to marijuana. There is increased sensitivity to impression, especially to colours. Peyote intoxication causes a peculiar vegetable consciousness or identification with the plant. Everything looks like a peyote plant. It is easy to understand why the Indians believe there is a resident spirit in the peyote cactus.

Overdose of peyote may lead to respiratory paralysis and death. I know of one case. There is no reason to believe that peyote is addicting.

Bannisteria caapi (Harmaline, Banisterine, Telepathine). —Bannisteria caapi is a fast growing vine. The active principle is apparently found throughout the wood of the fresh cut vine. The inner bark is considered most active, and the leaves are never used. It takes a considerable quantity of the vine to feel the full effects of the drug. About five pieces of vine each eight inches long are needed for one person. The vine is crushed and boiled for two or more hours with the leaves of a bush identified as *Palicourea sp. rubiaceae.*

Yage or Ayuahuaska (the most commonly used Indian names for Bannisteria caapi) is a hallucinating narcotic that produces a profound derangement of the senses. In overdose it is a convulsant poison. The antidote is a barbiturate or other strong, anti-convulsant sedative. Anyone taking Yage for the first time should have a sedative ready in the event of an overdose.

The hallucinating properties of Yage have led to its use by Medicine Men to potentiate their powers. They also use it as a cure-all in the treatment of various illnesses. Yage lowers the body temperature and consequently is of some use in the treatment of fever. It is a powerful antihelminthic, indicated for treatment of stomach or intestinal worms. Yage induces a state of conscious anaesthesia, and is used in rites where the initiates must undergo a painful ordeal like whipping with knotted vines, or exposure to the sting of ants.

So far as I could discover only the fresh cut vine is active. I found no way to dry, extract or preserve the active principal. No tinctures proved active. The dried vine is completely inert. The pharmacology of yage requires laboratory research. Since the crude extract is such a powerful, hallucinating narcotic, perhaps even more spectacular results could be obtained with synthetic variations. Certainly the matter warrants further research.†

I did not observe any ill effects that could be attributed to the use of Yage. The Medicine Men who use it continuously in line of duty seem to enjoy normal health. Tolerance is soon acquired so that one can drink the extract without nausea or other ill effect.

Yage is a unique narcotic. Yage intoxication is in some

† Since this was published I have discovered that the alkaloid of Bannisteria are closely related to LSD6, which has been used to produce experimental psychosis. I think they are up to LSD25 already.

respects similar to intoxication with hashish. In both instances there is a shift of viewpoint, an extension of consciousness beyond ordinary experience. But Yage produces a deeper derangement of the senses with actual hallucinations. Blue flashes in front of the eyes is peculiar to Yage intoxication.

There is a wide range of attitude in regard to Yage. Many Indians and most White users seem to regard it simply as another intoxicant like liquor. In other groups it has ritual use and significance. Among the Jivaro young men take Yage to contact the spirits of their ancestors and get a briefing for their future life. It is used during initiations to anaesthetize the initiates for painful ordeals. All Medicine Men use it in their practice to foretell the future, locate lost or stolen objects, name the perpetrator of a crime, to diagnose and treat illness.

The alcaloid of Bannisteria caapi was isolated in 1923 by Fisher Cardenas. He called the alcaloid Telepathine alternately Banisterine. Rumf showed that Telepathine was identical with Harmine, the alcaloid of Perganum Harmala.

Bannisteria caapi is evidently not habit forming.

Nutmeg.—Convicts and sailors sometimes have recourse to nutmeg. About a tablespoon is swallowed with water. Results are vaguely similar to marijuana with side effects of headache and nausea. Death would probably supervene before addiction if such addiction is possible. I have only taken nutmeg once.

There are a number of narcotics of the nutmeg family in use among the Indians of South America. They are usually administered by sniffing a dried powder of the plant. The Medicine Men take these noxious substances, and go into convulsive states. Their twitchings and mutterings are thought to have prophetic significance. A friend of mine was violently sick for three days after experimenting with a drug of the nutmeg family in South America.

Datura-scopolamine.—Morphine addicts are frequently poisoned by taking morphine in combination with scopolamine.

I once obtained some ampoules each of which contained one-sixth grain of morphine and one-hundreth grain of scopolamine. Thinking that one-hundreth grain was a negligible quantity, I took six ampoules in one injection. The result was a psychotic state lasting some hours during which I was opportunely restrained by my long suffering landlord. I remembered nothing the following day.

Drugs of the datura group are used by the Indians of South America and Mexico. Fatalities are said to be frequent.

Scopolamine has been used by the Russians as a confession drug with dubious results. The subject may be willing to reveal his secrets, but quite unable to remember them. Often cover story and secret information are inextricably garbled. I understand that mescaline has been very successful in extracting information from suspects.

Morphine addiction is a metabolic illness brought about by the use of morphine. In my opinion psychological treatment is not only useless it is contraindicated. Statistically the people who become addicted to morphine are those who have access to it: doctors, nurses, anyone in contact with black market sources. In Persia where opium is sold without control in opium shops, 70 per cent of the adult population is addicted. So we should psycho-analyse several million Persians to find out what deep conflicts and anxieties have driven them to the use of opium? I think not. According to my experience most addicts are not neurotic and do not need psychotherapy. Apomorphine treatment and access to apomorphine in the event of relapse would certainly give a higher percentage of permanent cures than any programme of " psychological rehabilitation."

Selected Grove Press Paperbacks

62480-7   ACKER, KATHY / Great Expectations: A Novel / $6.95
62433-5   BARASH, D. and LIPTON, J. / Stop Nuclear War! A Handbook / $7.95
17208-6   BECKETT, SAMUEL / Endgame / $3.50
17299-X   BECKETT, SAMUEL / Three Novels: Molloy, Malone Dies, The Unnamable / $6.95
17204-3   BECKETT, SAMUEL / Waiting for Godot / $3.95
17106-3   BRECHT, BERTOLT / Mother Courage and Her Children / $2.95
17108-X   BURROUGHS, WILLIAM S. / Naked Lunch / $4.95
17411-9   CLURMAN, HAROLD (Ed.) / Nine Plays of the Modern Theater (Waiting For Godot by Samuel Beckett, The Visit by Friedrich Durrenmatt, Tango by Slawomir Mrozek, The Caucasian Chalk Circle by Bertolt Brecht, The Balcony by Jean Genet, Rhinoceros by Eugene Ionesco, American Buffalo by David Mamet, The Birthday Party by Harold Pinter, Rosencrantz and Guildenstern Are Dead by Tom Stoppard) / $14.95
17327-9   FANON, FRANZ / The Wretched of the Earth / $4.95
17956-0   GETTLEMAN, MARVIN, et.al. eds. / El Salvador: Central America in the New Cold War / $9.95
62003-8   HITLER, ADOLF / Hitler's Secret Book / $7.95
17209-4   IONESCO, EUGENE / Four Plays (The Bald Soprano, The Lesson, The Chairs, and Jack, or The Submission) / $6.95
17226-4   IONESCO, EUGENE / Rhinoceros and Other Plays / $5.95
17016-4   MAMET, DAVID / American Buffalo / $4.95
62049-6   MAMET, DAVID / Glengarry Glen Ross / $6.95
17760-6   MILLER, HENRY / Tropic of Cancer / $4.95
17251-5   PINTER, HAROLD / The Homecoming / $5.95
17539-5   POMERANCE, BERNARD / The Elephant Man / $5.95
62498-X   ROSSET, PETER and VANDERMEER, JOHN / The Nicaragua Reader / $9.95
62009-7   SEGALL, J. PETER / Deduct This Book: How Not to Pay Taxes While Ronald Reagan is President / $6.95
17467-4   SELBY, HUBERT / Last Exit to Brooklyn / $3.95
17948-X   SHAWN, WALLACE, and GREGORY, ANDRE / My Dinner with Andre / $6.95
17797-5   SNOW, EDGAR / Red Star Over China / $9.95
17260-4   STOPPARD, TOM / Rosencrantz and Guildenstern Are Dead / $3.95
17474-7   SUZUKI, D.T. / Introduction to Zen Buddhism / $3.95
17969-2   TOOLE, JOHN KENNEDY / A Confederacy of Dunces / $4.50

GROVE PRESS, INC., 920 Broadway, New York, N.Y. 10010